Born in Dublin, **JENNY O'BRIEN** moved to Wales and then Guernsey, where she tries to find time to both read and write in between working as a nurse and ferrying around three teenagers.

In her spare time she can be found frowning at her wonky cakes and even wonkier breads. You'll be pleased to note she won't be entering Bake Off. She's also an all-year-round sea swimmer.

Also by Jenny O'Brien

The Stepsister

Silent Cry

JENNY O'BRIEN

ONE PLACE. MANY STORIES

HQ
An imprint of HarperCollins*Publishers* Ltd
1 London Bridge Street
London SE1 9GF

HarperCollins*Publishers*
1st Floor, Watermarque Building, Ringsend Road
Dublin 4, Ireland

8
First published in Great Britain by
HQ, an imprint of HarperCollins*Publishers* Ltd 2020

ISBN: 9780008390167

In memory of Jason Hopper

Prologue

Izzy
Five years ago

'Be careful. It's the first time you've been out with her by yourself.'

'Give over nagging, Izzy. We'll be fine, won't we, gorgeous?' Charlie said, bending on his haunches and gently running his finger down his daughter's plump cheek, her dark blue eyes staring back at him. 'We're going to let your mammy have some rest while we go to the shops. It's time we got better acquainted. I can tell you all about football and which team to support.'

'You will not. Don't listen, Alys. There's only one football team worth supporting and it's not his,' Izzy teased, feeling redundant now that Charlie had stolen her attention.

This would be the first time she'd be apart from her since the birth and already she could feel the bonds of motherhood straining at the thought of Alys being out of her sight, even if it was only for half an hour. It had only taken a week for her world to shrink to the boundary walls of the house. But she'd never been happier. Her eyes grazed the pair of them, and love filled every corner. But Charlie and Alys needed this time, both of them and a few minutes alone after another interrupted night's sleep

1

would be like a gift from the gods. Izzy had never felt so bone-achingly weary and, while she dreaded being apart, a rest would make all the difference.

'Now, what about a goodbye kiss from your pretty mam then?' Charlie said.

Pushing himself to standing, the car seat in the crook of his arm, he leant in for a kiss reminiscent of the best Hollywood romances.

'You daft thing,' she laughed. But secretly she was pleased, more than pleased.

She watched as he reversed the Mini into the road and continued watching until they were out of sight before returning to the warmth of the house. She slipped off her shoes by the front door and, fumbling into her slippers. headed for the kitchen. There was washing and ironing, not to mention food to prepare. There were so many things she knew she should be doing but she felt sick with tiredness. With a mug of tea in her hand, she returned to the sofa and, feet propped up on the end, rested back, allowing the silence envelop her.

There was always noise in the cottage. It wasn't Charlie's fault that he was one of those men you could hear long before you could see them: Charlie, her one-night-stand, who seemed to have taken up root in both her house and her heart. He was always clomping around the place with a heavy tread and if it wasn't him, it was one of his mates he'd invited back for her to feed. The house suddenly felt empty with the pervading sound of silence.

She'd close her eyes, just for five minutes … they'd be back soon.

The fire had died back to nothing, the embers just a pale glow in the grate. She turned her head towards the window, her hand instinctively pulling the woollen blanket around her shoulders, a shiver snaking its way across her spine. The last time she'd looked out, the sun had been streaming in through the pane but all that was visible now was the dense grey of twilight. The phone rang, slicing through her sudden fear. She struggled to sit, her neck stiff from the arm of the sofa. A million excuses chased through her mind.

They've been delayed, maybe had a puncture … or knowing Charlie, he's run out of petrol.

Her hand lifted the receiver to her ear before gently replacing it. She'd learnt the best way to treat cold callers was by doing exactly that. No comment. No words. Nothing.

She pulled the throw tighter over her shoulders, her eyes now on the clock on the mantelpiece, her mind in a tangle.

Two hours? How the hell could she have slept for so long? This was quickly followed by the worst thought of all: *He must have had an accident. Even now, he's in some anonymous hospital bed and as for Alys …*

Her stomach clenched when there was no need – she'd just ring his mobile. Reaching out a hand, she quickly tapped in his number.

The person you are trying to reach is currently unavailable. Please leave a message after the tone.

She was scared now, really scared. He never left his phone switched off even if it was only to check on the football scores. They'd been gone hours. She had no idea where the hell he could have taken her. Alys would need a feed and a nappy change. There was nowhere he'd go, not with a newborn.

Izzy heaved a sigh at her foolishness and, for one long moment, relished the feel of wool against skin as she tried to laugh her fears off. She wasn't his keeper. They'd got held up. Something had happened, something silly that she couldn't guess at and, in a minute, she'd hear the creak of the gate and the turn of the key.

The moment passed. The minutes continued ticking and her sliver of calm disintegrated.

3

In a sudden burst of movement, she leapt from the chair and ran up the stairs.

That's it. They came in earlier, hours earlier and even now they're both curled up in their beds, not wanting to wake me.

But Alys's cot was empty, apart from the pale-yellow blanket folded neatly over the end, just the way she'd left it that morning. Their bed was empty too, the duvet flung back any old how, the sheets cold, wrinkled, uninviting.

Outside. Maybe he pulled up and decided to close his eyes. Maybe it's like the last time when he forgot his keys and, if Alys has fallen asleep in the car, he might have decided not to wake me.

She remembered the last time. His sheepish grin when she shook him back into the land of the living, which developed into their first big row and ended in a swift coupling against the back of the sofa.

There was post on the mat but she just stepped over it. She wasn't in the mood for bills and flyers. She just needed to know that Alys was safe.

The air was cold, wiping the smile from her face. There was barely a glimmer of light as twilight switched to dusk. They were far enough away from everyone for darkness, when it hit, to mean exactly that. There wasn't even a visible moon or any stars to light the way. She took a second to drag air into her lungs, the smell from the winter-flowering jasmine around the door filling her senses, but there was no joy to be had from the scent. Her eyes adjusted enough to see the outline of the gate and the telegraph pole next to it. There was no car, no indication that he'd returned. There was nothing apart from the empty track leading up to the house.

Izzy stayed a while. Something was wrong, dreadfully wrong – something that she had no way of putting right.

She finally wandered back into the hall, the post in her hand, the throw trailing in her wake. She was cold down to the bone, but it wasn't the type of cold that the warmth from wool was going to solve. Her hand stretched towards the phone for a third time, her arm brushing against her breasts, now heavy with milk. She hesitated, her gaze lingering on the mail and the postcard on top. Was she overreacting? Was this the paranoid response of a new mum? Maybe. Possibly. Hopefully.

The card was plain white and, with no name or address scrawled on the front, must have been hand delivered. She flipped it over and all thoughts of a simple explanation died along with any hope in her heart.

I've got Alys. Don't try to find us, Charlie

Chapter 1

Izzy
Monday 23 December, 5.10 p.m. Swansea

It took one look, just one, for Izzy's world to shatter a second time.

To anyone else it was only a flicker, a face in the crowd but to her it was a face so intrinsically linked to her past that she paused in her fur-lined boots, unable to do more than stare at the woman disappearing across the street. It was all there in the angle of her head, the sway of her hips, the colour of her jet-black hair. It had been five years and yet it still felt just like yesterday.

Grace. Grace Madden.

A wave of ice-cold worked its way across her shoulders and down her spine, pinning her to the spot. She couldn't move even if her life depended on it. Instead, she watched, transfixed as Grace clambered into a waiting taxi before zooming into the distance. She was too late and yet what could she have done? Shout? Scream? Surely she could have done something instead of just standing there? The tears came in a sudden deluge. Tears for the opportunity she'd just lost.

'Are you all right, love? All this Christmas cheer getting to you?' The stranger's soft Welsh accent was a welcome interruption.

Izzy wiped a hand over her cheeks before scooping up her bags.

'I'm fine, just a little overcome,' she said, jolted out of her reverie. She was standing outside Costa, her gaze still lingering on the spot where she'd last seen her. Stepping out of his way with a brief smile, she headed inside to buy a coffee she didn't want simply because the tremors running up her legs made sitting an urgent necessity.

Costa was busy but she managed to secure a table right at the back and, pushing her coffee to one side, rested her head in her hands.

Was it even Grace? It certainly looked like her with her distinctive black hair sweeping her shoulders in sharp contrast to her pale face and razor cheekbones. But now, as the seconds ticked into minutes, she wasn't so sure. Bottle black was such a popular look these days and it wasn't as if she was that unique.

Squashing back tears, she reached for her cup with an unsteady hand and took tentative sips until the cup was drained. But still she sat, clenching it between her hands, trying to drag the strength up from somewhere to think about someone she hadn't thought of in a very long time. Grace, the woman she'd thought her best friend. A great friend she'd turned out to be leaving town at a time when she'd needed her the most – the weekend Alys disappeared. She hadn't even bothered to get in touch since. But now she was back.

Izzy frowned, trying to remember but suddenly the only thing she could think about was the glaring fact that Grace had chosen to leave the area at the same time Charlie had taken Alys. Now it seemed a little too convenient and, if she hadn't been on fistfuls of tranquilisers at the time, surely, she'd have forced the police to investigate this aspect of the case further.

She didn't know how long she sat, staring into the past. Time was irrelevant to someone like her. Time was irrelevant to someone who'd had the whole world in the palm of her hand only to lose it in an instant. She didn't know what pulled her out of her fugue. A rattle of cups? The door being pushed? The happy family of two-plus-two at the next table making more noise than sense?

In a spurt of energy, she picked up her scarf and wrapped it loosely around her neck, a quick look at her watch confirming that she'd spent far too long thinking about the past. She couldn't do happy families, not now. Now she had to leave, if only to catch the last train home. Spending the night in Swansea weighed down with shopping was the very last thing she wanted to face just before Christmas.

The local supermarket was packed, but it was always going to be at this time of the evening. Her mind was still buzzing with thoughts of Grace but she clamped them down under an iron lid. She would think about her but not now. Not here. Not yet. She'd get all her jobs out of the way before letting her creep back inside.

Head down, she avoided anyone and everyone. She wanted to buy what she needed before journeying home and slamming the door. Only then would she allow her thoughts to drift back into the past.

'Hello Izzy, long time no see.'

She looked up into the face of DI Rhys Walker, brother of Rebecca, an old friend from her school days, and the lead detective in the search for Alys. St David's wasn't the largest place in the world and she was always bumping into people she knew but not in Rhys's case. He was right when he said he hadn't seen her around but that was only because she'd managed to avoid him by ducking into whichever bar, shop or restaurant she'd happened to be standing outside.

She'd dealt with Rhys. She'd spent what felt like a lifetime holed up in Swansea Police Station going over the case. It was just her luck that he'd decided to commute when he'd been promoted rather than move out of St David's altogether. Every time she caught a glimpse of his burly frame around town, she had to shove her heart back down her throat with a thump. She'd had no choice but to deal with him then but now? Now she chose to avoid him and, if it hadn't been for spotting Grace, she'd have managed to avoid him again.

It wasn't that he was bad-looking, far from it. He wasn't that tall, probably five-ten but his well-muscled, powerful build made up for what he lacked in height. His dark brown hair used to be collar-length before police regulations dictated the short crop he was currently sporting. All in all, he was your boy-next-door type. A boy she'd grown up with through the years, despite him being six years older. They'd gone to the same school. They'd frequented the same cinemas and social venues. But he was a copper, only that.

She hopped from one foot to the other, her gaze flicking from her trolley to his and back again before landing on his ringless left hand. The last time she'd spoken to him he'd been single. But, by the state of his trolley, nearly overflowing with Christmas cheer, there was now bound to be a bride and a bundle of babies to complete his happiness. Well, bully for him. However, instead of passing the time of day, all she wanted was to hide under her duvet and think about the implications of seeing Grace again because, despite her misgivings, she was now one hundred per cent sure it was her.

He wasn't going anywhere. She could see it in the way his gaze drilled down through layers of skin, flesh and bone right to her heart, if indeed she still had that organ thumping inside her chest.

His hand fastened around the wire rim of her trolley before leaning in to inspect the contents. 'Not having turkey and all the trimmings?' he said, a frown replacing his smile.

Her gaze followed his and she saw what he saw: four rolls of

9

wrapping paper nudged up beside two bottles of plonk and one of whiskey, all topped off with a ready meal and a tub of chocolate ice cream. It was a lonely basket for a lonely woman, and it was also none of his bloody business.

'Yes, well. I'm not home for Christmas.'

'No? Where are you off to then?' His smile was back and she remembered again just what a nice bloke he was. 'I hope it's somewhere exciting?'

'Hardly! Only to my parents. And you? Do you have an exciting time planned?'

'Not really, although I do have Christmas off for a change.'

She held his gaze for a second before turning her attention back to the contents of his trolley and the large bag of Maris Pipers on top. Meeting him hadn't been as bad as she'd feared and the questions far less intrusive. But that wasn't surprising being as they were standing next to an old woman in a purple hat as she picked over the sprouts with a slow deliberation. She knew she should bat back a question about what he was up to with his full trolley. He certainly wasn't the only solitary man wandering around with a bemused look on his face while they searched for the cranberry sauce, but he was the only one she didn't want to get drawn into a conversation with. There was no way she was going to continue talking about turkey and the like. In truth, she didn't give a damn where he was spending his Christmas or with whom. She didn't give a damn whether he was planning to gorge himself silly on turkey or a plate of nut-roast with deep-fried falafel on the side. She just didn't care.

They'd given up. They'd given up searching after the first few weeks, but it wasn't something she'd ever be able to do. Charlie had stolen her child and then had the arrogance to post a card through her letterbox boasting what he'd done. What kind of man would be so cruel? Certainly not the kindly man hovering in front of her. She felt rejuvenated suddenly. Seeing Grace had rejuvenated her and changed something. Where before she'd been

10

prepared to let it ride, now she couldn't. For the first time in what felt like a very long time she was going to get off her behind and do something. The only question was what.

Her gaze shifted back to his face, an idea hovering. Should she tell him about seeing Grace in Swansea? Would he be interested after all this time? And finally, what good would it do? Before common sense interfered and stopped her, she leant forward, lowering her voice to a thin whisper.

'Actually, I'm pleased I've bumped into you. There's something I need to tell you.'

Chapter 2

Gaby
Tuesday 24 December, 11.50 a.m. Swansea Police Station

'You wanted to see me, Guv?'

'Ah, yes, DI Walker, come in and shut the door,' DCI Brazil-North said, lifting a hand and waving it in the direction of the only spare chair.

Rhys threw a brief smile in Gaby's direction before taking a seat and crossing his legs at the ankles.

So, this is my new boss. Not bad looking if you like square, rugby types … There are cogs there, many and complex – it would be foolish to underestimate him. Gaby frowned at the thought before returning her attention back to the woman behind the desk.

The DCI placed her pen down before lifting her head, her face an expressionless mask. 'I know it's Christmas Eve but I've asked DC Darin to drop in so I can introduce you. She'll be joining us from the Cardiff office in a couple of days and, with her arrival, I think a little reshuffle is in order. After the sterling effort you made inducting DC Abraham, I've decided to reward you with a new partner.' She leant forward, her elbows on the desk, her eyes flint. 'I don't want to hear a murmur of negativity towards our latest officer and I will hold you personally responsible if I do.' Her smile widened briefly to include Gaby. 'I hope you'll be very happy with us, DC Darin. The DI will keep a close eye and ensure you receive a warm welcome from *all* members of the team.

Leaning back in her chair, she picked up her pen, again focusing on the document in front of her.

'Ma'am, if I could have a brief word in private?'

There was an awkward silence where Gaby took to examining her nails, her attention now on the man at her side and what he was about to say. Surely he wouldn't refuse to mentor her? But after what had happened in Cardiff, she wouldn't put anything past her esteemed fellow colleagues. At least in the beginning they'd been welcoming. It was only later when they realised she wouldn't be party to a cover-up that they'd turned nasty. It had taken strength of character and a bucketload of chocolate for her to deflect the bullet they'd carved with her name, rank and number. The strength of character remained. Gaby sat and waited, the silence lengthening, her clear nail polish not bright enough to hold her gaze for more than about five seconds.

'An officer of your experience should know that there are no secrets between partners. Say your piece. I'm sure DC Darin will keep your confidence,' DCI Brazil-North finally replied, still staring down at the document in front of her.

'It's about the Baby Grant case, ma'am.'

'Oh God, really?' She placed her pen down carefully before raising her head. 'This had better be good, Walker. The force spent millions the first time round scouring the globe and they didn't come up with anything other than censure from the public and politicians alike. You know as well as I do that the possibility of her still being alive is non-existent?'

'That's as may be, ma'am. But I bumped into the mother in the supermarket yesterday – she's adamant she's in possession of new evidence that will make a huge difference to the case.'

'I'd forgotten that you still live in St David's – a hell of a trek to work and back.'

'But great to get away from it all.'

'Mmm. So, what new evidence?'

'Grace Madden seems to have appeared back on the scene. Miss Grant's convinced of it. It was actually quite sad seeing her like that with her meal for one,' he said with a little shake of his head. 'She can't move on with her life until she gets some news, one way or the other. You might remember that both the baby and boyfriend disappeared around the same time as the friend – it was all highly suspicious.'

'I know all that.' Her tone was as glacial as her look. 'I also know to the pound just how much it cost the branch in terms of man hours searching for Madden and the boyfriend. So, she's turned up, has she?' She picked up her pen and scribbled something in the margin of her notebook.

'Well, not quite but the mother seems to think that she spotted her yesterday.'

'I don't need to hear any more, Rhys. There's not a lot we can do until after all the festivities are over. When you get back tell the team to have a sniff around but don't spend long on it and be discreet. The very last thing we want is to alert the media. It was like a circus last time.'

Chapter 3

Izzy
Wednesday 25 December, 2.27 p.m. St David's

Izzy's parents had prepared enough food to feed an army and not the five adults and two children present. In the old days she would have been more than happy to clear her plate but that was before food had toppled off her list of things that were important. Now, a tightening waistband meant she placed her knife and fork neatly in the centre of her plate before finishing her meal. Her sister and brother-in-law, Bethan and Oscar, were still grazing and, with every additional sausage wrapped in bacon and extra spud, they were each getting a nod of approval but she couldn't change back into the girl she once was no matter how much her mother wished it.

She pushed her chair back, unable to stand it any longer, her mind on Grace and the glimpse she'd caught of her darting out of the Royal Arcade and into the waiting taxi along St Mary's Street. All she wanted was some peace to think it through but that wasn't going to happen anytime soon.

Her eyes flicked between Mam, Dad and the kids. 'Anyone for coffee or is it tea all round, as usual?' she said, trying to push the day forward. There was still pudding to get through: brandy custard to accompany the Christmas pudding for the adults and gooey chocolate cake for the boys.

She headed into the kitchen and filled the kettle before starting on the saucepans, her gaze drawn to the window and the view out across St David's Head and the sea beyond. While she loved her family, these long, drawn out parties were always a chore and this one seemed more of a chore than usual. She hadn't slept a wink since returning from Swansea and five minutes alone, even if it meant starting on the pile of washing up, was all she needed. But, with the sound of the door opening behind her, she wasn't even going to be allowed that.

'Where did you go to make that tea then? China?' Bethan said, placing a pile of crockery on the table before starting to scrape plates into the food waste bin.

'It's just coming. You know Mam likes it strong enough to strip the hairs off Dad's chest.' Izzy caught her sister's eye, trying and failing to dampen down the fit of giggles at the thought of their dad, who had only a few strands of grey left on his scalp, let alone on his chest.

Bethan lifted a clean tea towel from the hook to the left of the sink and started to dry a glass. 'So, how are you really doing, sis?'

'Oh, the usual. You know.'

'No, I don't know, not really! I don't know how you manage to get out of bed in the morning or even sleep at night. If something like that had happened to either Gareth or Dylan, I think I'd have—' She stopped suddenly, her cheeks pale, confusion and embarrassment stamped across her face in equal measures.

Izzy stared at her for a moment, memories of the time she most wanted to forget tumbling across her mind: the suicide attempt. It took her almost a year to shake off both the depression and the psychiatrists, not to mention the constant attention from her parents checking to see if she was all right. But the truth, a truth she'd never admitted to anyone, was that swallowing

16

those sleeping tablets was only a half-hearted attempt. It was just a cry for help. Did they honestly think she wouldn't have done it if she'd really meant to? Did they think she'd have picked up the phone when they'd made their nightly call if she hadn't wanted to be saved? Dying would have been an easy but unfulfilling outcome. She still needed to know what had happened to her daughter.

'Come on. If you carry on you'll have us both in tears,' she said, managing a small smile. 'Let's leave Oscar and the parents to fend for themselves for a while. It's *James Bond* on the TV and I must have seen it a million times already. What we need is a romp on the beach with the dogs. The kids are going square-eyed in front of their iPads. You're going to rue the day you ever agreed to buy them.'

Porthclais beach was one of their favourite haunts as youngsters. It was low tide and the dogs raced through puddles with their tongues out and tails wagging. They'd even brought a football and, with the boys happily playing an impromptu game, Izzy and Bethan sat on the end of the harbour wall, watching the antics unfold when the dogs finally discovered there was a ball game underway and no one had invited them to play.

Gazing at the boys, they started a rambling conversation about how Mam and Dad were faring now that the chip shop was a distant memory.

'They still worry about you, you know. It's all very well spending all your time working,' said Bethan.

'I don't view spinning wool as really working and, as for knitting – it's how I relax.'

'You know what I mean. Setting up your own cottage industry is admirable, and we couldn't be prouder of the way you've managed to create a niche for your handmade knits. But you can't blame Mam and Dad for wanting to see you settled with a man at your side and perhaps another—'

17

Izzy grabbed her hand, stemming her flow of words. Her sister meant well. They all meant well. But she didn't want another child. Children weren't like cars that could be traded in for a newer model. There was nothing wrong with Alys. She was the most perfect baby in the world and all Izzy wanted was for her to be back where she belonged. She couldn't give a toss about what happened to Charlie. Over the years she'd come to realise that even when he was at his most romantic, there'd always been a barrier when he'd tried to inveigle his way into her heart. The bullies had done a great job of fine-tuning her lack of self-confidence. Their taunts had made it impossible for her to believe that a good-looking bloke like Charlie could just suddenly drop at her feet. It was only after Alys's disappearance that she realised just how right she'd been.

'Shush, Bethan. You know that's not going to happen.' She managed a laugh. 'I'm far too busy with the business to be worried about another man and anyway, one Charlie in my life is more than enough, thank you very much.'

'But what about—'

'I'm not missing out,' she said firmly. 'I have you batting for me and the most amazing pair of nephews.' Her eyes were now on the football tug-of-war between Gareth and Arthur, the older of the two dogs.

'Oh, I nearly forgot. I bumped into Rebecca last week.'

'Really?' Izzy managed to suppress a groan, knowing only too well that any comment made about her best friend would lead straight to Rhys. Bethan just wouldn't let it rest.

'She was with her brother. He asked after you, by the way. I always knew he had a soft spot for you and this just proves it.'

'Really?' she repeated, squashing her temper back down where it belonged. She wasn't interested in Rhys like that and, after all that had happened, he was the very last man she'd look at. But how did she go about telling her well-meaning sister?

She looked up from where she'd been staring at her boots and caught the beam on her sister's face. 'What?'

'You and Rhys Walker. I remember the way you used to look at him when he was a bobby round St David's. And the way he used to return that look, come to that.'

'That was a very long time ago. I'll admit I used to think he was cute in that uniform but he's with someone now and anyway, even if he wasn't, I'm not interested.'

Bethan pulled a frown. 'Rebecca never mentioned it and he certainly didn't look married.'

'Ha, why do you automatically assume that he's married and, even if he was, it's not as if he's going to wear a *do not touch* label; not all men wear wedding rings.'

'Oh, you know what I mean. I always hoped you'd get together.'

'You're as bad as Mam. I don't need a man in my life and, if I did, it wouldn't be someone like him. He really is the eponymous Mr Boring.' She stood and whistled for the dogs. 'Come on, let's get the boys home. I hope you've worked up an appetite for supper.'

'Do you have to go back so early? I thought we'd get to spend most of the day together,' Mam said with a scowl. 'And what your dad and I are going to do with all this turkey, I don't know.'

'I'm sorry. But I still have a couple of orders to finish in time for New Year's Eve and I'm behind as it is. And there's Bucket to consider too,' she said, slinging her bag across her shoulder. 'The neighbours are very good but you know what he's like around strangers. What about I come round during the week for one of your "Turkish curries"? But no chips on the side like last time, mind.'

Izzy placed her pile of presents in the boot before turning and enveloping her parents in deep hugs. The van, a vintage VW camper complete with flower motifs, was a recent but necessary addition. The Mini disappeared on the same morning as Charlie and Alys and, just like them, it had never turned up, despite a lengthy search. She had great hopes that one day it would appear in the small ads but there hadn't been even one reported sighting since that fateful morning when he'd backed out of the driveway.

The house felt cold and unloved after a night away. She glanced at the wood-burner and the pile of logs stacked in the corner, but she was far too wound up to even strike a match. Instead, she left her coat on and wandered into the kitchen to flick on the kettle. There was no sign of her snow-white moggy, Bucket. But staying out late was nothing unusual. The fields behind the cottage were alive with all sorts of interesting creatures to keep him occupied, many of which he saw fit to drag through the cat-flap whatever the time. He'd appear when he was ready with a sharp meow and a fine line in ignoring the hand that fed him.

Mug in hand, she picked up her laptop from the table and carried it across to the sofa. If she was honest, the reason for not staying later at her parents had been nothing to do with business. No one would expect her to read her emails on a bank holiday and, if she'd been that desperate, she could have always checked her orders on her phone, despite her dad's aversion to any and all things technological. He'd put a blanket-ban on the use of mobiles in the house except for the making and receiving of calls. After the initial annoyance and anxiety of not being able to check her device, it was actually a welcome relief to keep it in the bottom of her bag. No, the real reason she'd headed off early was because of Grace. Ever since seeing her, memories of their friendship had been uppermost in her mind.

Her fingers wandered over the keyboard, typing in Grace's name – something she should have done years ago but she hadn't been in a fit state at the time. With a missing boyfriend and baby she had far too much to think about, and it wasn't as if a nine months' pregnant woman could be tied up in Alys's disappearance.

Izzy lifted her hand to her forehead, the start of a headache looming. Memories from that time were hazy but she'd just assumed that Grace had just upped and left. That it was something to do with her husband, Geraint Madden, a man she'd never met. He must have returned and whisked her away. People lost touch all the time and she could be forgiven in not following it up what with everything else going on. Grace had got tucked away in the back of her mind and she'd never bothered to pull her out again.

Her first name, Grace, wasn't that unusual – an old-fashioned name but one that had been growing steadily in popularity. They'd even had one in her class at school. But despite that, she was confident she'd be able to find her online. Most people had an internet presence of some sort.

Izzy spent the next half hour trawling through Google, her tea growing cold by her side. But even though she found enough Graces to fill a football stadium, none of them seemed to be the right one. With the thought of her still lingering she snapped the laptop shut and headed back into the kitchen just in time to hear the cat flap rattle. Crouching down, she filled Bucket's dish with his favourite cat food before switching the kettle on again and reaching for a camomile tea bag. There was also her mother's homemade Christmas cake beckoning to her from the shelf and, before she knew it, she'd cut herself a large slice.

She dropped her spoon in the sink before carrying her mug and plate back into the lounge, Bucket trailing her heels. The evening wasn't going as she'd planned. She thought by now she'd have a telephone number or a place of work …

There were jobs she could have been getting on with like packing up the latest orders ready for posting to America. She also needed to add to her pile of felt for more berets. But she wasn't in the mood for any of it. Seeing Grace had unsettled her, and she didn't know why. Common sense told her she should just let it go, that she should let her go. She obviously didn't want to be found or she'd have signed up to Facebook. But, for some reason, Izzy's stubborn streak wasn't letting common sense have a look in. She was of a mind to carry on with her search.

Bucket disturbed her thoughts by jumping up on her knee, his loud purr a comfort, and her thoughts shifted away from Grace and to the question that had been lingering ever since that day in Swansea. Ever since that glimpse of black hair framing her pale face.

Had she given up too quickly on her daughter? She'd never forgotten her. She was always there. The girl she could see out of the corner of her eye. The girl being hoisted into the shopping trolley, a stuffed tiger clenched between chubby fingers. Any girl with blonde hair and dark blue eyes got a second look even though she knew she wouldn't be able to recognise her now. Eyes changed colour. Hair darkened. Features altered. She wouldn't recognise her even if she was standing next to her.

She rubbed Bucket behind his ears, dipping her mind into the past. She'd carried on actively searching for Alys throughout that first year. It was all about Alys, never Charlie. She couldn't bear to hear his name let alone remember the good times they'd had together. It was all about finding her child. She'd hated him then and she still hated him for what he'd done to her, for what he was still doing. The only time she'd had any feeling without hatred at its heart, was the day she took the bus into Fishguard to track down his mother and stepfather. Then she'd felt sympathy for him and only then. When he'd refused to talk about his reasons for leaving home she'd been too busy with her own life to question him. But one look at the rundown semi and the foul-mouthed pair who called themselves his parents and everything made sense. She stayed long enough to find out that he hadn't taken his passport before hurrying away to catch the next bus home.

It felt as if she'd been treading water those first twelve months, neither moving forwards or back. But the stress and strain eventually took their toll and, after the incident with the sleeping pills, she'd had to come to a decision, the hardest decision she'd ever had to make: her daughter or her? If she carried on with her obsession she'd end up, if not dead then in some mental institution. So, she stopped haranguing the police on a daily basis. She stopped contacting them at all. Instead, she joined a local knitting group and soon the day-to-day act of living inured her to any thoughts other than the most superficial.

The temperature plummeted as late afternoon slipped into evening. Izzy finally put a light to the stove before sitting back on her heels, her eyes mesmerised by the flames catching the scrunched-up newspaper and stretching out towards the kindling, her thoughts continuing into the past …

Chapter 4

Izzy
Five years ago

August must surely be the worst of months in which to find yourself pregnant.

She laughed at the thought. It wasn't as if she'd just opened her eyes to being five months into this mistake of all mistakes. It wasn't as if she hadn't slept with Charlie, knowing full well she was taking a huge risk. It wasn't as if she didn't know the facts of life. No, not those – the other facts. The fact that if a bad thing was going to befall anyone around here it was always going to befall her. Before she'd left school all her classmates had been messing about with boys and had never gotten caught, which in a way had led her into a false sense of security. After all, as the least popular girl around, the likelihood of anyone asking her back to their place was zero. And yet, within six months, she was the one explaining to her parents what a mess she'd made of things.

She was hot, sweaty and, with four months left to run, she could only expect more of the same. Picking up her bag, she headed for the car, all the time muttering at the injustice of it all.

He gets to have a Saturday morning lie-in with a cup of tea brought to him in bed, more fool me, while I get to drive to the church hall on the other side of St David's for the first of my ante-natal sessions. You would have thought he'd have wanted to accompany me like any other expectant father ... that's the biggest joke of all.

She remembered his words. 'But, Izzy, why did you have to make it Saturday? And anyway, I'll be the only man there.' He'd given her one of his little-boy-lost looks, the same one that had first attracted her to him when their eyes had met across a crowded room.

Yeah, corny as hell – it would have been romantic except that the room was the local chippy and she was the one serving him. If she'd had more sense she'd have realised what he was really after: extra fries and, as he'd just missed his last bus, a bed for the night. She should have known it was too good to be true. Who in their right mind chatted up the chip shop owner's daughter after she'd spent four hours behind the deep-fat-fryer? She could almost taste the grease and, truth be told, the very last thing she was looking for was a man unless he came with a hot shower and a foot massage. But he came in just before closing and one look into his deep blue eyes and they both got a lot more than they'd bargained for, her hand instinctively reaching for the excess flesh hanging over the top of her leggings.

Now here she was, trying to squeeze into a parking space, thankful for once that she was the proud owner of a clapped-out Mini with over 100,000 miles on the clock and not some people carrier. But getting out was more awkward. Her waist had exploded over recent weeks but that was hardly surprising given her job. The problem with working in a chip shop was that she was always hungry. It never used to matter before she'd fallen pregnant. She'd eaten what she wanted and had never gained even an ounce – now she was plain fat. She was just thankful that Charlie had stayed around for as long as he had. He wasn't perfect but then neither was she.

Izzy pulled a grimace at the sight of the four other women present, three of whom were accompanied by their partners. She'd always hated walking into a room by herself and, as she was the last one to arrive, she was forced to take a chair by the type of person she usually avoided. She scanned the woman's perfect hair and perfect make-up, all set off by a cutesy designer maternity dress sprinkled with little white daisies. She'd even managed to cope with heels but then her ankles and feet were as nature intended and not swollen lumps of salami more suited to the deli counter at the local supermarket.

After a talk on healthy eating and tips on how to continue exercising, Carys, the midwife, called a short break and within minutes the three couples were chatting like old friends.

'Hi, I'm Grace, pleased to meet you.'

Izzy looked up, surprised that anyone was bothering to speak to her, let alone the perfect woman sitting next to her.

'Izzy and likewise,' she said, offering a smile.

'So, is this your first then?'

'Yes, and probably my last at this rate.'

'Whys that?' Her heavily pencilled eyebrows swept upwards.

'Oh, you don't want to hear all about my troubles. What about you?'

Grace held out her left hand, displaying a shiny, plain gold band on her ring finger. 'I've only just moved to the area. My husband is sorting out the sale of our house and then he'll be joining me,' she said with a smile. 'What about a spot of lunch after we've finished – you can tell me all about living in St David's?'

The choice wasn't a difficult one. Lunch with Grace or popping into the chip shop and being roped into helping, despite it being her day off.

'You were telling me about why this might be your only child?' Grace said, sitting back in her chair and placing her hands protectively over her small baby bump.

'It wasn't planned or anything. I'm lucky he stayed around – it wasn't meant to be more than a one-night stand.'

'How exciting. He must really love you if he's prepared to start a family straight away.'

'Mmm, I don't know about that.' Izzy placed her half-finished burger back on her plate, trying to ignore the remainder of the chips. Charlie was far from perfect, unlike Grace's husband, Geraint, a corporate lawyer. But she decided not to spoil Grace's dreams of a happy-ever-after because that's the one thing her life wasn't. With Charlie still out of work, life was a daily struggle with only one wage coming in and adding a baby to the mix was going to be tougher still. She had no idea why he stayed but if she continued treating him the way she did, he'd leave. Then what would she do? She'd be left alone with a baby to look after.

'You're so lucky,' Grace continued. 'It took me ages to get pregnant and all you had to do was look at a bloke and your ovaries started twitching.'

'Yeah, well, they can twitch all they like. After this bundle of joy is born, I'm going on a strict diet and on the pill. Charlie won't recognise me,' Izzy added, reaching for another chip.

'I'm sure he loves you just the way you are,' Grace said, lifting her bag onto her lap and pulling out her purse. 'How about a coffee at my place? It's so much better than the instant they have on the menu. I don't mind having to forgo wine, but decent coffee is a must.'

Grace's apartment, along New Street, was a temporary measure until her husband could join her. The coffee table in her plain white lounge was testament to that, littered as it was with details of dream farmhouses in and around the Pembrokeshire area.

'I'll bet you're all organised for the birth,' Grace said, handing her a mug of coffee before pushing a plate of chocolate biscuits in Izzy's direction.

'Well, we've had the nursery painted and bought a few outfits but, apart from that …' She scrolled through the photos on her phone to the one of the nursery before handing it to her.

'Lovely colour, yellow.' Grace went to hand it back only to pause. 'Is there one of Charlie on here?'

'There's one of him paddling,' Izzy said, taking the phone back to search for the right photo.

Up until a few weeks ago she'd always joined him on his daily trip to the beach but that was out of the question now. Sunbathing in a size twelve swimsuit was totally different to the size she'd exploded to. Now she just rolled over in bed when she heard the door close behind him on his way out for a morning swim or whatever it was he got up to. He said he was trying to get a job and she'd like to believe him. A job would make all the difference and not just because of the money. He was drifting and with nothing to focus his attention on apart from her, she was afraid he'd soon realise that he could do an awful lot better.

'Oh, not bad,' Grace said, interrupting her thoughts, her eyes on his toned abs and flat stomach. 'There's something a little Ryan Gosling about him, especially around the eyes. Not a patch on my Geraint, of course.' Her attention shifted to the framed black-and-white photograph above the mantelpiece. 'But then again, beauty is in the eye of the beholder as they say. Help yourself to a biscuit.' She stretched out her forefinger and tapped on the edge of the plate.

'I really shouldn't. I'm too fat as it is.'

'Nonsense. It's important to eat properly in these last few months. Anyway, you'll lose it when the baby's born, all that running about.'

'I'm not so sure. I can't seem to stop eating since I got caught.'

'I wouldn't worry too much – some men prefer bigger girls.'

'How can he love a blob like me?' Izzy sniffed, rubbing the back of her hand across her cheeks. 'As soon as the baby is born and the sleepless nights kick in, he'll up and leave for something slimmer and prettier and there's nothing I can do to stop him.

He'll dump me and I'll end up a single mum on benefits – another social statistic without two pennies to rub together.' She blushed scarlet, not quite believing she'd told someone she'd only just met all that but, somehow it felt right.

'I'm sure it's not as bad as all that. You're a very pretty girl, you know. A bit of make-up and toning after the baby is born and you'll be fine. More than fine. And if Charlie does stray it's probably not the end of the world,' Grace said, her face hardening. 'He obviously doesn't deserve you. There's nothing worse than being dependent on one man for everything. If anything happened to Geraint, God forbid, I'd be upset for a while, but I'd soon find someone else to fill the gap in my bed as well as my heart.'

Chapter 5

Gaby
Friday 27 December, 8.45 a.m. Swansea Police Station

'DI Walker, if you have a minute. I'd like a word about the Grant case,' Gaby said, as soon as she spotted him heading towards the coffee pot in the squad room.

'Certainly, let's go into one of the interview rooms. The downside of an open-plan office.'

Arriving for the first day in a new job straight after Christmas had to be the worst possible of starts. She'd only made it back to her flat late last night after a morning travelling back from Liverpool. In fact, it would have been better all round for everyone if she'd given Christmas a miss but that was something her mother would never have allowed. She might be the largest of disappointments but her presence was still demanded in the family home despite her mother's thin mouth and harsh words.

She felt sick with apprehension. This was meant to be a new start, another one, and yet she was about to do the one thing she'd promised she wouldn't. She was about to interfere.

'Call me Rhys, just not when the guv is in earshot. What is it, er – Gaby? Unusual name, by the way.'

'I'll take that as a compliment,' she said with a smile. 'It's short for Gabriella, after my Italian grandmother.'

'Indeed. Well, Gabriella Darin, what nugget of wisdom do you have to impart?'

He pushed the door open and gestured for her to enter first. She could feel his gaze wandering over her plain grey jacket and skirt and down to her feet, laced into sensible low-heeled shoes and she tried not to show that she'd noticed. Instead, she gritted her teeth and bit back a snappy comment. This was her new boss after all and it would serve her well if, just for once, she managed to keep her mouth shut.

'Take a seat, Gaby.' Rhys pulled out a chair and waited until she'd sat down.

'Well, sir – Rhys. When I heard you speaking with the boss about the Grant case, I decided to look it up and—'

'And solve what's had the whole of the force, from John O'Groats to Land's End, stumped for years?' he said, his voice dry.

She parked her face in neutral before replying. 'It's not that.' She chose her next words carefully. 'Why did no one think to suspect the mother? Surely she has to be the prime suspect?'

'Simply because she didn't do it.'

'But how could you know that? She had the best motive after all.'

'And that motive was?'

'Why, jealousy, of course,' she said, on a roll. 'She finds out her boyfriend, a boyfriend she's only been with a few months, has been bonking her best friend, leaving her all alone to cope with a newborn.'

His eyes wavered, drifting down to the empty table and she just knew he was going to palm her off with some sort of hogwash drivel. She pressed her lips together and waited, her fingers curling into her palms.

'Look, I appreciate your enthusiasm and all that but you weren't on the case from day one. You didn't have to witness the loss of hope on her face when we turned up at her door. You weren't involved in the hours upon hours of legwork as we followed up on every lead, however tenuous. We turned over every stone within a ten-mile radius and didn't find even one measly clue as to their whereabouts. He's abroad by now, probably in some South American country where we'll never find them.'

'Or dead?'

He paused, his eyes trained on the wall behind her head, before he brought his gaze back to meet hers. 'Yes, of course. Or dead. I'm surprised you opted for jealousy as the motive, Gaby. Why not something juicy, like a crime of passion?'

She ignored that. After all, the odds were she'd read the same crime psychology books as him. There was a wealth of reasons why people went on to commit murder: passion, greed, revenge, jealousy, anger. In this type of case, jealousy was statistically the most likely, something he would have known, so any reply on her part was irrelevant.

'What about the card then?'

He steepled his fingers under his chin. 'You have been busy. What do you know about the card … er … Gaby?'

'She found it thrust under her door that first day – the card that engineered one of the largest police hunts Wales has seen in years, a police hunt that turned up zilch.' She settled back in the chair, her legs tucked underneath, her expression expectant.

'Look, you're new here and keen as they come but I know she didn't do it. Parental abduction is such a heinous crime but for it to happen to a newborn was virtually unheard of. It's still unheard of. We carried out the investigation by the book. No.' He brushed his hand across his face, presumably marshalling his thoughts. 'We had no book to follow. We wrote the book on parental abduction of a newborn. We covered every angle …'

He paused for breath. 'Now that we have Grace Madden back on the scene we're going to bloody well search for her until we find her. We tried the last time and failed.' He stared into the distance a moment, a frown appearing. 'We couldn't even find the husband and Geraint Madden is a whole lot more unusual a name than Grace. When we've found them we'll have another think. Detective work is a little like being given a jigsaw puzzle for Christmas only to find that, when you open the box, the manufacturer has forgotten to give you any of the pieces. The clues drop out of the sky in a random snow-shower. There's no pattern. No uniformity. Up until now we've had nothing to go on other than the most valuable commodity of all. A copper's instinct.'

She watched him push himself up from the chair and shove his car keys in his pocket. Suddenly she was disappointed in him. She didn't know why.

'Come on. I'll introduce you to the team.' He hesitated, his eyes locking with hers and she could almost see the dark of his pupil dilating under her gaze. 'I'm not going to beat around any bushes, Gaby. Life isn't perfect, and a squad room is less perfect than most places. I can't fight your battles for you. But whatever happens outside of this room, do me two favours; keep your chin up and keep me informed.'

'Morning everyone. This is DC Gabriella Darin, newly transferred from Swansea. I'm sure you'll all wish her a great big Welsh welcome,' Rhys said, strolling to the front of the room to join DCI Brazil-North.

The squad room was crowded but then it was 9 a.m. after a two-day break. Everyone was scrambling around for a place to sit before the morning briefing, but no one paused to even look in her direction let alone offer her a smile. She scanned the sea of faces in their various forms. These were her colleagues, the ones meant to watch her back. These were the people she was meant to trust with her life. If they were anything like the lot in Cardiff she wasn't even going to be able to trust them with a smile. Instead, she bit down hard on her lower lip, the dull, metallic taste of blood a welcome distraction. She'd thought Cardiff was bad, but they'd liked her at the start. It was only after, when they'd found out about— she shook her head. Cardiff was in her past and that was where she intended to keep it.

Her gaze slid to the far corner and the shy smile focused in her direction, and she took it in the same way a drowning man gasps for breath. Squaring her shoulders, she managed to catch the woman's eye, just to confirm that the smile was meant for her, before crossing the room, well aware of all eyes following her progress.

'Hey.'

'Hey back. I'm Amy, Amy Potter, the family liaison officer. Pull up a chair and take the weight off.'

'Thanks, everyone calls me Gaby,' she said, looking at the slim, youthful blonde before quickly twisting in her chair to check out the other members of the team.

There were twelve in total, mostly men and all doing a fair job at not looking her in the eye. She was good at her job, bloody good, something they'd learn the hard way.

Amy leant forward, placing a hand on her arm. 'Don't mind this lot of Neanderthals. They'll come around after they've gotten used to you.' She pulled her hand back, her eyes now facing front, before whispering under her breath. 'Shush. Brazil-North doesn't take any prisoners.'

'When you're quite ready, DS Potter, DI Walker would like to update you on the Grant case.'

A collective groan spread across the room only to stop abruptly at the sound of the DCI banging the heel of her hand against the table.

'I know we've been here before, many times. But there's a new development. Over to you, Rhys.'

His gaze wandered over each and every one of them before finally starting to speak, his brow wrinkled. 'There's been a new sighting of Grace Madden. It's not likely that a nine months' pregnant woman would have been involved but there are questions that still need to be answered. We need to discover why she disappeared so soon after Charlie Dawson abducted Baby Grant. You must admit it's all a bit too convenient. So I'd like to hear some ideas as to why Madden should suddenly turn up in Swansea?'

'What about shopping?' a large man standing at the back shouted, causing the room to erupt into laughter.

'Very funny, Bill. To buy what exactly? If you don't fancy a trip to the Quadrant Shopping Centre then I suggest you shut it.' He scanned the room again before continuing, 'I'm as fed up as you are that, after five years, we're still no further forward in knowing what happened to the pair of them. So, why after so long would the friend suddenly appear on the scene or is it a harmless coincidence? There's always been that unanswered question of whether Dawson was having an affair and if so, who with? It's something we've been unable to either prove or otherwise. And what about Madden's child? He or she'd be about the same age as Alys Grant by now.'

'So, that's school age. I'll do a quick trawl of the local schools and nurseries to see if anything gets spat out,' Bill said, probably in an effort to reprieve himself.

'Good idea. We don't have the resources to spend too much time on this so just carry on with what you're doing for now. We'll catch up on Monday unless there's any further developments.' He turned away, making for the door, tilting his head in Gaby's direction.

'Good luck,' Amy whispered into her ear. 'He looks in a mood. We always thought he had a thing for the mother – this won't help.'

Gaby nodded her head before threading her way through the chairs, her eyes focused on the door and the back of his broad shoulders.

So he had a thing for Isabelle Grant, did he? Good to know and perhaps useful to the investigation.

She put on a sudden burst of speed to catch him up, her mind carefully shelving that nugget of information for when she had more time to examine it. Her instinct was telling her if they found Grace Madden, Charlie and Alys would be close behind.

Chapter 6

Izzy
Friday 27 December, 9.45 a.m. Abereiddy

Izzy couldn't settle. There was work to be done. Her website to update and orders to get ready. But instead of entering her workroom she sat in the lounge in front of the fire with her cat on her lap, reluctant to do any of the jobs mounting up. Grace Madden was the key to the mess that was her life. The only problem was she didn't know what to do about it. She'd passed it on to Rhys but she knew from experience that finding her wouldn't be a priority for the police. If they couldn't find her five years ago the trail would be stone cold by now.

It took Bucket jumping down to interrupt where her thoughts were taking her, his deep-amber, unblinking glare trained on her face. Reaching down a hand she dragged it across his back, relishing in the soft silkiness of his fur. Sometimes it felt as if he was her only friend. He was certainly her most loyal. She'd found him hiding in an old bucket within weeks of losing Alys. In those dark days she'd roamed the countryside searching for clues, whatever the weather, and it was like an omen finding him curled up, covered in fleas. He was battle-scarred too with a torn ear and scratched face - who knew what kind of life he'd had to endure before she happened upon him. They were alike, muddling through from day to day. His needs were simple. Plain food and warmth and for that she got more purrs than she could cope with and a warm body to tuck up to at night.

'All right, boy, I'm coming.' She followed him into the kitchen and to where he was now staring into his bowl. It was like a personal affront for him to find his food bowl empty. She still couldn't face the thought of cooking a meal and even had to hold her nose to prevent the smell of fish turning her stomach. Food didn't interest her in the same way it had during her pregnancy. Her thoughts returned to the size she'd once exploded to – there was nothing like a heavy dose of tragedy to make the pounds slip away. She was thinner now than she'd ever been but no happier. She used to think that the width of her waist and the breadth of her hips were in direct correlation to her happiness, but it hadn't worked out like that. All those months obsessing about her weight … She'd been at her fattest when she'd been with Charlie and yet he'd said he loved her for her pretty smile and sparkling eyes – well, that's what he used to tell her. Now she struggled to remember those glossy shiny words. She certainly didn't believe them.

She wandered back into the lounge, placing a fresh drink on the coffee table before adding a couple of logs to the wood burner and sitting in her favourite chair. There had to be a way to find Grace.

Chapter 7

Izzy
Five years ago

Izzy pulled back her wardrobe door, sweeping a hand at the array of misshapen T-shirts, leggings and granny cardigans neatly lined up.

'I've got nothing to wear and I so want to look my best,' she moaned, pulling at the T-shirt that only half covered her belly before glancing across at her friend's neat little bump.

Grace patted her hand. 'It won't be for much longer. Only one week to go and it could be early,' she said, arching her left eyebrow. 'What about your maternity jeans and that pretty blue blouse with the embroidery around the neck?' She drew out the hangers and held them up for inspection.

'I suppose they'll do,' Izzy said, placing her hands to her lower back and stretching.

'Have you been having any more pain than usual? That's normally the first sign.'

'Only after last night's curry,' she said with a grin. 'Dad does a wicked chicken vindaloo.'

'What, with chips on the side?' Grace teased.

Izzy smiled back where before she'd have taken it to heart but Grace was different. She'd only known her a few weeks but in that time she'd become one of her best friends, if not the best. Charlie continued to refuse to attend parenting classes, but it didn't matter so much now she knew that Grace would be there. Life seemed to be settling down into a pattern and one she wasn't unhappy with. Charlie had managed to surprise her by picking up a job. It wasn't much, just manning the pumps at the local petrol station, but it was a start. There was now a spring in his step and that morning he'd even swung her around in the kitchen before planting a big kiss against her mouth, just like he'd used to in the early days.

'I'm taking my two best girls out for a slap-up meal tonight as it's payday,' he said, bending down and pressing a kiss against her belly.

'You daft thing.' But she was secretly pleased, more than pleased. She'd thought they were floating, drifting apart at a time when she needed him more than ever but apparently not. Maybe there was hope for them yet.

She smiled again, a slow lingering smile that must have highlighted her happiness because Grace paused, her eyes scanning her face with a frown, any trace of laughter now wiped clean.

'What?'

'I'm not sure whether I should tell you.'

'Tell me what?' Izzy picked up her mug and took a sip, all her attention focused on the woman opposite. Grace obviously had something she was determined to tell her, something she wasn't going to like.

'If you knew something, something important about someone … something that might cause them distress, what would you do, knowing full well it could be the end of their friendship?'

Izzy dropped her gaze and took a moment to place her mug on the bedtable, careful to push it away from the edge before finally raising her head. She had no need to explain who she was talking about because of course she was talking about her. Something that could ruin their friendship – it must be something to do with Charlie.

'Just tell me.'

'If you're sure you're willing to hear?'

'You can't start something and not finish it,' she snapped, wanting to get whatever Grace had to say out into the open so she could deal with it. She shifted her hand to her belly, smoothing her palm across the taut bump, the discomfort from yesterday starting up again with a vengeance. Perhaps she should phone the midwife but first she needed to hear what Grace had to say.

'You know I had to go into Swansea yesterday?'

'Yes, you said already.'

'Well …' She brushed her hair back with a restless hand. 'I decided to pop into one of the cafés along the Waterfront and Charlie was there.'

Now she had her attention, all of it. Her gaze shifted from her hand to Grace's face, all thought of her belly ache pushed to the corner of her mind. 'Charlie? My Charlie? But you've never met him. How would you—?'

'Remember you showed me his photo on your phone. It's a good likeness.'

'You must be mistaken.' She sank down on to the side of the bed. 'He left early to work at the garage—'

'Okay. Sorry, but I was so sure, the man I saw even had a birthmark in the centre of his cheek … Maybe it was just someone that looked like him,' she said, picking up her mug and taking a deep sip.

Izzy felt the colour drain from her face and the room start to spin. She couldn't speak. She couldn't think and suddenly the burning pain she'd been feeling since last night surged, causing her to clutch at her belly. There was more, of course there was, and she steeled herself, her nails digging deep into her palms, her breath coming out in a long gasp.

'Go on.'

'I don't get it?' Grace's eyes widened.

'Tell me the rest then.'

'Izzy, I—'

'Tell me the rest, goddammit or I'll ring him up and ask him.'

Grace swallowed hard, her eyes wavering but Izzy had no sympathy. Her so-called best friend was about to smash her fairy tale into smithereens. It wasn't much of a fairy tale but, at least it was hers. It was all she had. It was all she'd ever wanted, her hand instinctively gripping the side of the mattress as another wave of pain wracked though her body.

'He was with a woman.'

'Is that all?' she said, letting air seep out of her lungs. 'He has loads of female friends. They all hang around in a crowd. Just because—'

'Listen Izzy, he was all over her like a rash. It was embarrassing. In the end the waitress had to come over and ask them to leave.'

She stared back, her mouth slightly open. Why would Grace do this to her? She'd thought her a friend, her best friend. A kindred spirit if you like. But now it was as if the blinkers had fallen away and she was seeing Grace for the very first time and she didn't like what she saw. Why tell her now about Charlie? Just what was she trying to achieve?

Bracing her hands on the bed she pushed herself to standing. She had to get out of the room or she'd scream. She'd scream and never stop. But something was wrong, very wrong as the spasm of pain intensified. She closed her eyes briefly before opening them and staring across at the woman she could barely recognise.

'What is it, Izzy? What's wrong?'

Chapter 8

Izzy
Friday 27 December, 10.00 a.m. Abereiddy

She blinked rapidly, running that last conversation over in the quiet of her mind. She needed to think about the one thing that was bothering her.

The birthmark.

Her forehead pleated as she struggled to think. She remembered telling the police about Grace's insistence that Charlie was having an affair. That was one of the things that had instigated them trying to find her. But had she ever told them about the birthmark? She knew there'd been something that hadn't made sense at the time, but she couldn't work it out and she'd quickly forgotten under the weight of everything else. Her waters breaking. The frantic rush to hospital. The long, drawn-out labour culminating in an emergency caesarean section.

The issue of how Grace had recognised Charlie from a photograph she'd only glimpsed months before, a photograph that hadn't included his defining feature, was swept away on a tidal wave of pain, joy and then deceit. The birthmark wasn't big or anything. In fact, she'd thought it cute. It was an integral part of him which she loved along with his cheeky smile and twinkly blue eyes. But Charlie had hated it with a passion. He'd even considered having it removed when he had enough money to pay for the surgery. He was always insistent that any photos had to be taken from what he termed *his good side* – she knew from experience that he'd only delete any snaps where it featured.

She felt her eyes prick. Even after all this time the thought of his betrayal still hurt. She'd hoped by now she'd be immune to the memory of his two-timing ways, but love wasn't like that. She didn't love him anymore. Instead she hated him with every waking breath. But, in the dark recesses and in her dreams, she still remembered how it was. She still remembered how they were. She'd have bet anything that he was genuine and she'd have lost. No. She did lose. She'd lost everything.

The birthmark, she knew it must be important and, after five years of an already exhaustive search there wasn't going to be much new to go on. But this time it was going to be different. This time she wasn't going to search for Charlie. This time she was going to expend her energies on trying to find Grace, if only to ask her straight out if she'd been sleeping with her boyfriend. Time was against her. Grace had probably forgotten all about their little friendship but, what the hell. She wasn't looking for anything apart from the truth and she certainly didn't need her in her life, not now. All she wanted was to stare her in the face while she asked her the question that had been waiting five years.

What bloke would cheat on a nine months' pregnant woman with another one? But what other answer could there be?

Chapter 9

Izzy
Friday 27 December, 3.15 p.m. Withybush Hospital

Being in the Midwifery Suite for the first time since losing Alys was right up there with getting a tooth pulled. The last time, she'd left the suite and been escorted to the Mini with a wreath of smiles, Charlie by her side, his knuckles gleaming white as he clutched onto the car seat with both hands. A new baby was a celebration just as a lost baby was a tragedy.

But Alys wasn't missing, or that's what Izzy kept trying to tell herself. She'd just lost her way and it was up to the person that loved her the most to find her.

She eventually tracked down Carys, the lead midwife, in her office, a shoebox of a room with breastfeeding posters on the walls. She could tell straight away that she remembered her. But that was hardly surprising. The story had made the front of the *South Wales Echo* within a day and the front of all the nationals by the end of that first week.

She took her time settling in her seat before lifting her bag onto her lap, more for something to hold onto than anything. Heaving a sigh, she told herself she could do this. She was here to find out about Grace, and she wasn't leaving until Carys had told her everything she knew.

Five minutes of wrangling and word games later, and Izzy's temper had started to rise. She didn't care about patient confidentiality and it wasn't as if there was anything confidential in the questions she was asking. All she wanted was some clue that could lead her to Grace. She wasn't fussy – anything would do.

She hadn't seen Grace since her friend had popped into the hospital with the cutest toy rabbit for Alys. There was no note, no text or message after to let her know she'd upped and left town and Izzy was too tied up with Alys and then her abduction to think anything of it. But now she needed to know and Carys wasn't prepared to help.

'But it's not as if I'm asking you to divulge anything secret. I know she was living in that new block of flats opposite the bus station.'

'I don't know anything about that,' she said, not quite meeting her eye. 'Have you thought to ask the other women attending the sessions? Maybe they can help.'

The other couples? Izzy closed her eyes briefly, trying to picture them through the veil of time that had turned them into dim shadows – it was useless. She could scarcely remember what they looked like let alone conjure up a name.

'No, sorry. I wouldn't know where to start.'

Carys stared back, her smile softening. 'How about if I tell you how the sessions are organised? That part is public knowledge and there may be something to help. The way the group works is by months, so all expectant mothers and their partners are invited to sessions, four calendar months before their baby's due date.'

'And who invites them?' Izzy said, returning the smile, relieved that she wasn't going to be turned away with nothing.

'Through their GP initially. So, your friend would have had to register with a doctor's surgery when she moved into the area.'

Carys flicked a look at her watch before shuffling the folders in front of her. 'I do hope you find her. We were all devastated when it happened.'

Izzy made her way to the door, offering a brief thanks. Carys had been more helpful than she could have been in the circumstances and it certainly wasn't her fault that Charlie had done what he had. She just hoped and prayed that she'd be able to find Grace after a gap of five years. She'd as good as told her he was having an affair. She hadn't believed her at the time. Now the only question in her mind was – who with?

'Hello, I'd like to make an appointment.'

'Name?'

'Madden, Mrs Grace Madden.'

'I'm sorry. I can't seem to find your details on the system. Which doctor did you say you were with?'

Izzy's fingers curled around the receiver briefly before slotting it back into place, though what she really wanted to do was smash it to smithereens. She'd tried all the doctor's practices in and around the St David's area only to draw a complete blank. How on earth did Grace get to hear about the parenting sessions if she hadn't registered with a GP? It was all a mystery and one she intended to solve.

'Finished on the phone, love? You stop there and I'll go and make you your favourite drink. There's no need to rush off. It seems an age since we had a good old natter.'

She was around at Mam's, simply because, after leaving the hospital, she'd been too wound up to make her way back home.

'But I was only here a couple of days ago,' she said, throwing her a smile over one shoulder. 'What more could you possibly want to discuss?'

'Nothing in particular and anyway, Christmas doesn't really count. All that food is conducive to a bout of indigestion and not a good chat,' her mam said with a grin, pushing a mug of chocolate into her hands, topped with marshmallows and cream. 'Just the way you like it.'

Perhaps when she was fifteen but now wasn't the time to say anything. Her mam was always trying to feed her up and today Izzy was just going to give in. She loved her really and, in a world that was suddenly feeling all a bit strange, that was the most important thing.

'Thanks Mam, love you,' she said, lifting the mug and letting the explosion of sugar assault her tongue with all the finesse of a sledgehammer. After all, there was nothing quite like chocolate to lift the spirits and it was meant to be good for you, although perhaps not with quite so many marshmallows.

'Love you back,' she replied, and they shared a smile as the years fell away. The drifting apart since losing Alys seemed to fade and it was just like it was in the old days before Charlie, before everything.

Hot chocolate finished, they hugged the table with their elbows, their knees nearly touching under the warped Formica, the same table Izzy used to sit at to do her homework. The same table she'd laughed and cried all over with this woman by her side. Her mother's periwinkle-blue eyes were a little dimmed by time, the skin edged with wrinkles. Her hair was still a deep auburn mainly thanks to her fortnightly visit to the hairdresser. She put Izzy to shame with her smart matching lambs-wool jumper and skirt, the diamond hoop earrings Dad had bought her for their twenty-fifth wedding anniversary glittering in the weak sun. But now wasn't the time to bemoan the state of her own wardrobe. Izzy had more important things to think about.

'Mam, did you ever hear me speaking about a Grace Madden?'

She'd finally decided to share her concerns with someone and who better than her mother. Bethan was too tied up with the farm and the boys and there was no one else.

'You mean that stuck-up piece that dropped you when Alys went missing?'

Izzy placed her mug back on the table with a careful hand before meeting her gaze. 'That's unlike you. You're usually the most mild-mannered woman I know,' she said, a frown appearing.

'Well, what of it? It's true. I'll never know what you saw in her. Your dad and I couldn't have been happier when she did a runner. You're so much better with that nice Rebecca Walker for a friend. A bad influence is what that Madden woman was with her airs and fake tan to match her fake accent.'

'You never said.'

'What do you expect? You had more than your hands full with Charlie and then the baby.' She leant forward and pressed her hand. 'Not a day goes by when I don't think of Alys and I still hope that Charlie will come to his senses and get in touch.' She shook her head, rooting for the tissue that always lived up the sleeve of her jumper. 'You've gone and locked yourself away in that house of my mother's and we barely see you.'

'I'm busy with the business.'

Her mam sat back in her chair. 'Really? Busy all day every day? We only live a few miles down the road and, if that's too far, we're on the end of the phone. It's always us that have to do the running. I don't mean to nag, love, but it's been as hard for us as it has for you. Not only have we lost Alys we also seem to have lost you in the process. You've changed from a fun-loving girl to a shadow where there's work and little else. Charlie was a nice enough lad, but the world is jam-packed with men and here you are living the life of a nun.'

'How do you know I'm not out with a different man each night of the week?' Izzy said, managing to conjure up a weak smile.

'Well, are you?'

Izzy blushed, shaking her head.

'Just promise me you'll try and think on what I've said. Your dad and I are worried about you.' She went to push herself up from the table only to pause, her hands squared flat against the top. 'Come on, enough of this talk. You were telling me about Grace?'

'I saw her last week in Swansea,' Izzy said, choosing her words carefully. 'I saw her and now I don't know what to think.'

'I don't know what you mean? I thought she left the area.' Her mam narrowed her eyes. 'I think that's what you told me.'

'I'm not sure it's that simple, Mam,' she said finally. 'The truth is she just disappeared without a trace, around the same time as Charlie and Alys.

'But why would she?'

'I don't know. But there's one thing for sure. I intend to find out.'

It was nearly nine o'clock by the time Izzy finally got up to leave.

'You'll be careful on the roads, won't you? You're sure you don't want to stay the night?'

'I can't, Mam, Bucket would never forgive me,' she said, dragging her into a hug before heading out to the van.

She'd always hated driving at night, especially at this time of year when the only light was from the odd house along the barely inhabited stretch of A487. But, for once, she didn't spare a thought for the journey ahead. If the car broke down, she'd just phone someone. It wasn't as if it was a long trip or anything, and her mind was too full of the past to be bothered by something so inconsequential.

She couldn't get the three of them out of her head: Charlie, Alys and Grace. She also couldn't stop thinking about her own paltry existence. It suddenly felt as if she'd let life slip her by while she set up her business and expanded her customer base. Her life had turned into a pale image of what it could have been. Instead of having a family, all she thought about was where the wool for her next design was coming from and how best to photograph her latest project. She was a one-woman master-crafter with a strong online following and a growing business. If things carried on she'd have to take on more than the handful of local women she already employed to help her turn her hand-spun wool into works of art. She'd pushed aside all thought of what her life was meant to be. She'd turned her back on trying to meet another man just as she'd turned her back on trying to find Alys …

Maybe some music would help to keep her brain from performing somersaults. She turned on the radio and started fiddling with the dial to find a station playing the latest tunes, anything to keep her thoughts at bay. But they wouldn't be quietened. She tried to convince herself that she hadn't forgotten, that she hadn't given up on Alys, but it was all a lie. She should have still been out there everyday hunting the streets and banging on every door. If she could turn back the clock, there were so many things she'd change. Her life had gone off on a tangent where work had tried to fill the place of her child.

She blinked rapidly, before flipping the radio off. Listening to Adele telling her how much she missed her was just what she didn't need – she had enough darkness in her soul without her interference. She was pleased beyond belief when she finally reached the turning for home – the tangled ivy, twisting up the brickwork, glistening in the light cast from her headlamps.

A sigh escaped. She wasn't one of those romantics that found enchantment around every corner, but this house was so much more than simply bricks glued with mortar. It was both her haven and refuge. The place she used to come every Wednesday when Granny picked her and her sister up from school. She'd let them dump their bags and shoes by the back door before trailing through to the kitchen for homemade Welsh cakes, still hot from the griddle.

She slammed the door closed on her memories and placed her shoes in the basket before hanging her coat and beret on the old mahogany hat stand. The front door opened straight into the lounge, which meant she had to be extra tidy in case of impromptu visitors. Bucket jumped down from the back of the sofa to wrap himself around her ankles, a deep purr and gentle meow telling her in no uncertain terms that he was hungry.

'All right, boy. Time for supper.' But before she made her way into the kitchen, Izzy ran through the list of evening checks she'd carried out by rote ever since she'd moved in.

Van locked and keys in the bowl on the table. Front door locked and security chain fastened. Windows secure in the lounge although, as she hadn't opened them in what felt like months, there was little chance of them having been left open. But that didn't stop her from checking. She couldn't remember the number of times she'd snuggled up in bed only to remember she'd forgotten to check one of the windows or doors.

Izzy eyed her mobile, sitting on the table. She really should phone Rebecca for a catch-up. It was funny in a way that she now counted Rebecca, a friend from her school days and the antithesis of Grace, as her closest friend. But Rebecca understood her where Grace never had. Izzy wasn't interested in make-up or trying to make the best of herself. She dressed how she wanted and relished nothing more than the thought of her own company. When they met they talked non-stop but they'd often go days or even weeks without a word. She took a step forward only to pause and head for the stairs. For once she felt in need of a chat – the only thing stopping her was the fact that Rebecca was Rhys's little sister.

The house boasted three bedrooms, all situated in the roof space, so boiling in summer and far too cold and expensive to heat in winter. She ignored the room on the left; it held too many bitter memories of those first two exciting days after her home-coming. Oh, there weren't many. Alys had never spent a night there, her place being in the crib by her side of the bed. But it was where she'd changed her nappy, the changing table angled under the window in the eaves so that she could stare out at the rolling hills behind. It was where she'd stored her tiny selection of clothes – clothes she'd finally bundled up into sacks and dropped off at the local charity shop. The room might be empty of everything associated with Alys, but it would never be empty to her.

Lying back in bed, her hands behind her head and Bucket by her feet, Izzy's thoughts continued to interrupt any idea of rest. With the arrival of Grace things were changing, small things like Mam telling her what she thought for once. She hoped the change continued because returning to a life where work played the dominant part wasn't going to be enough anymore.

Chapter 10

Gaby
Friday 27 December, 6.05 p.m. The King's Arms

'So, what was that you were saying about Rhys and Isabelle Grant?'

'Shush, keep your voice down. If either Bill or Shea hear, I'll be mincemeat.'

Gaby and Amy were sitting around a large table in the back of the pub, nursing large glasses of Chenin Blanc while Bill and Shea hugged pints of lager to their chests, all their attention on the game of rugby on the TV screen hanging on the wall.

'Sorry,' Gaby said, taking a large sip of wine before placing it carefully back on the table. She'd been looking forward to joining Amy for a drink ever since she'd suggested it in the office earlier. It was just her luck that a couple of the other detectives had decided to tag along at the last minute.

'There's no need to apologise,' Amy said, lowering her voice to a whisper, her eyes flickering to the men opposite. 'I just wouldn't put it past either of them to let Rhys know that we've been gossiping about him.'

'Fat chance of that.'

'Exactly. As if we don't have better things to gossip about.' Amy nudged her with her elbow, her eyes gleaming, all her attention now focused on the couple of hunks walking across the bar. 'You can have the balding one on the right.'

'Great!'

Gaby was surprised by how nice it was sitting there, the warmth from the log fire adding an extra layer of atmosphere to the traditional pub with oak beams strung with an assortment of golden horse brasses. She'd never been one for close female friendships. For a start she'd always been too tied up with work. She'd been a loner as a child and that had continued into adulthood. But Amy seemed different. Maybe it was because of her career choice as family liaison officer but, whatever the reason, she appeared to have an insight and perception far in excess of her years. From the look of her clear skin and bright gaze, she'd guess her at being mid-twenties – so probably a good five years younger than her own twenty-nine years – but with a maturity of twice that age.

She drained the rest of her glass and, lifting her black leather bag, stood to her feet. 'We still have half an hour before the taxi comes – fancy another?'

'Why not. I'll give you a hand.' Amy turned to Bill and Shea. 'The same again, boys?'

'Now, where were we? Oh, yes – Rhys and Isabelle Grant.'

Within seconds of them arriving at the bar, a pair of leggy blondes descended as if out of nowhere and whisked both men away from under Amy's nose. But she just shrugged her shoulders with a laugh before hopping onto one of their vacated bar stools and throwing Gaby a smile.

'You win some …' she said, rolling her eyes before picking up her glass and taking a sip. 'Oh yes. Rhys.' Her voice dropped a level. 'I'm not sure how the rumour started, probably right from the beginning of Baby Grant's disappearance although, now I come to think of it, he wasn't even part of the initial investigation. It was meant to be Bill's case, but Rhys's old man soon changed that.'

'Rhys's old man,' Gaby repeated, peering at her over the top of her glass. Of all the things she'd expected her to say that wasn't one of them,

'The DCI,' Amy replied, lowering her voice. 'I thought you would have known. Brazil-North has only been here about three years. Up until then Elijah Walker was the guv and a right stickler too. Ex-military. You know the type. Very strict on the uniform. He even had us lining up for daily inspections. The whole station breathed a sigh of relief when he decided to take early retirement and move to Yorkshire. Well anyway, I'd only just joined straight from university and was completely wet behind the ears but even I could see that his father was booting Rhys up the rungs of the ladder super quick.' She threw a quick glance across at Bill and Shea before continuing. 'Not that he wasn't up for it. From the beginning I was struck by the hours he was spending on the case. Okay, so his father was right behind him making sure he did a proper job but he barely left his desk in the early days and when she tried to top herself—'

'What?' Gaby said, her eyes widening. 'Why didn't anyone tell me? I know there are a few boxes left to work through but ...'

'Sorry, I thought they had. It was kept out of the papers, thanks to Rhys. She was crazy with grief, around the station all the time even when she wasn't needed. Not eating. Not sleeping. Not washing. A disaster on legs. She had to be driven back home most days that first year. And he was always there for her. Never a harsh word. It was tea and sympathy laced with that little extra something he couldn't hide no matter how hard he tried. We all knew that it wasn't about finding Alys. It was all about finding Izzy's child, only that. I know that sounds like the same thing but, believe me, it's not. If there was a reward for effort he'd have won it hands down,' she said, gesturing to the barman. 'It was personal and, despite the five-year gap, it's still personal.' She rummaged around in her bag for her purse before withdrawing a twenty. 'He won't give up unless we find her and, of course, what real chance is there after all this time?'

Gaby shifted back on the bar stool, mulling over Amy's words. Rhys was quite a bit older than Izzy Grant, ten years or more and yet he'd never married. Was that the reason for him nearly barking at her when she'd asked about the case? Unrequited love. She frowned, her thoughts stepping into the cesspool that she still struggled to cope with. But with her, it hadn't been unrequited. Her hands clenched, her nails biting deep as a picture of Leigh Clark escaped the locked compartment of her mind. Leigh Clark, the tall, broad-shouldered man she'd given her heart to in Cardiff only to find that it wasn't love, not on his part. It had taken a visit from his heavily pregnant wife for Gaby to come to her senses. With her personal life imploding along with her professional one, she'd had no choice but to leave.

Chapter 11

Izzy
Monday 30 December, 10.10 a.m. Abereiddy

The morning arrived all too quickly and, as a start to the week, it was a bad one – a bad one that persisted when Izzy found the boiler had decided to play up. She should have given up on the day there and then. After all, what harm could come to her if she stayed hidden in bed with the curtains closed and the phone unplugged? She was just about to follow up on the idea when the doorbell rang.

Pulling the door open, she found it was the one person she couldn't cope with, even now. But policemen were well-versed in the art of getting members of the public to do exactly what they wanted and within seconds Rhys and his sidekick had invited themselves in for a coffee and a chat.

'Sorry it's so early but a copper's time is never their own. This is DC Darin, by the way,' he said, waving a hand in the direction of the woman with him.

DC Darin followed him in, stooping to pick something up from the doormat before setting it on top of the table. 'The postman comes early around here,' she said, nodding to the card lying face up with a picture of the Eiffel Tower staring out.

'No, not really. I must have missed it when I came in last night.' Izzy frowned. She didn't know anyone in France, and certainly not someone that would bother to send her a card unless …? No. She shook her head. That was ridiculous. There was no way he'd … not after a break of five years.

'Are you all right?' Rhys said, interrupting her train of thought. 'You're awfully pale.'

'I'm fine, just a little tired.' Her gaze shifted from the card and back to his face. 'There's no news about the investigation, I suppose?'

'No, I'm afraid not.' His voice was kind, his smile kinder. 'But we haven't given up and, with this new development, who knows what's around the corner? Now, what about a cuppa for a couple of hard-working detectives?'

She looked at him properly for the first time; the boyish good looks that had made him so popular with the ladies were still very much in evidence. As Rebecca's best friend, she'd spent large amounts of time sitting at their kitchen table struggling with her homework and she'd gotten used to the sight of him leaving the house dressed up for the evening. Being ten years older he'd seemed so mature to a shy inexperienced teenager and way out of her league. The last five years had been kind to him. His brown hair had darkened, but it was still thick and with a tendency to curl despite the short cut. He looked tired, shadows pressed into his skin and a smattering of stubble embracing his chin. But it was his eyes she focused on the longest. She'd used to think his gaze lingered longer than normal in her direction but, of course, she must have been imagining it. She grimaced. Who was she kidding?

'You sit down by the wood burner,' she said, gesturing to the sofa in front of the stove. 'The boiler's playing up again but the fire's all ready.' She threw them both a smile before kneeling and striking a match.

'I didn't think people lit fires these days?'

'I'd probably freeze if I ripped it out. The boiler's broken more times than it's fixed.'

'I'll take a look before I leave if you like? I'm quite handy with a spanner.'

I'll just bet you are, Rhys Walker, but I don't want you in my house any longer than necessary despite your good looks and charm.

'No, it's fine but thanks anyway. I've already phoned a plumber.' She pinned another smile in place before heading into the kitchen to put the kettle on and search for the chocolate biscuits she kept in the back of the cupboard for when Bethan came to visit with the boys.

Sitting around drinking tea, she tried to forge a new compartment in her brain, a compartment she couldn't quite seem to squeeze him into, no matter how hard she shoved. It had been four years since the weekly updates and progress reports and in that time he'd shifted back from *cop on the case* to *Rebecca's brother*. Now he was back with the notebook open on his knee and an expression on his face that shouted business.

'I'd like to revisit what you told me in the supermarket. How sure are you that it was Grace Madden? After all, it's been five years since you've seen her.'

'As sure as I can be unless she has a twin.' She smiled but there was no humour in the stretch of her lips. 'For months we lived in each other's pockets. Not a day went past without her either phoning or dropping in on me. In those last weeks, up to the birth, I was closer to her than my mother or maybe even Charlie.'

She paused, staring into the distance, reliving that last moment in Swansea. Closing her eyes, she could still see the long trench coat she'd been wearing, the thick swathe of hair as she opened the door to the taxi. She opened her eyes with a snap, remembering something she'd almost forgotten. 'And anyway, she recognised me.'

He leant forward, his gaze pinned to hers. 'She recognised you?' he repeated, his voice sharp.

'Yes. Just before the taxi pulled away. Her eyes met mine through the back window. She definitely knew it was me.'

'And yet she didn't stop the taxi from pulling into the traffic? She didn't leap out of the back to be reunited?'

'No, why would she? After all, she was the one that broke up the friendship, not the other way round.'

'And you? You didn't call her name, shout even? You didn't race across to the taxi to confront her?' He held her gaze. 'Here's the woman that you now suspect … well … I'm not quite sure of what exactly but, maybe someone involved in Alys's disappearance and you didn't—'

'There wasn't time,' she interrupted. 'It all happened within the blink of an eye. One second she was there and the next the taxi had pulled out into the traffic. If I had the time again don't you think I'd have tried to do something? But after five years of silence it was too much of a shock for me to process.'

I know I'm over-explaining but they think I'm at fault here. They think I could have done more and doesn't a large part of me agree? Izzy's gaze landed on DC Darin who was staring back. Assessing. Evaluating. Blaming. *She thinks I'm lying. She thinks I've made it up.* Izzy blinked hard. *Dear God, they probably think I'm trying to jump-start the case back into life. He doesn't know me very well if that's what he thinks.*

She stood, gathering the mugs and plate onto the tray, her eyes now unable to meet theirs. She'd had enough of them making her feel as if she was in the wrong. She wouldn't be so rude as to ask them to leave but she hoped they'd get the message.

'Well, if that's all … I've a lot to get through now Christmas is over,' she said, standing there, the tray held in a death grip.

'Just a couple more questions, if you don't mind.' Rhys flipped through his notebook only to pause and stare at his writing before lifting his head. 'I know this is difficult but one of the leads we followed up in the initial investigation involved a comment you made about Grace Madden and Charlie having an affair?'

Placing the tray back on the table with elaborate care she sat back on the edge of her chair, suddenly deflated. 'That's not quite right.' She shook her head in an effort to gather her thoughts. 'Grace told me she'd seen Charlie with another woman. I didn't believe her at the time …'

'Why was that?' Rhys interrupted, continuing to study her face.

'Charlie has a small birthmark right here,' she said, raising a finger to the centre of her cheek. 'Something she said she'd noticed in the café. There's no way she could have known unless she knew him …' Her voice stuttered to a halt.

He dropped his gaze to his notes for a second time, flicking through the sheets. 'A birthmark? I don't seem to remember—?'

'Oh, you're confusing me. I don't remember what I said back then and what I didn't,' she said, starting to stand. 'It wasn't big or anything, less than the size of a penny but to Charlie it could have filled his whole face. He hated it so much – I doubt there's a photo in existence where it features.'

'Okay, there's no need to worry. I remember it was a difficult time.' He smiled briefly. 'So to recap – what you're saying is that, at the time, you didn't think he could have been having an affair, but now you've remembered about the birthmark and you're questioning how she could have known about it. Is that right?'

She looked at him for a moment before nodding her head.

'Izzy, I'm sorry for having to ask such difficult questions but I hope you realise we do need to ask them?'

She couldn't speak, not with images of Charlie and Grace cavorting around her head in a variety of positions. She couldn't do anything other than drop back in the chair with another nod of her head before closing her eyes. She'd brought this on herself. If she hadn't gone to Swansea that day. If she hadn't bumped into Rhys in the supermarket … She heaved a sigh before opening her eyes and meeting his gaze. The stark fact was she still needed to find out the truth even if it ended up breaking her. She still needed to find Alys.

She swallowed before speaking. 'It doesn't matter. I'll answer anything. I'll put up with anything. But I have to know what happened to be able to move on.'

'We know you do,' DC Darin said, speaking for the first time. 'And with this new information, I'm hopeful there'll be a break-through.'

Izzy took in her warm smile and deep brown eyes, encased in the longest eyelashes she'd ever seen. She'd thought that this new detective would be like all the rest of St David's but that didn't appear to be the case. Oh, she'd heard the rumours, it was impossible to live in such a small rural community and not – the barely concealed whispers speculating about what she'd done with the bodies. The people Izzy used to think of as friends, who now crossed the road instead of having to face her in the street. She used to think that life was difficult while growing up – she'd had no idea just how hard it was going to get. But the one thing she wasn't was a coward. She needed to know what had happened to Alys no matter how hard it turned out to be.

'Thank you,' she said, her voice catching in her throat. She stood again and headed back to the table, idly picking up the postcard and turning it over, more for something to do while they shrugged into their coats. She didn't know anyone on holiday and certainly not in France—

Chapter 12

Izzy

'I don't understand …?'

She woke up to find she was back in her chair with her head between her knees, the feeling of a handprint between her shoulders as if someone had just removed it. There was a buzzing noise in her ears like the trill of a thousand bees and a sensation that something had just happened. She had the puzzle in front of her, the vital clue missing.

'You collapsed, Izzy,' Rhys said, close to her ear. 'But I'm not really surprised. Were you going to tell us about the cards or just continue trying to act detective? I honestly thought better of you than that.'

She raised her head and stared at where he was resting back on his heels by her feet. He was so close she could smell the light trace of his aftershave, something musky. He was certainly close enough for her to see the disdain marring his features. Switching her gaze, she noted the expression stamped on DC Darin's face. There was comfort and concern there, only that. So, what was the reason for his sudden anger?

'I'm sorry, I don't know what—?'

'The cards, Izzy,' he enunciated clearly as if speaking to a child, tilting his head towards the postcard now lying on the corner of the table. 'Just how many have you received?'

'I've received none apart from that first one and now this. Why would you even think I'd keep something as important as that a secret?' she said, waiting for the world to stop spinning and the nausea to settle.

'I think she's telling the truth, boss.' DC Darin's soft sensible words, with the trace of Liverpool curdling the vowels, were a welcome relief.

Rhys's eyes drilled down before shifting away, the sound of a sigh hissing between his teeth. 'Okay. I'm sorry if I upset you.' His attention was back on the card. 'It's unlikely they'll be able to get any prints but there's always a chance.'

He picked it up with the tip of his nails. 'I don't suppose you have a freezer bag in the kitchen?'

She stood only to find him by her side, his free hand on the curve of her waist. 'Hey, go easy. You'll probably feel woozy for a couple of minutes.'

'Woozy?' Her eyes dropped to his fingers where he'd gripped onto her skin, his knuckles white against the green of her jumper.

'You fainted.'

'I've never fainted in my life,' she snapped, jerking away from his hand, the feel of his fingers still imprinted on her flesh.

'No? Well, there's always a first time for everything.'

He trailed after her into the kitchen and watched as she rummaged in the drawer under the hob, leaving DC Darin alone in the lounge. Izzy watched him ease the card into the bag with a finesse that belied the size of his hands. When he'd sealed it closed, she stretched out her arm. She knew what it said. One look and the short sentence was indelibly stamped across her mind. But she still wanted to read it again.

Alys is fine – don't try to find us.
Charlie.

'Why would he write to me now – it's been five years? I don't understand …?'

'No, neither do I,' he said softly. He walked back towards the sink and picked up the kettle. 'You're as white as a sheet which, more than anything, proves you're telling the truth. I'm sorry for thinking otherwise. Put it down to lack of sleep. Come on, let's have another cuppa and talk sensibly about what's just happened.'

She wanted him to go. Oh, not the woman. She was fine, comforting even. She hadn't got a lot to say for herself, but she probably couldn't get a word in with a dynamic boss like Rhys around. No, it was Rhys that was the problem. She wasn't in the mood for spending time with a man who suddenly appeared to be around every corner. She hadn't had any dealings with him in years and yet here he was asking more questions, questions she was finding difficult to answer. Okay, so it was her fault he was here, but she hadn't realised he'd still be taking such an active interest in the day-to-day running of the investigation. She'd just assumed he'd have a cushy desk job by now instead of being the one to turn up on her doorstep.

He placed a mug in front of her and she lifted it to her lips, curling her fingers through the handle. He was right. A mug of tea was just what she needed and she rested her head back, starting to relax. He threw another log on the wood burner and she sat, staring at the flames creeping over the wood with a soothing intensity. He chose the chair opposite and, making himself comfortable, continued studying the card. She frowned at his sudden level of interest. There was nothing to see apart from a cheap card with a picture of the Eiffel Tower, similar to millions of other cards sent around the globe every year. So, what did he find so exciting about the back of this one?

'Surely you must know it off by heart?'

He placed the card on the table beside him before raising his head, his hand pulling his phone out of his pocket.

'Hmm, it's not the card so much as the postal mark,' he said, all his attention now on his screen as he scrolled through the device.

'It was sent from Paris, obviously. Why else would the postcard be of the Eiffel Tower?'

'Not necessarily. France is broken down into numerical regions and Paris, I seem to remember, is number 75 whereas this postal mark has a pretty clear 62 stamped on …' He paused, switching off his phone with a puzzled frown.

'Well?'

'Well, it's time we were making tracks. I'm sure you have lots to do,' he said with a smile – one that didn't quite reach his eyes.

The door finally closed behind them, leaving her with a confusing list of feelings to dwell on. The postcard had thrown her. Why now, for heaven's sake, after all this time? Her hand crept to her throat as a new thought crossed the border of her mind. Perhaps someone was playing a sick joke.

Chapter 13

Gaby

'You shouldn't make promises you might be unable to keep,' Rhys said, as soon as they'd reached the car.

Gaby spent a moment pulling her skirt over her knees before replying. 'Excuse me?'

'You as good as promised her we'd find her daughter.' She felt his gaze flickering in her direction. 'So, what do you think you can bring to the table that we haven't already?' he said, starting the engine. 'We've been trying for five years and come up with zilch, simply because there are no clues.'

'Well, we have more leads now. The card and this Grace Madden.'

'Pah. The card could be from anybody. Yes, it's nice to think it's from Charlie and he's holed up in France. But it doesn't make sense.'

She picked up the card from where he'd placed it on the dashboard and turned it over. 'There's something about this whole situation that doesn't make sense. Why leave it so long? What has changed to make a card appear out of the blue like that? It doesn't fit with any of the profiling carried out on missing person cases,'

68

she said, not really expecting him to answer. 'Something must have happened to prompt the card but what? The obvious answer is Grace Madden being back on the scene but what reason could she have unless she's still in touch with Charlie?'

She ran through the words again but there was nothing … No leads. No new clues. The postmark, their best bet, was smudged as if the card had passed through many hands. She reached for her phone and clicked on the International Postal Database, her gaze narrowing. Why would someone go to all the trouble of buying a postcard in Paris only to post it someplace else?

Shifting in her seat she was suddenly aware that Rhys hadn't said a word for a good few minutes. Her eyes shifted to his face and the grim set of his jaw. She'd give quite a lot to know what he was thinking. Instead, she decided to ask him a question. 'I thought it was posted in Paris but now I'm not so sure. What did your search turn up because, all I'm getting is a place called Coquelles?'

'You know what your problem is, don't you?' Rhys said, throwing her a look before returning his attention back to the road.

'What?'

'You don't take enough holidays.'

'What's that got to do with anything?'

'Because, Gaby, then you'd know that Coquelles is just south west of Calais and where the Channel Tunnel terminates.'

Gaby shot him a look. 'So what you're saying is that someone jumped on the Chunnel and got out at Calais to post the card only to return on the next train? Can they even do that?'

'You'd better believe it.'

'It sounds all a bit cloak and dagger if you ask me. Why go to all that trouble just for a card? It's not as if it said anything.'

'But it did the job, didn't it? Izzy Grant was beside herself.'

'Which proves that she couldn't have been involved.'

'I hate to say I told you so but …'

She thumped him gently on the arm, turning her attention back to the card. 'So, do you think it's a coincidence that the wording on the card is so like the first one Izzy received or that its arrival coincides with Grace appearing back on the scene?'

'That's why Grace Madden is significant. We failed to find her the first time round,' he said, braking sharply to avoid the transit van who'd just pulled over into the fast lane without indicating. 'Check back through the files but I seem to remember the search stopped with the husband.'

Chapter 14

Izzy
Thursday 2 January, 8.35 p.m. Abereiddy

'I've been admiring that all evening,' Pat said, pausing to take a sip from her glass of lemonade.

'It's something I started ages ago.' Izzy replied, spending a couple of minutes hooking back the stitch she'd just dropped. 'I don't think I'll be adding it to the range anytime soon.' Her fingers ran over the gossamer-thin lace pattern in muted shades of rich cream.

She was no more in the mood to entertain than she was to leave the safety of her workroom. But she was running a business and with a business came responsibilities or, in this case, the five local women she employed to help her meet her orders. They met up twice a month at the cottage, which was a bit of a chore but so much easier than having to drive round to each of their homes to drop off supplies, collect completed projects and organise payment. With the wood burner roaring and wine and nibbles on the side they '*knitted and bitched*' to their hearts content while they discussed all things wool-related and beyond.

'It's lovely, reminds me of those Shetland lace, "wedding ring" shawls,' Pat said, weaving a new strand of grey wool into the back of the patchwork scarf she was working on.

'Well, that's the idea although I've no plans on getting married any time soon.'

Izzy spread the circle she was working on across her knees, the cream a stark contrast to the brown of her leggings. She'd started the shawl when she'd found out she was pregnant with Alys – not a wedding shawl, but a christening one made from the finest wool she could find at the time. However, she'd never gotten around to finishing it, something she regretted with an ache that went right through like a blade. But the arrival of the postcard had brought a renewed sense of hope. Her daughter was still alive, and Izzy was more determined than ever to find her.

'Perhaps we could use the idea in one of our berets?' Pat said, thinking aloud. 'We could use the basic felt design but add a lace overlay in a contrasting colour – you know, the kind of thing a trendy teen might wear?'

Izzy lifted her head, a smile breaking. 'I just knew there was a reason I asked you to be a member of the group. That's bloody brilliant.'

Pat was the only accountant she knew. Not only was she a fantastic knitter, she also helped to keep the books in order and therefore her little business afloat. It was always a source of amazement that she was so talented. Sitting there in her blue suit, the jacket casually flung across the back of her chair, she didn't look as if she could thread a needle let alone produce the quality scarves she delivered week after week.

Izzy surveyed the room, deep in thought. Of all the people there, she was the only one that didn't seem to fit. There was Marjory, a fifty-something divorcee with no kids, who spent her days in a typing pool and her evenings watching soaps while she speed-knitted her way through their range of baby blankets.

Sitting beside her was Janice, married with two kids at university, who could knit a beret a night to supplement their living expenses. Paula and Mary, seated at the table, were so similar with their short grey hair and uniform of gathered skirts and patterned blouses that Izzy had to think twice before saying their names. Pensioners in their eighties, they used the extra income for treats and holidays.

But Pat was different. She could afford not to work in the evenings. As a twenty-something stunning blonde with one of those round, voluptuous figures that had men swallowing hard and women sharpening their claws, she should have been able to find something better to do with her spare time. And yet here she was, every second Thursday, being her greatest prop.

'My pleasure.' Pat twisted her wrist and, staring down at the time on her dainty gold watch, promptly rolled up her half-finished scarf. 'I'm sorry to break up the party but I've an early start tomorrow. There's nothing I hate more than rush hour traffic.'

'Oh, where are you off to?' Izzy asked, folding up the shawl between a couple of acid-free sheets of tissue paper. 'Perhaps you'll be able to pop into the sales?'

'I wish. I'm on an all-day audit in Swansea without even a break for lunch.'

Izzy threw her a look. 'That's not right, surely? You have to eat.'

'They have ways and means, Izzy. It's called a couple of cheap sandwiches, a brown banana and inferior powdered coffee on tap.'

She chanced joining her in a laugh, not quite sure whether she was joking or not – she could never quite tell with Pat.

'Why don't you come with me? I'll get to share the journey with a fellow knitter and, instead of getting strange looks from the natives, we can have a natter about lacy berets and the like. I might even be able to take a lunch break if I say that I'm meeting a friend. Then I'll be able to join you for a little retail therapy.'

'That's a good idea,' she said. *And while I'm at it I'll be able to pick your brains about what the hell I'm going to do next!*

Chapter 15

Gaby
Friday 3 January, 9 a.m. Swansea Police Station

The squad room had all the usual coppers for the regular nine o'clock mop-up meeting. But, apart from a quick peep over at Bill's face, Gaby kept her eyes on the wall above their heads. She knew they all thought the case should be shelved. They all thought that Alys wasn't going to turn up, not now. The men and women on the team were clearly divided into two camps and yet they were united on this: neither one believed that Alys would ever be seen again.

The more hardened officers, who'd been around the longest and had seen and heard it all before, believed that something sinister had happened, something sinister on that first day. Whether Charlie had gone off the rails or whether some horrible accident had befallen them were both at the top of their list of possible scenarios. The second group took her disappearance at face value, an opinion heavily fuelled by the wording on that first postcard. But, whatever their thoughts, the case had been knocking around the station far too long and with too few leads to be thought anything more than a nuisance. It would take a miracle to solve.

'I'd just like to give you an update on Alys Grant …'

'Really! We've had more updates than almost any other case I can remember,' Bill said, rubbing his fingers between his eyes.

'Come on, Bill, you know this is important. This case, more than any other, remains a blot on all of our books.'

'But DI Walker …' Michele interrupted.

Gaby eyed the petite redhead with interest, keen to see how Rhys managed dissent within the ranks.

'Don't "But DI Walker" me. I don't want to hear it. There's been another postcard and therefore new evidence – evidence which we can't discount.'

'Probably some copycat pervert trying to shake things up. You watch. She'll get a ransom note next.'

'After five years? I don't think so.' He turned back to Bill, who was doing a good impression of someone fascinated by their fingernails. 'What did forensics come up with?'

'Not a sausage, apart from the thousand or so postal officials that appear to have handled the card. As you suspected, it was posted in Northern France, which makes me think that someone hopped on the Eurostar with the sole purpose of posting the card – it's unlikely they live there.' He flipped through the pages of his notepad. 'The results from the stamp are back but again it's a non-starter. No DNA traces to be found.' He snapped his pad closed and returned it to his back pocket. 'Whoever sent it did their homework.'

Gaby's brow wrinkled. That was the part of the investigation that worried her, that and the little question of why. Why go to so much trouble five years after Alys's disappearance? Nothing else had changed as far as she knew or, if it had, no one was saying. Despite her optimism of earlier this was a difficult case with no new leads worth following because, as a lead, the second card was useless. All it had achieved was upset for the mother, but perhaps that was the intention all along.

Gaby had spent most of yesterday going back through some of the many box files on the disappearance, in the hope of coming up with something but Rhys, for all his laid-back demeanour, had followed procedure to the letter. He'd led the six-man team over that first year and had done everything he could within his disposal. The case was faultless except for the one obvious short-coming: their failure to find Baby Grant. The failure to find Grace Madden was also something Gaby was interested in, especially after that comment about the trail ending with the husband. She'd tried to find a weakness, some slip-up or omission that she could focus on. She wasn't being overly critical *per se*. She just wanted to see if an independent eye could, in any way, work out what had or hadn't been done that could have had an impact on the unsatisfactory outcome. She still had a few boxes left to go through but, up to now, it had been a textbook portrayal of what to do in a missing person case, particularly when the missing person just so happened to be an infant.

'Okay, so has anyone any bright ideas about why someone would send another card after a five-year gap – other than a crank?' Rhys said.

She swallowed hard; her mouth was open before she had time to tape it shut.

'I think you're approaching this from the wrong direction, if you don't mind me saying, sir.'

The sound of chairs shifting was almost deafening but she just ignored the attention. She was part of the team, whether they liked it or not.

'Go on, Darin. I'm listening.'

'Well, we need to put ourselves in Charlie Dawson's shoes. He's holed up with his daughter somewhere, happy as you like because he's managed to disappear off the face of the planet. He wouldn't need to send a card. A card is a risk, and a huge one at that. Someone might see him post it, perhaps even Alys, who'd be five by now and presumably at the age where she's learning to read and write. So, what's changed to make him feel the need to send the card to Alys's mother? What's happened to make him feel threatened?'

'And …? How would you start going about finding out just what's got him twitched?'

'I'd start with the mother and work my way through all of her relatives and then his. Also, I wouldn't put it past her to do some amateur sleuthing.'

'Really? And you'd know because …?' Rhys said, throwing her a questioning look.

'If you think they're better at detecting in Cardiff perhaps you should think about going back,' Bill snapped.

'You're out of order, DS Davis. Any more comments like that and I'll be calling you into my office,' the DCI said before throwing Gaby a thin-lipped smile.

The guv wasn't happy with either of them but she'd known what she was taking on when she'd agreed, albeit reluctantly, to her transfer. Gaby wasn't known for her finesse, but finesse didn't get results. Tackling investigations head on got results, only that.

She turned her attention back to Rhys while he delegated work, but she wasn't really listening. The mother had convinced her of her innocence but that was only part of the picture. Just what had Isabelle Grant been up to and what difference could she have made?

Someone somewhere had stood on a nerve and, if they continued, God only knew what might happen.

Chapter 16

Izzy
Friday 3 January, 9.05 a.m. M4

Pat wasn't wrong about the motorway being gridlocked. By the looks of the number of cars on the road everyone had had the same idea for a little splurge in the January sales.

'Have you decided where you want to go for lunch? There's a good pizza restaurant along Oxford Street?' Pat said, pulling into a car park along Oystermouth Road.

'That'll be fine.'

After parting from Pat, instead of making her way into town Izzy headed for the Swansea Central Library. She had three hours to waste and little idea on what to squander them on as the thought of shopping left her cold. What she really wanted to do was to continue her search for Grace and where better than the library.

While that second postcard worried her it wasn't the main concern. It was the thought that Grace could have been carrying on behind her back with Charlie all the time she was pregnant with Alys. She frowned. Common sense dictated that, as an idea, it was a bloody stupid one. If he was going to play away surely he would have looked for someone with a little less baggage than a heavily pregnant, married woman? Her frown deepened at the thought. Even if it was true, what on earth had made Grace mention the birthmark at all? The most annoying thing in all this was if it hadn't been for her waters breaking, she'd have been able to ask her.

It was all very well having a plan to find Grace. It was the execution that she was floundering on. How did you go about finding someone who clearly didn't want to be found? She looked at the large grey building in front of her then walked in.

'Hello, how can I help?'

A blush scored her cheeks and she hoped that the woman manning the desk wasn't as scary as she looked. She reminded her a little of the headteacher at their secondary school with her neat chestnut bob and carefully made-up face. Miss Fenshaw was a pussycat underneath her perfectly manufactured image of efficiency. She only hoped this woman proved to be the same.

Throwing her a smile, she said, 'I'm trying to find out as much information about a missing person as I can but I'm not sure where to start?'

'What about our online archive of local newspapers? It's the best place to begin if you know the dates in question.' She smiled back, her white teeth at war with the gentle wrinkles radiating from the corners of her eyes. 'There's also the National Archives. If you have a name and date of birth you'll be able to find birth, marriage and death certificates.'

And it was as easy as that. It took hardly any effort in front of a computer terminal to pull up all the relevant newspaper articles from those dark days, days she didn't remember, not really. She certainly hadn't been in any fit state to read the newspapers or speak to any of the trillion reporters banging on her door. She'd been on antidepressants by then and had spent the best part of a year in a haze of regret washed down with a large dose of guilt. *What if* was her mantra. *What if* she'd been nicer to him? *What if* he'd loved her a little more and his lover a little less? Yes, lover, because underneath it all she still thought there was another woman involved. The only question in her mind now on that score was whether it was Grace or someone else.

But there was one final *what if* that lingered longer and louder than all the rest. *What if* Alys had slept through the night? What if she'd been the perfect baby who'd slept longer than the measly two hours between feeds? Would she have gone with them? She shook her head. No, she couldn't think that. She couldn't apportion blame to a week-old baby. All the blame fell squarely at Charlie's door.

She worked her way through the articles, searching for any new pieces of information but there was nothing. The early news items were full of photos, her fingertip tracing over the image of Alys's face blown up to front page size – the same photo she wished a good night to each evening. She didn't remember her now, not really. When she dragged up a mental image it wasn't her. It was her image in this photo. She didn't have that many. A few taken in hospital but when they'd arrived home it was all so new, so bone-achingly challenging to go so long without sleep that she'd forgotten about her promise to take as many photos as she could. So, she was left with about twenty images to remind her of that first week – twenty images of Alys's little life apart from her first Baby-gro, squirrelled away in the bottom drawer of her chest of drawers.

It only took a few days for the story to shift from the front page to the middle before fizzling out to nothing. There were a few sightings from as far away as Edinburgh but after a couple of weeks, everyone lost interest, even the police, as greater crimes took precedence. Alys's father had kidnapped her. But she was safe or, at least, that's what the postcard had said. It hadn't said why he'd taken her but there must have been a reason. It didn't take long for loyalties to waver and attention to turn to an alternative reality – one which focused on why he'd felt the need to remove his daughter from her mother.

Her neck was starting to ache along with her back. She pushed back from the screen and stretched her arms up to the ceiling before pulling out a bottle of water from the top of her bag and taking a sneaky sip. There was a chocolate bar too but she ignored it. Instead, she returned her attention to the screen, her fingers hovering over the keys. She'd learnt nothing new, nothing at all. It felt as if she was reading someone else's story. The tragedy seemed removed somehow now that she knew the ending, not that it was an ending she could ever accept. It was impossible to disappear without a trace. They'd just been looking in all the wrong places.

She shifted in her chair, deciding to check to see if there was any information on Charlie. Within seconds, she'd pulled up Google. She'd searched for him before many times. She'd trawled the internet. She still trawled every few weeks just to see if there were any new sightings or mentions. He'd probably changed his name and maybe even his appearance but that didn't stop her from searching Facebook, Twitter and web forums for anything that might ring some bells. After a few minutes she leant back in her chair, disappointed yet again at the lack of anything new and, glancing at her watch, she decided on a different tactic.

With help from the librarian's instructions, she quickly found her way into the National Archives. It was time to try and find Grace.

Birth certificates, such simple little things, were a minefield of information, something she'd never really thought about until just now. She blinked at the computer screen and the long list of Grace Maddens even as she wondered what she was trying to achieve with the search. So what if they'd been friends? It was only for a few months and people drifted apart all the time. She didn't know what her sudden fascination was with someone who'd walked out of her life. It was unlikely Grace had been involved with Charlie and, with her own pregnancy to deal with, why on earth would she want to bring up another woman's child?

There was nothing like a heavy dose of introspection to turn the facts on their side. Izzy rested her chin in her hand, staring at the long list of Grace Madden's on the screen in front of her. She had no idea of how to narrow the list down or even why she should be trying. The truth was, she'd become obsessed with someone from her past, someone who had little meaning or relevance.

She shook her head, dislodging the thought. She still had time for one final search but that was all. When she left the building, she'd give up on Grace and leave the police to the job they were paid for.

Her hand hovered over the keys but instead of searching for Grace, she forced her fingers to press a different arrangement of letters. She'd concentrate her search on someone else, someone different albeit linked.

Her gaze rested on the name in front of her. Geraint Madden. Her ponytail felt greasy under her hand as she reached up to massage her suddenly aching scalp, her eyes still focused on the list in front of her. There were few Geraints to choose from, but which one? A fifty-year old, born in South Africa? Or maybe the twenty-two-year old living in South Shields? No, not possible. She added them both to her mental list of rejects along with any Geraint Madden over the age of forty-five and under thirty. She was only left with one possibility. Geraint Timothy Madden, age thirty-nine, and born in Carmarthen.

She sat back, the water curdling in her stomach. She'd been hoping for something definite: a date of birth, a marriage certificate, an area to search so that she could accidently-on-purpose bump into Grace and finally confirm what she knew to be true – that she hadn't been involved in their disappearance. But that wasn't a conversation that was going to happen anytime soon. That wasn't a conversation that was going to happen at all.

Turning away from the screen she slipped her arms into the sleeves of her jacket and picked up her bag before heading out of the building. The last hope for a happy resolution to this puzzle, which ended in her hugging Alys to her breast, had just fizzled out to nothing. If the details she'd just jotted down on a scrap of paper were for the right Geraint Madden, then he'd died the same year of Alys's disappearance.

Chapter 17

Izzy

'There seems to be a distinct lack of anything that even looks like a shopping bag to me,' Pat said, her eyes glued to Izzy's empty hands. 'I would never have thought you a fussy shopper but ...'

'I sort of got caught up with something – sorry I'm a bit late.' Izzy slipped her phone into her pocket, the sight and smell of food a welcome distraction from the text she'd just received from Rebecca. She wanted nothing more than to pop around on the way home and share her fears with her best friend over a bottle of wine. In truth, the only thing stopping her was the thought of Rhys getting to hear about it. She'd trust Rebecca with her life. She'd certainly trusted her with all her secrets. But that wasn't enough to stop a little earworm of suspicion that Rebecca was trying to set her up with her brother.

'No problem. I've ordered extra-large glasses of Chardonnay. You know it's going to be a bad day when the customer hands you a mountain of shoeboxes.'

'What type of shoes?'

'Not the type I wear.' And they both took a moment to admire her spiky stilettoes before turning their attention to the waitress approaching their table.

They'd reached the steaming mugs of coffee stage, in place of the dessert they were both determined to avoid, before the conversation rewound to that of earlier.

'So, how did you amuse yourself then while I've been slaving away?'

'Oh, nothing really. Just this and that,' she said, picking up her mug and playing for time.

The truth was she wasn't sure how much to divulge, if indeed anything. After all, while friendly they weren't actually friends and the trip to Swansea and then lunch was the first time she'd spent any time with Pat outside of the business. She didn't know that much about her apart from the basics, like where she lived. She also knew that she had an on-off boyfriend called Harry, an accountant with the same firm. But none of that added up to very much. Alys was someone she never discussed outside of her immediate family. There was nothing to say. Conversations started never got finished, embarrassment pushing away any words. What was there to say other than *sorry*?

She placed the mug back on the table. 'I was trying to trace an old friend, so I popped into the library.'

'And?' Pat said, her eyes sharp over the rim of her mug.

'And, nothing. The only person with the same name died …' She paused, seeing again in her mind's eye the death certificate as if it was right there in front of her. 'It can't be the same person.'

'Well, that's easy to check,' Pat said, glancing down at the bill. 'There'll be parish records and maybe even a grave. Not that I fancy trailing round graveyards, especially in these heels.' She drained her mug before placing it next to Izzy's with a gentle clatter. 'Now, this is on me. No arguments. After all those shoe-boxes, I'm just going to add it to my expenses.'

Outside, the shadows cast by the clouds overhead caused them to quicken their step. Izzy walked Pat back to the office and, with a brief hug, told her she'd make her own way back to St David's. That was true enough but first she was going to blow her savings by taking a taxi to Carmarthen and the grave-yard behind the local Methodist church where Geraint was meant to be buried.

An hour later found Izzy wandering up and down the carefully manicured strips of grass that separated the graves, trying not to get too upset at the letters etched into a variety of headstones. She paused beside a granite angel, her gaze skimming over the words, before squeezing her eyes tight to blacken out the image. Her life was hard enough without having to read about other people's tragedies.

It was cold and damp, and Izzy was regretting that she hadn't remembered to bring an umbrella as cold drizzle inveigled its way down the neck of her jacket. Turning up the collar, she hunched her shoulders and tucked her hands deep within her pockets before continuing to follow the well-laid paths, some of the lichen-covered headstones so old that she could barely make out their inscriptions. She shouldn't be here. She should have taken Pat up on her offer of a lift home and found a different way of finding out about Geraint. The Internet. The phone. Even Rhys, for God's sake. There were so many other ways than standing surrounded by the rank smell of death and decay.

'Hello there. Can I be of any help?'

He came out of nowhere, chasing the air from her lungs and her heart from her chest. She'd been priming herself to give up, to flee from both her thoughts and the graveyard. There was no point in looking any further. She'd phone up the station on her return and pass all the information over to Rhys to sift through. Now, she didn't know what to think.

She focused on his face, noting the kindly smile and twinkling eyes. But it was the sight of the dog collar circling his neck that gave her a good indication that he was someone she could trust – that would have to be good enough for now.

'I'm looking for a grave.' She could have bitten off her tongue as soon as the words were out. What else would she be looking for in a graveyard at this time of day?

'Ah, yes. I thought you might be,' he said, his eyes scrunched up at the corners. 'Well, there are hundreds to choose from. I'm Reverend Simpson, by the way – Bartholomeus Simpson but most people call me—'

'Bart?' Her lips pulled into a grin.

'That's it exactly,' he said, shaking his head. 'It's not fair, is it? I did think of complaining to a higher authority. It's not as if it's the best of names for a member of the cloth but it is what it is.'

He waved his umbrella in a wide arc, indicating the scope of her task. 'Perhaps I could be of assistance? What year did this person pass away? The gravestones are in some sort of year order,' he added, dragging out a handkerchief from his pocket with his free hand, one of those old linen ones that had been pressed into submission by a determined hand.

'Five years ago, a Geraint Madden.'

He lifted his head and his hand paused in the act of wiping his nose. 'Sadly, I remember that one,' he said, again shaking his head. 'I always seem to remember the tragedies for some reason. But one-hundred-year-old grandparents that died in their sleep after a life of good living, pah – I never remember those.'

The grave was larger than she'd imagined, larger and with a plain headstone. Someone came to tend the earth, someone that cared if the sight of the large daisy-like flowers in full bloom were anything to go by. The writing was brief – just a name and a date. The date hit her where the National Archives had failed to make an impression.

Geraint Timothy Madden

6th March 1979 to 28th August 2014

A month before she'd first met Grace.

Chapter 18

Gaby
Friday 3 January, 4.45 p.m. Swansea Police Station

'So this is what you do with yourself when you're not at your desk?'

Gaby looked up from behind the pile of boxes she'd been ploughing through for most of the day, throwing an extra wide smile at the welcome interruption. Apart from a quick break for lunch, she'd been at it nonstop since the morning meeting and she was heartily sick of the whole thing. She wished she'd never heard of Alys and Isabelle Grant. She wished she'd never heard of Swansea and as for bloody DI Rhys Walker. If she had to try and decipher one more word of his small cramped handwriting she'd scream.

'Hello Amy. I do hope you've had a more productive day than me,' she said, pushing away the current box file and standing. 'I have never been so bored. So much time spent with little or no result is not my idea of fun.'

'That bad, hey?' Amy picked up the neat pile of notes Gaby had made. 'What were you hoping for? Rhys is a good copper. It's unlikely he'd have missed anything.'

Gaby frowned. 'I hope he doesn't think I'm checking up on him. It's just that with such a big investigation I was eager for some more clues.'

Amy patted her on the arm. 'I'm sure he won't think that and if he had he could easily have found you something else to do.' She threw a look over her shoulder before lowering her voice. 'The Archives Officer has his ears tuned. So have you found anything?'

'Nothing that we can use,' she said, placing a pile of loose papers into the box and closing the lid. 'But the paucity of clues is telling.'

'How come?'

'It tells me that the person responsible was very clever. It's easy to make someone disappear but not without leaving some kind of footprint. There's nothing. No CCTV. No monetary trail. Even the car disappeared.' She stood and pulled her shoulders back before arranging the box files in a neat pile. 'We're not dealing with someone making a spur-of-the-moment decision. The baby snatch was orchestrated to the nth degree. Charlie Dawson was nineteen at the time and with only a part-time job manning the pumps at the local petrol station. I've checked his schooling records, Amy. He left at sixteen and flitted in and out of tempo-rary work, never staying in the same position for more than a few months. By all accounts, Izzy and Alys were the making of him. Rhys interviewed all his family and friends and the consensus was that he wouldn't just up and leave like that.'

'But if Charlie didn't take her when who?' Amy asked, her eyes wide.

'Someone clever. Very clever indeed.' Gaby glanced at her watch before picking up her keys and mug. 'It's nearly time to knock off. Are you up to anything later?'

'If you can count Netflix being up to anything.'

'What about coming around to mine? I have the makings of spaghetti carbonara in the fridge.'

Gaby rented a small one-bedroomed fisherman's cottage in Mumbles, a quaint village situated on the western end of Swansea Bay and only a twenty-minute drive from the police station.

The whitewashed cottage had no garden, its front door opening onto a small square-shaped lounge with a tiny kitchen and shower room leading off. A wrought iron spiral staircase coiled its way to a large bedroom tucked under the eaves with blackened beams and a view across to the pier and lighthouse.

'You make yourself comfortable while I open a bottle.' Gaby said, switching on the lamp in the corner. 'Red or white?'

'White please.' Amy took off her coat and placed it on the stand beside the door before settling on the red corduroy-covered sofa and slipping off her shoes. 'What an amazing place. However did you find it?'

'Internet search and luck. It's too small for more than a single person and, as I have no thoughts on that score, I snapped it up.' Gaby set a large glass of wine in front of her and a small dish full of Mini Cheddars. 'Don't worry about driving by the way. The sofa pulls out if you decide to stay over. I can easily loan you a T-shirt and a spare toothbrush.'

'I might just take you up on that. I still live with my parents, worse luck. I had been hoping that my knight would have popped by to whisk me off my feet but no such luck.'

'Well, anytime you need a place to kip the sofa has your name on it.'

'What about you?' Amy cradled her glass between her fingers and took a deep sip. 'What brings you to Swansea? The men not handsome enough in Cardiff?' She paused, her colour rising. 'Oh God, sorry. Or women? I hope I haven't just put my foot in it.'

Gaby eyed her over the top of her drink, struggling to hide a smile. 'No rapid removing of feet needed. I'm heterosexual or, at least I was. After my last relationship I think I'm going to be nothing for quite a while. If I can make such a mess of things, I'm better off on my own.'

'You and me both.' Amy reached for the bottle and topped up her glass before pushing it towards Gaby. 'Here's to tossers.' She lifted her glass in mock salute and said, 'So what did yours do then? Mine, for what it's worth, dumped me after five years. He said that he wasn't ready to settle down. What he really meant was that he wasn't ready to settle down with me – I saw the announcement of his engagement in the paper last week.'

'Oh Amy …'

'It's okay. I'm over it now,' she said, the sad smile telling Gaby a very different story. 'He has a nice nine-to-five job at the post office and if I'm honest, the strain of having to always apologise when work interfered with his plans was becoming a real bore. He's engaged to someone that works with him. She's been chasing him for ages. They'll have nice boring little lives to look forward to instead of the excitement of a career in law enforcement,' she added, rolling her eyes.

This share and tell was new to Gaby and something she wasn't comfortable with. Growing up in Liverpool to strait-laced Italian parents, she'd always struggled with forging friendships. But she liked Amy, she liked her a lot. They were similar in many ways. They were both intelligent, career-minded women who cared deeply for the work they'd signed their lives over to. Men were important but not at the expense of their jobs.

'Mine was called Leigh,' she said, but there was no sign of a smile on her face. 'I met him when he serviced my car. I should have known then that there was something iffy about him, the size of the bill for an oil change and tyre check.' She stared at the grate and the fireplace that she'd been told not to light by the landlord due to the continual problem of birds' nests. 'Even then I wouldn't have accepted his invite but things weren't going too well at work and –' she lifted her head briefly '– loathe that I am to admit it, I was lonely. It didn't strike me at the time that he always chose out of the way corners to meet. Never anything central. Never anything near to where he lived. He'd always make excuses about the state of his flat and, stupid of me now, but I never twigged. He told me he loved me and I believed him. He could have told me the moon was made of cheddar and I would have handed him a cheese knife and plate. His wife was six months' pregnant when we met and nine when she finally realised what he'd been up to with his supposed overtime.' Gaby leant forward and, grabbing a handful of Mini Cheddars, started to work her way through them, one by one. 'She came to the station and accosted me in front of all the other officers, which made an already intolerable situation unbearable. Of course, I never saw him again. I never answered his calls. His declaration of undying love wasn't worth the breath he'd used to say the words. I was called into the super's office and torn down more than a few stripes for bringing my "tawdry personal life", as he called it, into the department. Six weeks later work blew up big time and I was forced to leave.' She pushed the now half empty bowl of cheese biscuits in Amy's direction and picked up her glass. 'This is a new start for me, Amy, in more ways than one. I need to make it work. You said that for Rhys the case is all about finding Izzy's daughter. For me I just need to solve a case, any case, in order to prove to myself that I still can. Otherwise I'll head back to Liverpool with my tail between my legs and spend the rest of my life working as a waitress in my parents' Italian restaurant.' She laughed. 'When you taste my pasta, you'll realise why they don't allow me anywhere near the kitchen.'

Chapter 19

Izzy
Friday 3 January, 4.50 p.m. Carmarthen Rectory

The manse was cold, despite the three-bar electric fire and mug of tea warming her palms. Izzy had suspected that Reverend Simpson was kind when she'd met him but for him to invite her into his home, a stranger, and all because she'd lost her footing and would have fallen onto the grave if he hadn't stretched out an arm and managed to save her.

'Thank you again for—'

'Don't mention it. A misspent youth on the rugger field as a boy,' he said, bending his arm to show off his muscles.

'Well, I can't tell you how grateful I am. I could have damaged the grave – it doesn't bear thinking about.'

'More like given yourself a black eye. Those headstones are built to last against all weathers. A young slip of a girl like you isn't going to be more than a wisp of air to a ruddy great lump of rock like that.'

She laughed at the analogy. She'd never been a young slip of a girl, and certainly not these days with the odd grey hair starting to shine through the brown, but she appreciated his attempt at trying to make light of what was proving to be one of the most difficult situations.

Settling back in her chair, she couldn't stop her thoughts from returning to Geraint's grave. There was something about being faced with a fact head-on for it to really sink in. A stark entry on a computer screen was one thing but to see a name, a name she'd heard so many times, etched into stone was something completely different. There could be no mistake. It wasn't as if it was a common Welsh name. She had no idea how many Geraint Maddens there actually were hanging round Wales but there was no way it was going to run into the thousands or even hundreds. The other thing about all of this, of course, was that Grace had lied. She'd lied about their life together. All the times they'd talked never once had she let slip that her glamorous life was a façade – that Geraint was already cold in the ground by the time they'd met at that first parenting class.

Izzy lifted her head, trying to focus on the man opposite instead of her thoughts. There'd be plenty of time for that later.

'So, I gather he was a friend then?' he finally said. 'Such a tragic case.'

'Yes. Tragic.' She'd finished her tea and, leaning forward, went to place her mug on the table before standing. 'Well, I've kept you long enough—'

'No, you stay right where you are,' he interrupted. 'You look as if you've seen a ghost. It's still raining so there's no rush. How about another cuppa?'

She threw him a little smile of thanks before resting back in her chair and closing her eyes, the noise of the mugs rattling against the tin tray comforting somehow in a world that was suddenly not comforting at all. All the times she'd thought of Grace she'd imagined her happily married to Geraint, but he'd been dead all along.

Reverend Simpson walked back into the room, pressing

another mug into her hand before placing a plate of freshly buttered toast on the mahogany coffee table.

'Tuck in, I missed lunch and I hate eating alone.'

She wasn't hungry even though she hadn't managed to finish her lunch. She felt as if she'd never be hungry again. But, after a pause, she picked up a slice just to be sociable and a comfortable silence ensued, something she welcomed. It wasn't that she didn't want to tell him about Grace. It was just that she didn't want to admit she'd been taken in by all her lies. She was still trying to work it out. She was still trying to find a reason for Grace's pretence but there wasn't one that made any sense.

The silence stretched, not an awkward one but one she was destined to fill. She swept her tongue over her teeth and swallowed the last of the toast.

'I didn't know Geraint, as such. It was more his wife, Grace.'

'Ah, I was wondering if it was something like that. Such a wonderful woman and her daughter is a delight. She brings her here every Sunday, despite the weather. The service wouldn't be the same without little Daisy.'

'Her daughter?' Her voice was barely a whisper.

'Yes. Daisy Madden. She's a sweet little thing. Such a tragedy having to raise her without her father around.'

She could feel his gaze on her, but she kept her eyes trained on the tips of her boots, stained from all that trampling around the graveyard. The very last thing she'd expected to hear about after finding Geraint's grave was Grace's child. She hadn't forgotten about Grace being pregnant, but it was something she hadn't allowed herself to dwell on – not with her own sadness lingering in the shadows.

She swallowed hard before lifting her head. 'What happened, that is, if you don't mind me asking? We sort of lost touch when she moved out of the area.'

He nodded before speaking. 'A car accident. What else? Nowadays people speed along with no thought for anyone other than themselves. I remember, back in the Seventies, a thirty-mile speed limit meant just that, and people wouldn't even think of driving without insurance,' he said, his mouth a thin line. 'I wasn't here then, but it was in all the local papers. They had to switch off his life support machine in the end. The baby was a blessing, a huge blessing.'

She wanted to hear more. She wanted to hear it all. She wanted to know where it had happened and when. Was Grace even there at the time or did she have to wait for that knock on the door? It wasn't that Izzy was being macabre. But his words had conveyed a picture in her head, almost a movie scene with Grace sitting at his side, holding onto his hand, forced to watch his life slipping away, her belly swollen and taut.

Frowning, her mind travelled back to the date on the headstone. All this had happened weeks before they'd first met. Grace's bump wouldn't have been anything like the balloon proportions her imagination had conjured up. Maybe she was being too harsh on her. Maybe, instead of deliberately setting out to bend the truth, it was all too new, too painful to discuss. No wonder she hadn't wanted to stay in touch. So much heartache. So much grief.

Despite his hospitality and kindness, now she needed to be alone. She had lots to think about. New things that she could never have imagined when she'd set out this morning. That little saying came into her mind – be careful what you wish for. She'd never really had any serious ideas about Grace and Charlie being an item and this news pretty much confirmed it. The birthmark was a niggle, only that.

She bent down and scooped up her scarf from where she'd dropped it on top of her bag and wound it around her neck, her thoughts in freefall. Life had played a trick on Grace in the same way it had her. There had been no *happy ever after* for either of them and, with that realisation, she finally let go of any last vestiges of hope of ever finding Alys. In truth, she'd known within the first few weeks of her being taken that the chances were dwindling, that everyone had given up hope, everyone apart from her. No one ever talked about her daughter anymore. She was the elephant in the room, a topic to be avoided at all cost.

Izzy felt empty all of a sudden. Hollow. Barren. It was as if a big hand had descended out of the air and removed a vital chunk. The final chunk. She'd made one last push to find her daughter and she'd failed. There was nothing left.

She said her goodbyes, full of thanks but keen not to miss the 17.59 train to Haverfordwest, the nearest station to St David's. The reverend had been a huge help but also, in a way, the instigator of her sudden inertia. However, he wasn't to blame. After all, she was the one who'd decided to visit the library just as she was the one who'd traced his obituary and final resting place. No one had forced her to follow the breadcrumb trail to Geraint's grave. She had no one to blame but herself.

The afternoon had slid into evening, the light shifting from grey to black. She wasn't squeamish, far from it. She'd never have survived even one night alone in the cottage if she suffered from nerves. But she was far from happy retracing her footprints across the graveyard, the reality of all those dead bodies never far from her thoughts.

Chapter 20

Izzy

Sunday 5 January, 4.50 p.m. Carmarthen Church

Leaving St David's for the third time in two weeks was something of a record. Most days Izzy didn't even get in her car to drive the short distance into town. Her needs were small and, with a milkman still delivering fresh milk and eggs, there was little reason for her to leave the comfort and security of her home. But, unlike the last time, this time she wasn't going back into Swansea – this time she was retracing her footsteps back to Carmarthen Rectory or, more specifically, back to the church.

It was a long time since she'd attended a church service just for the sake of it. In recent years there'd usually been either a couple or a coffin to force the issue. But today was different. Today she'd decided to sit in on the service, while she watched and waited for any sign of Grace. She was here to make her peace with the person who'd been chipping away at her thoughts for days.

The church was packed, with room at the back only but that suited her fine. She didn't want to be noticed. She didn't want to be watched. She was there to observe. Her plan had been to turn up just before the heavy wooden doors closed and sneak into a seat at the back. She didn't want to scare Grace. She didn't even particularly want to speak to her just yet. All she wanted was to find a pillar to lean against and hope that, when she finally found her, she'd know what to do.

There was no pillar to hand. She was squeezed up against the end of the pew, her left thigh squashed flat by the woman next to her. But she hardly noticed. All her attention was focused on scanning the rows ahead for any sight of ink-black hair, cut into a sharp shoulder-length bob. They were halfway through the last hymn before she finally decided to give up. There were just too many people scattered about for her to see and it wasn't as if she was even sure she'd be there.

With the final chords of 'Bread of Heaven' still ringing in her ears, the woman beside her snapped her hymn book closed and Izzy followed her example, her mind jerking in a new direction; her reluctance to visit the police station to let them know she had a good idea where to find Grace. She'd had more than her fill of coppers over the years and none of it good. The truth was they'd failed her daughter. If they'd acted quicker instead of waiting for Charlie to return on that first day then they might just have been able to stop him from leaving the area. If they couldn't find her when the trail was red-hot, what chance did they have after five years? No, she'd been right not to tell them about today. This was her way of making amends for giving up on her daughter. She should have kept banging on Rhys's door at every opportunity, keeping the investigation in the forefront of everyone's mind, but it had been too difficult that first year. After she'd finally been released from hospital following the overdose, her mother had encouraged her to take up knitting again as a way to keep the depression at bay while Bethan talked her into attending night classes given by a local textile artist. It wasn't planned but using her brain and her hands made it easier to sleep and, with each successive day, she got dragged further into the world of wool production and designing. As a coping strategy it worked. It worked too well. It pushed all thoughts of Alys to a place in her mind where she could survive her loss, but it also stopped her from searching.

Izzy finally stood up, offering the impatient woman beside her a small smile that wasn't returned. But stroppy parishioners were the least of her worries … She turned back to face the aisle and the first person she saw was Grace.

'How did you find me?'

'It wasn't hard in the end, not really.'

'But after all these years?'

Izzy eyed her over the top of her cup before dropping her gaze to Daisy, considering her reply. The child picked up a yellow crayon and started filling in the sun, her pink tongue clasped between tiny white teeth.

It still hurt to see children the same age as Alys. It hurt like a bitch and it probably always would but she was learning. It was mainly down to Bethan and her drip drip approach of getting *Aunty Izzy* involved in Dylan and Gareth's lives that finally meant she could find enjoyment in watching a small child wrapped up in their imagination. The yellow was soon discarded only to be replaced by blue as she started on the sky, her chubby fingers gripping the crayon with a fierce determination.

'Well, I wasn't looking for the first five,' she finally said, running her tongue over dry lips. 'Life sort of took over and got in the way.'

Izzy placed her cup back on its saucer with a sigh. Now what? The distance between them stretched immeasurably and seemed a lot greater than the years since they'd last met probably, in part, because they had more skeletons in their combined cupboards than the graveyard they'd just left. What had been the point in finding her? Raking over old ground wasn't going to help find Alys – it was only going to cause upset. The last few years hadn't exactly been a barrel of laughs for either of them. She was well aware that Grace had lost her husband under the most horrific of circumstances and in a way that left no room for hope. There was nothing more final than death.

'Oh, when did you start?'

It was Izzy's turn to frown. She paused in the act of sipping her drink, taking a moment to repeat the question in her head because, as questions went, it didn't make sense. Surely the question of when she'd started searching was the wrong one? Surely it was more relevant to know why? Placing her elbows on the table, she decided to be completely honest. She had nothing to hide and she certainly didn't want to be caught out in a lie.

'I saw you,' she said, raising her head and looking her in the eye. 'Christmas shopping, you know. I thought you'd spotted me?' Her voice held a question.

'No. I would have stopped if I had. I have no reason to ignore you.'

Izzy lifted her spoon and added sugar to her coffee, despite not having taken sugar in drinks since she was six. She knew Grace was lying. The image of the shock on her face, framed by that taxi window, was as clear now as when it had happened. She'd like to question her further but, suddenly she was too scared. One wrong word and she could destroy the only opportunity she might have of finding out what had happened.

They continued sitting opposite each other, but it was like having coffee with a stranger. The reality was that they had nothing in common and nothing to say to each other. Their friendship, which had meant so much, had disappeared. She flushed, remembering that she hadn't even commiserated about the death of her husband. While their friendship might lie in tatters the very least she could do was go through the motions.

'I haven't said how sorry I am about your loss.'

Facial expressions are a funny thing. Izzy used to be able to

103

tell every thought written across Charlie's face – he was far from complex. If he had a full belly and enough money for a beer with the lads on a Friday night he was easy-going to the extreme. He never shouted or got cross. He never seemed to worry about anything or anyone unless it had football in the title. Even now she still didn't know how he'd managed to steal Alys out from under her nose without her guessing that something was up.

With Grace it was different. Izzy had never been able to read her, not even a flicker. That day when she'd mentioned the possibility of Charlie having an affair, she hadn't seen it coming. For all she'd known, Grace could have been about to tell her about a hike in the price of fish. It was a bombshell completely out of the blue. Izzy could only imagine Grace's anger and sorrow at the loss of Geraint in the same way that she'd been prey to both those feelings following Alys's abduction. But for her to smile? Her smile was confusing and totally out of keeping with the conversation to date. She fiddled with the spoon again, her thoughts trying to puzzle it out. The look had disappeared. Had it ever been there, or had she imagined it? There was nothing funny about the death of a husband. Nothing at all.

'You don't have to say sorry. You never even met him.'

Izzy set her spoon aside and, taking her courage in both hands, said. 'Well, that's hardly surprising is it? How could I possibly have met him?' She watched what little colour Grace had disappear leaving thick foundation and a clown-like blush in its place. 'I don't know what game you've been playing,' she went on to say. 'But it's over. Caput. Finished. I also don't want to make a scene, but I will if I have to because finding Alys is all I care about. You have to admit that leaving as you did, so soon after her disappearance, seems a little too convenient?'

Grace threw her a nervous look, her eyes briefly on Daisy who was busy colouring in some grass. 'I couldn't cope, all right? You're strong but I'm not. When I heard about what had happened to you I flung all my stuff into the back of the car and scarpered.'

Izzy leant forward. 'But why the need to lie about your husband? I just don't get it.'

'Geraint didn't want children when it was my dearest wish.' Her lips became a thin line. 'We very nearly split when he discovered I was pregnant and when he died I lost it completely. His friends ... his family.' She spread her hands wide. 'I just wanted to curl up and join him after the accident but there was the baby to consider so I hopped in the car and left to find a new life, a life without him.' She touched her hand, giving it a little squeeze. 'I know I let you down. But it was a time I couldn't speak about. To speak about it would have made it real. And then when you lost Alys, it felt as if life was repeating itself.'

Izzy stared back, shaking her head. 'I still don't understand. You never struck me as the emotional sort. I even remember you telling me once that if something happened to Geraint you'd soon find another man to fill your bed. So, what's happened to change that? Why the devoted widow act? The way the minister spoke it's as if you've attached yourself to a ghost.'

'I don't have any choice. His parents ...' She pressed her fingers under her eyes, careful not to disturb her make-up. 'You think all this comes for free,' she said, waving her hands at her Chanel handbag, with gold rings stacked on every finger. 'All this, my sweet, comes at a price – their price. As soon as I had Daisy, my life, my freedom was curtailed. They tracked me down and threatened me with all sorts.'

'But there's nothing they can do, surely?'

'Oh, isn't there?' She glared across the table; her hands curled into tight fists. 'Izzy, we're different, you and me. You've always been the nice girl. Me, I'm not so nice. There are things I've done, things I'm not proud of but Daisy ... Daisy is my life and I'll do anything I can to hold onto her even if it means acting something I'm not.' She tucked her scarf more firmly around her neck before draining her cup. 'It's time I left. Don't try to get in touch again, my dear. I'm not worth it.'

'Hold on a minute,' Izzy said, trying to equate the hard woman opposite with the Grace she once thought she knew but it was like having the blinkers removed. Her friend had been a mirage, only that. She hadn't known her, not really. She'd been young and gullible and had fallen for everything she'd said. She lifted her chin, her gaze hardening.

'There's one thing I need to ask, just one and after, I promise, I won't try to get in touch again. The birthmark on Charlie's cheek. How did you know it was there because it sure as hell wasn't in any photo I ever showed you?'

Grace stared back, her gaze unwavering, her voice soft. 'Izzy, I like you. Ever since that first day I thought now there's a girl, a nice girl who's never hurt anyone, a girl that deserves the best. Charlie wasn't fit to wipe your boots let alone share your life and your bed.' She paused, swiping back her hair. 'That story about him and his girlfriend in a café somewhere in Wales was made up. A very poor attempt to warn you that he wasn't all he seemed.'

'And the birthmark?' Izzy whispered.

'I knew he had a mole because I saw it before, during and after we … when we—' She stood abruptly, starting to gather up Daisy's crayons, stuffing them any old how into her little *Peppa Pig* rucksack before reaching for their coats. 'You shouldn't have asked. You should have left it as it was.'

'Don't you see I had to know?' Izzy's frown deepened. 'When? When did you and he …?'

'If it's of any consolation it was before we met, maybe even before you fell pregnant.' She stood there, one hand holding loosely onto Daisy's, the other fiddling with her keys. 'It was nothing. It meant nothing,' she said and, with one final look, turned on her heel and hurried out of the café.

Chapter 21

Gaby

Wednesday 8 January, 9.05 a.m. Swansea Police Station

Gaby wasn't in the best of moods but, after another three days stuck going through box files in the Archives, no one could blame her. If DI Walker had his way she'd still be there instead of taking up her usual seat in the squad room for the morning briefing. She could see it in the frown pooling and the jut of his chin when she'd shuffled into the room, a mug in one hand and her notebook in the other. He'd be even less pleased when he realised that the search had been a complete waste of her time. She cradled her mug in her hands, winking across at Amy over the brim before returning her gaze forward to where he was pacing the length of the room like a caged panther. He had something on his mind. She had no idea what.

'I intend to ask Miss Grant to drop into the station later – she deserves to know that the card is a complete waste of time.' He ran his hand through his hair, the frown deepening. 'I take it that there're no further developments?'

There was a lot Gaby could say in reply but for once she decided to take the sensible option and keep her mouth closed.

She'd spent all her time pretty much since Friday squirrelled away dissecting the case with only the grumpy Archives Officer for company and all she'd come up with were a load of questions and nobody she could ask that wouldn't bite her head off in the process. Bill Davis was the obvious choice but, she didn't need a degree in human relationships to realise that for some reason, she'd be the last person he'd ever agree to help.

In the old days she'd have made more of an effort to try and rectify what was wrong with their working relationship. She'd have pulled their interactions to bits and tried to change whatever it was about her that ticked all of his wrong boxes. But that was before Cardiff and before Leigh. That was before she'd learnt that there were some people that would never like her and her *giving a damn* was the reaction they were probably looking for. She'd obviously never be able to please him but, as long as she did her job, there was nothing he could really do about it.

She took a sip of her drink before settling it beside her notepad and returning to the short list of questions she'd been jotting down, like the reasons for the particular search area following Alys's disappearance. If she wasn't assured that both Bill and Rhys would explode, she'd have spoken up when asked but she decided to wait, for once, to see just what the rest of the team came up with.

Rhys paused a moment, his gaze resting on the top of her head but she pursed her lips in an attempt at keeping the stream of words from escaping. He turned away finally, focusing on the other members of the team.

'Bill, Michele. You were going to do a background on Miss Grant. What have you come up with?'

'Nothing that seems to involve her in any wrongdoing,' Michele said, darting a look towards Bill and where he was busily writing in his notebook. 'Apart from keeping herself busy with the business, there's not a lot going on with her life. I've checked out her website and been in touch with some of her supply chain. She doesn't appear on any of our databases as a person of interest and hasn't even picked up a parking ticket or speeding fine. There are no bills outstanding just as there's no indication that she's come into possession of a large influx of cash. She owns the cottage outright, left it by her grandmother a couple of years before the disappearance but that's the only thing out of the ordinary.'

'What about her personal life?'

'There's nothing to report but then again she appears to be a very private person so, unless we put a tail on her, we wouldn't know necessarily exactly what she gets up to. But, on paper at least, she appears to be exactly what she seems. A single woman still struggling with the loss of her child.'

Gaby opened her mouth only to close it again, the thought wrapping itself around her mind. There was one course of action no one had suggested and she couldn't think why not – it was one of the first things she'd thought of. She glanced at her watch, planning the rest of her morning even as Rhys started giving out orders. Getting access to the travel records for the Eurostar wasn't something she'd be able to manage without a court order but, with a little bit of luck and quite a bit of nerve she might just be able to blag herself a copy from some undiscerning minor official. She was as certain as she could be that she'd come across a name that she recognised. The only question now was which one.

Chapter 22

The office was just how she remembered, maybe a little untidier. Maybe the shelves were a little fuller, but it was still the long narrow office with the same desk, chair and filing cabinets. Even the blind looked the same, the cream slats discoloured yellow with age.

She focused on his expression as he walked across the room and the lack of anything even approaching a smile. After yesterday's disastrous meeting with Grace, she'd been hoping for a miracle. But the lack of a smile was as good an indication as any that she was going to be disappointed. And with that thought, she was suddenly angrier than she'd been in a long time. She knew it wasn't his fault and that he was probably doing everything he could but reason and good sense flew out of the window. She didn't care if he'd worked on the case night and day for the last five years. She didn't care if he'd slept in his office and eaten at his desk. They'd left her hanging with nothing and now, when there was the possibility of a breakthrough, they'd decided to what? To invite her in for a cosy little chat and break the bad news that the postcard was just that – some crappy dead-end clue leading nowhere.

Her gaze flickered from his face and back to the postcard, propped up against the keyboard, before speaking. 'So, the card is useless then. You could have just told me over the phone instead of dragging me all this way and on the bus too,' she said, folding her arms across her chest. 'I have orders to compile, a business to run. But not only that – you made me build my hopes up only to have them—'

'I'm sorry,' he interrupted. 'You should have said.'

'And what good would that have done? You'd still have dragged me here and for what? Go on. Tell me it's different this time. Tell me that, after all these years, you finally have some idea as to what actually happened to my daughter.'

'I can't tell you that,' he said, not quite meeting her gaze. 'I don't have any news – not in the way you mean.'

'Then why the hell did you invite me here? You have no idea how traumatic it is.' She could feel tears pressing under her lids and she just knew she was about to make the biggest fool of herself, and in front of him too.

She'd taken pride in her ability to hold her feelings at bay. It wasn't as if she hadn't had plenty of opportunity over the years to learn how to control her emotions. Oh, not initially. She couldn't remember the first few weeks after the disappearance and she had no intention of trying. But she soon learnt how upsetting others found grief. Grief was all very well but only when it was the dignified sort. A gentle sniff. A surreptitious eye wipe with the corner of a tissue. Real sorrow was all snot and snivelling. It was red-rimmed eyes and the gut-wrenching ache that started in the belly only to lodge in the back of the throat. There was nothing glamorous about someone in the throes of misery, nothing at all.

Her legs felt weak and, taking a couple of steps, she lowered herself into the nearest chair. All she wanted to do was hide in a corner and give way to her feelings but not now and certainly not in front of him.

He must have had some training or something because, apart from a bundle of tissues hastily thrust into her lap, he left her to manage alone. If he'd said anything, if he'd tried to touch her or offer any kind of sympathy, she'd have stood up and walked out of the room, no matter the reason for the appointment. She felt like the blunt end of a battering-ram. With a little push she'd keel over and give way to the grief that was bubbling just under the surface. But, left to her own devices, she managed to divert the tears with a loud blow of her nose and a few hearty breaths that would do any Channel swimmer proud.

With her emotions in check, she stuffed the spare tissues up her sleeve and lifted her head only to find him staring, the bland expression back.

'Feeling better now?'

'I didn't mean to snap. Too many more disappointments like this and I'll end up in the funny farm.' She heaved a sigh, wishing her voice didn't sound so much like a squeak. 'Just do me a favour, would you? Next time you have news, if there is a next time, just blurt it out. Skirting around the issue only ends up in me building my hopes up and—'

'Of course. Adding to your hurt is the very last thing I want.'

'I know. I'm sorry – there was no need to take my disappointment out on you. It's just sometimes the whole situation gets the better of me. I know you're trying to do your best. So, why am I here? It must be nearly your lunchbreak.'

'Lunch. What's that?' he said on a laugh.

'You should eat, you know.'

Well, I will, after.' He paused, dragging his hand through his hair. 'The card, as I think you've already guessed, wasn't the eureka moment we'd all been hoping for. There's no way to trace it back and no clues to who sent it. But the issue isn't so much the card. It's more a case of *why now*?'

'I don't understand?'

He cleared his throat. 'The thing about criminals is there's always a reason behind what they do. They wouldn't do it otherwise. Sending a card to you is a risk, a huge one. There's CCTV cameras in the most unlikely of places and with so many crime shows on Netflix, everyone's an amateur detective.' He rubbed his chin. 'There's always the possibility, of course, that it was sent by someone up to mischief – someone with more time on their hands than they know what to do with and a keen sense of causing the greatest upset and damage they can. So, the reason you're here is to have a think about what you've been doing or not doing over the last few weeks. What's different, if anything? Have you spoken to anyone or received any phone calls?' His eyes fixed on her face. 'We need help with this, Izzy, and you're the only one that we can turn to. Try and think. What happened, if anything, that's different?'

'Apart from spotting Grace in Swansea and the postcard, there's been nothing,' she said, struggling not to let her voice rise. 'Work has been busy, more than busy. I've spent nearly every day stuck in my workroom dyeing and spinning wool.'

'Nearly? So, what did you do on the day or days that you weren't working?'

'I went into Swansea for lunch with a friend, but that was after I received the card so probably not relevant.'

She didn't know why she didn't tell him about the trip to the church unless it was the sneaky feeling that he wouldn't be very happy that she'd decided to interfere with the investigation. But it wasn't as if she'd committed any crime in looking up an old friend except perhaps when she'd impersonated Grace in those calls to the doctor's surgeries, a blush scoring her cheeks. She bit her lower lip, remembering his comment about everyone acting like an amateur detective. What he didn't know couldn't worry him and, after yesterday, she was pretty sure her sleuthing days were over. Her brow wrinkled at the line he was taking.

She'd thought, after all this time, that they'd have wiped her own name off the list of suspects but obviously not. He probably imagined that she had both the time and inclination to travel around Wales and France dishing out postcards like Smarties. Lifting her hands, she traced her fingers under her eyes before dropping them back onto her lap and meeting his gaze as he continued to speak.

'And there's nothing else you can remember?'

'That's right.' She picked up her bag and, reaching for her coat, said, 'Is that all?'

'No.' His smile was brief and his words came as a surprise. 'What about lunch?'

'When you said you knew a little place where we wouldn't be seen together, I did at least think it would be warm and as for the menu … it's a little limited, don't you think?'

'There's nothing wrong with cheese and pickle sandwiches and the lack of variety surely has to be compensated somewhat by the view across St Non's Bay,' he said, fiddling with the radio. 'And anyway I feel I owe you after making you come all the way out to Swansea. It's a nice change to get away from my desk and dropping you home at the same time seemed the right thing to do. It's just a shame I can't do anything about the weather.' He stretched out a hand and turned up the heater. 'Is that better?'

'Perfect, thank you. So, what's with all the secrecy then? I was only joking about not wanting to be seen with you.'

'I'm glad to hear it!' he said. 'It's not so much about not wanting to be seen together. I just can't afford to be seen in your company outside of the investigation.'

'I don't understand?'

'There's a word for detectives that fraternise with members of the public directly involved in a case – it's not a pleasant one.'

'Is that what this is called – fraternising? I thought we were just having lunch. I wouldn't have come if I'd known you were going to read something more into it, like *fraternising*,' she said, half in jest, half serious.

'It's not me, all right. It's everyone on the team.'

'Everyone on the team?'

He must have heard the surprise in her voice, but he remained silent, his fingers drumming against the steering wheel. She turned her head away from the sound, trying to focus on the view ahead, the remains of her sandwich pushed back into its plastic wrapper.

What harm could it do sharing lunch if we're not doing anything we shouldn't?

The thought slid out of nowhere, pushing everything else aside and leaving chaos in its wake as she examined this new idea from all sides. Did she really want to sit munching on a sandwich while she passed the time of day with Rhys? And if not, what else would she rather be doing? After all, time was precious. She'd spent the last five years being defined by her loss. She was the woman who'd lost both her partner and her baby and had nearly gone mad in the process. She was also the woman who'd crawled her way back from the edge and learnt to live with the past by throwing herself into the present. But the truth was, she didn't want to be that woman anymore. Alys had gone. If she was being completely honest, she now knew she'd never find her. Grace was a final farewell if you like: her last chance at trying to change what she'd always feared to be the truth. She hoped Alys was still alive, but she couldn't even be sure of that now.

She threw him a quick look before returning to gaze out of the window, more confused than ever. While she suspected that Rhys liked her in *that way* it wasn't something she'd given a great deal of thought to. He'd just been Rebecca's older brother and not someone she'd ever think to go out with, even if he'd asked. He went to the same parties, but he was the sensible one, the one that offered to drive them home, the one that was always there, just on the outside of all the fun. If he asked her out now, what would her answer be? In truth, she didn't know. She didn't fancy him, not in the way she'd fancied Charlie. But look how that relationship had turned out. Perhaps she should settle for the next best thing – someone solid and reliable. Someone respected in the community. Someone with a good job. Someone who apparently wanted to shift their acquaintance up a notch.

'Come on, lets stretch our legs,' Rhys said, interrupting her musings with a click of her seatbelt and the sound of his door opening. 'I'll be stuck behind my desk for the rest of the afternoon and it will be too dark when I get home to do anything other than slob out in front of the telly.' He dragged his coat from the back seat before heading round the bonnet to open her door.

She followed him because it would be rude not to, but she ignored his hand, instead tucking hers inside her pockets and pretending to look at the view. She couldn't remember the last time she'd bothered to walk along the path up to St Non's Chapel and then onto the coastal path to stare down at the beach beyond. There was no one about but that was hardly surprising considering it was January and, if not actually raining, then seriously thinking about it. He couldn't have thought of a less deserted place to take her for lunch if being discovered was what he was worried about.

On reaching the chapel, she moved away from his side and over to the well. It was more a hole in the ground really but a place filled with memories, happy ones. Mam used to take Bethan and her on their birthdays, rain, hail or shine. 'Throw a coin and make a wish,' she used to say. 'But mind you don't tell anyone or it won't come true.'

Izzy's eyes filled, as she remembered all the wishes over the years. A new doll for her collection and, later, a new doll's outfit. The wishes changed in both quality and quantity as she'd grown-up and still she'd never told a soul, not even Bethan despite the teasing. The last time she'd visited the well had been in the weeks following Alys's disappearance. She'd known it was madness but desperation was an unpredictable ally and, during those dark days, she'd been prepared to try anything.

Searching in her jacket for a coin revealed a torn tissue, a parking stub and fluff from the tumble drier.

'I'll just nip back to the car.'

'There's no need,' he said, holding out a pound coin between his thumb and forefinger, a smile breaking across his face.

'But I can't take your money.'

'Why not? Mine's as good as any and it won't affect anything. In fact, I think I might just have a go myself.' His voice trailed off as he put his hand back in his pocket for more coins.

'Ha, why would someone like you need a wish?'

He paused, his gaze roaming over her face before answering. 'You should know better than asking that, Isabelle Grant. If I tell it won't come true,' he said, his words mirroring her thoughts. 'Go on, you first.'

Izzy turned back to the well. The coin felt warm against her palm from where it had retained the heat from his body. Plucking it between her fingers and, eyes closed, she dropped it down the shaft, listening for the faint sound of it banging against the side, all her thoughts and prayers now tied up in that little gold disk. But, after losing all hope, she wished for closure. Only that.

Chapter 23

Izzy

'Oh shit.'

'Excuse me?'

Rhys had just turned left onto the A487 and towards Abereiddy when he'd suddenly swerved to avoid a screaming car heading in the opposite direction.

'Sorry for swearing and all that but –' he crunched the gears '– that was my boss.'

'So? What's that got to do with anything? Surely he can't be annoyed that you actually took a lunchbreak for once?'

'He just so happens to be a she and she has every right to be annoyed with me. I was meant to cover the office over lunch and here I am off galivanting with a witness,' he said, glancing in her direction before negotiating the tight turning into her driveway and switching off the engine.

'But she probably didn't even see you?'

'But she'd have recognised the car, Izzy. The truth is I shouldn't have left the office or dragged you into my mess. At the very least she'll give me a bollocking,' his eyes darkening.

'And the very worst?'

'She's within her rights to pull me off the case if she did see you in the car.'

Izzy opened her mouth to speak only to close it again at the sound of his mobile screeching into life. She watched as he unclipped it from his belt before lifting it to his ear, his face inscrutable, his one syllable replies giving no clue as to who was on the other end.

Finally, conversation over, his gaze slid to hers, his face still an unreadable mask. 'I'm sorry but I need to go. There's … Something's come up. I'll be in touch soon.' He lifted his hand to her cheek, his palm cold against her suddenly warm skin. 'Thank you for sharing my lunch. It was the best cheese and pickle sandwich I've had in a long while.'

He waited for her to climb out of the car and slam the door, but she could tell he was keen to be on his way. Within seconds of her feet touching the ground he'd conducted a smart three-point turn before heading back in the direction they'd just come.

She could ignore the sound of the bell and even the rattle of the knocker. After all, there was an art to dyeing fleece and if each step wasn't followed to the letter it would only be fit for the bin. What with wool washing and soaking to aid the uptake of the nettle dye, she wasn't even aware that she hadn't eaten since that cheese sandwich with Rhys. There had been a scratch at the door a few hours ago, which necessitated a quick break to feed a disgruntled Bucket but, apart from that, she'd been too busy to think about anything other than the task at hand. It was when a sharp tap at the window had her nearly jumping out of her socks that she finally lifted her head from the wool in front of her.

'I'll be there in a jiffy.'

Setting aside the now forest-green wool on top of her drying table she headed out of the workroom, stripping off the industrial looking gloves and apron along the way. She couldn't think of who might be calling, her eyes trained on the wall clock ticking its way towards 9 p.m. The only people who ever came knocking on her door, apart from the postman, were members of her knitting team and the next meeting wasn't scheduled until next week.

As a single woman living in the back of beyond, she made sure to fasten the security chain before twisting the latch. Pulling open the door, she was surprised to see Rhys and that other officer standing on her front step.

'Can we come in?'

Or what? Or I'll just say no and then watch you walk away?

'Well, it's a little late, don't you think? Couldn't it wait until the morning, whatever it is?'

'Come on, Izzy, open the door. It's freezing out here. This is important.'

She'd already started to unclip the chain only to pause at his words, her fingers resting on the brass hook, her gaze staring at what little of his face she could make out in the reflected light from the hall. If it was urgent that could only mean one thing. A breakthrough. The very thing she'd been hoping for. The only thing she'd been hoping for. She clamped the edge of the door between her fingers, trying to control the sudden tremor racing down her spine. She needed to know what he had to say but suddenly she was afraid. She'd waited so long for news, too long. It could only be bad.

She wrenched back the chain and pulled the door wide open, expecting them to step inside but they made no attempt to move despite the cold seeping in from all sides.

'Izzy, don't get your hopes up. It's far too early for that. But I need to tell you that we've found your car.'

Chapter 24

Izzy

Of all the things she'd expected him to say that was the very last. She'd almost given up hope of hearing those words. She'd waited for years to hear something about the car. She'd scoured the papers and hounded the police, glancing at each Mini to see if the bump on the fender, where Charlie had reversed into a lamppost, was still there.

It was quite easy to hide a person especially if that person didn't want to be found. But hiding a car was more difficult or that's what she kept telling herself. Oh, it was easy enough to change the appearance. A respray job was one of the easiest things but changing the chassis number was much more difficult and even if they'd managed to remove it, she still had the logbook with a list of all the scratches and dents noted down in her neat handwriting.

She directed them to the sofa while she sat on the arm of the chair opposite, waiting for him to speak.

'A couple of cliff jumpers over from Swansea thought they'd do some practice dives in the Blue Lagoon. One of them spotted something unusual.'

'But why now?' she interrupted.

'No one knows. Just luck, I guess,' he said. 'One of the lads decided to take note of the number plate and call it into the station.'

Her eyes widened at his words. All this time. All those searches for nothing because her car had only been a stone's throw away in the bottom of the lagoon. She'd always known, deep down, that there could be no happy resolution to Alys's disappearance. Grace Madden was a red herring, a mirage she'd conjured up from nowhere in a desperate attempt to find a conclusion to her story.

She fumbled up her sleeve and withdrew a tissue, determined to remain in control of her emotions until she was alone. There were lots of questions just bubbling under and rattling the lid of her mind. Who were they? What had made them decide to dive the lagoon at this time of year? But, by the set of his jaw, she knew Rhys wasn't going to tell her much more.

'I'd like to see exactly where they found it.'

'We can't allow that. There's nothing to see anyway, not until tomorrow,' he said, shaking his head. 'Things won't start moving until the morning.'

'I'm not a child, Rhys. It's not up to you to allow me or not and if you don't take me, I'll go by myself as soon as you've gone. I know I have a torch lurking somewhere,' she said, flicking her head in the direction of the kitchen, her eyes never leaving his face. 'I'd rather not go alone but I will if I have to.'

It was a very different walk down to the Blue Lagoon with only the beam from his high-powered torch to light the way. The darkness enveloped everything in its gloomy shroud of blacks and greys, and she knew she'd never have had the nerve to make the journey alone. But he didn't know what it was like to have hoped and dreaded for this moment in equal measures only to realise that your worst fears had been realised. There was a finality about the situation. Everything was now out of her control.

The first thing she noticed, arriving at the top of the lagoon was the cordon of yellow tape. They'd even managed to erect a large white tent – tell-tale signs that things were different now. A solitary policeman, huddled in his thick reflective jacket, was the only other person present. Presumably he was there minding the crime scene. Was it a crime scene? How could a place of beauty hold so many dark secrets?

'All right, Ben. Anything happening?' Rhys said.

'No sir. The crane will be arriving first thing tomorrow to—'

'Right, that's fine. Phone me if there's anything, anything at all. I'll get Ellis to relieve you at 2 a.m.'

'What time will the crane be arriving?' Izzy said.

'It's really not advisable that you attend.'

'I don't care what you think is advisable or not, Rhys,' She flapped her arms against her sides to keep warm. 'This is my child we're talking about. So, what time?'

'It's going to be a circus down here,' he hissed, probably aware that the police officer was still within ear shot. 'We've tried to keep it away from the media but there's always someone down at the station who blabs to someone and, before we know where we are, we have the newspapers on top of us, not to mention TV crews.' He led her away from the quarry and they retraced their footsteps back to the cottage, his arm an immovable force on her elbow. 'They'll all want an interview, a little slice of the action and with every slice a little part of you will be chipped off. You'll feel sullied, dirty even, when none of this is your fault. We've known each other a long time, you and me and I know that's not what you want to hear,' he added, tightening his grip. 'I can't stop you from coming. I can't even begin to imagine what this must be like for you. But I went into the force straight from school, which means I've been involved in quite a few high-profile cases like this one. In the name of kindness and trying to help, they'll strip you down to the bone. And, when it's all over, they'll walk away and leave you and your family to pick up the pieces.'

They'd reached her front door, DC Darin following them like a faithful shadow. Izzy had listened to everything he'd said but it didn't change anything. Whatever he or anyone else said she was still going to be there at first light to see her car being lifted from its resting place.

'I know you're right. You're a good man trying to make the best of a bad job, but I don't care about the rest of them. Let them do their worst because, whatever happens tomorrow, the worst has already happened.'

She inserted her key into the lock and, with a brief wave of goodbye, slipped inside before shutting and locking the door. Making her way into the lounge she sank down on the rug, her thoughts in meltdown. All this time she'd thought that Charlie had taken Alys. She'd thought he'd stolen her from right under her nose for reason or reasons unknown to start a new life. That he'd taken the car initially to either sell or abandon somewhere far away from the cottage. But that was wrong. That wasn't how it'd happened. He certainly wouldn't have had any reason to dump it in the lagoon. She was going to have to take a scrubbing brush to those thoughts and start again. Just what could have happened for him to ditch what was, after all, a perfectly good car?

Chapter 25

Izzy
Thursday 9 January, 8.50 a.m. The Blue Lagoon,
Abereiddy

Rhys had been right in everything he'd said. The area round the Blue Lagoon was standing room only with both the media and nosey parkers vying for best position. Izzy had phoned her parents to alert them to what was happening and to plead with them to stay away, using all the arguments Rhys had tried and failed to use on her. So she stood alone apart from Rhys who seemed to have glued himself to her side.

In a repeat of last night, Rhys and DC Darin had arrived on her doorstep at first light and this time they'd both tried to persuade her to stay at home. But she'd managed to stop their arguments by stuffing a bacon sandwich and a mug of tea into their hands with a smile. Working at the chip shop all those years had some advantages. She'd learnt that it was much harder for a customer to argue when they were faced with an extra slab of succulent battered cod straight from the fryer.

She'd dressed down for the occasion, donning an old black coat and beanie pulled low. Yes, it was a sort of disguise, but it wasn't going to fool anyone, not today. She could almost smell the stench of vultures circling. But these vultures fed on a different kind of flesh. Their meat was the misery and unhappiness of others and the one thing she was determined not to do was get involved with them on any level. Rhys, give him his due, probably had a million things to do other than accompany her but, in a funny way, she welcomed his support – having a wall of muscle between her and the crowd made a huge difference to the situation.

In hindsight, she shouldn't have come. In hindsight she should have stayed in front of the fire with Bucket cuddled to her chest while she waited for events to unfold. But it was far too late to turn away with all eyes now on the centre of the lagoon.

The crane towered overhead, its bright yellow paintwork in stark contrast to the beauty of the breached quarry. There was plenty of activity with chains being dropped into the water for divers to secure around the car. Finally, with a cacophony of noise, the crane screeched into action, its rubber tyres straining under the pressure from its heavy load, the chain swinging in the wind that had built up overnight. Cameras flashed but, instead of noise, a curious silence descended as everyone watched for the first glimpse of the weed and barnacle-covered lump of metal finally emerging from its watery grave.

Izzy found it hard to imagine that it was the same vehicle her dad had bought her when she'd passed her driving test; the same car she'd used to beetle around St David's and beyond. The blob of murky green bore no resemblance to her trusty car and her thoughts plummeted at the idea of any useful clues being found within.

There was one question she hadn't asked Rhys even though it had been puzzling her since last night and that was why the hell Charlie had gone to such lengths to hide the car so near to home. It wasn't as if he was flush with cash, far from it and, apart from his wallet, he'd taken nothing with him. The only thing that fit was a wealthy girlfriend but there was no evidence. Finding the car now just didn't make any sense.

Rhys wandered away to have a chat with a couple of officers, leaving Izzy in the care of DC Darin.

'Are you sure you want to stay?' she asked, laying a tentative hand on her arm. 'There won't be much more to see. The lads from forensics are waiting to examine the—' she stopped abruptly, not that Izzy noticed.

Izzy wasn't listening to a word she'd been saying because she'd just seen something. She'd just seen the one thing that she hadn't expected, the one thing that made a travesty of the last five years. She opened her mouth to speak, but there were no words – there was nothing left apart from hot tears dragged from the depths.

She pulled away from DC Darin's arm, needing to be alone, if only to gather her breath, her mind awash with images flooding in from the past. Images of her precious Alys: the feel of her soft skin, the warm milky smell mingling with Johnson's Baby Bath. She leant over; her hands braced against her knees, and dragged air into her lungs. She shouldn't have come. She should have—

'Miss Grant, could we have a word? I'm Lou Sanders from *The Herald*. What are your thoughts now that your car has been found?'

'Leave her alone. Can't you see she doesn't want to speak to you?' DC Darin said, shifting in front of Izzy.

'And you are?' the reporter said, tilting her head.

'Detective Constable Gabriella Darin and, if you don't want to find yourself at the centre of a complaint to the Independent Press Standards Organisation, then I suggest you find someone else to harass.'

Gaby took hold of Izzy's elbow, leading her across the path and towards one of the police vehicles before settling her in the passenger seat and asking the police officer standing guard for the keys.

'Well, what was that all about, hmm?' she said, her voice soft. She turned the key in the ignition, switching on the heater before continuing. 'You've remembered something, haven't you?'

Izzy could feel her eyes skimming across the side of her face, but she couldn't find the words to tell her about the car seat. It wasn't anything special, just a basic blue and grey check with studded blue handle but it was all they could afford at the time. And it was this handle that she could still see in her mind's eye through the window, water streaming out through the gaping holes; just a shadow really of the shape etched against black. She still remembered laughing as they'd struggled to work out which way to strap it into the car, the instructions coming in every language under the sun except the one they could both understand. It didn't make any sense that Charlie would have taken the baby and left the car seat – unless it wasn't good enough? It all came back to the possibility of him having a wealthy girlfriend. It was the only reason she could think of for him abandoning what was, after all, a perfectly good piece of equipment.

Her eyes snagged on the detective sitting quietly by her side. She was nice, this DC Darin, with her dark eyes and thick plait. Izzy hadn't liked her at first. She hadn't known what to think. Liking shouldn't come into it, of course. But it did. It was all about trust at the end of the day. She had to trust her to find out what had happened. She had to confide every detail of Charlie and their life together, no matter how stupid or insignificant. Izzy compressed her lips. She'd done that already. She'd spent hours holed up at the station rehashing again and again the minutiae of their lives. But she'd obviously forgotten something because otherwise they wouldn't still be missing.

Izzy opened her mouth to speak only to close it at the sight of Rhys bearing down.

'What's up?' he said, his attention on DC Darin.

'She got a bit upset when the car appeared. Not only that –

Lou Sanders from the press had a go so I thought it would be best to hide out here for a while.

'Good idea. Hop in the back, Gaby. I'll drive.'

'But I want to stay,' Izzy interrupted. 'I can't leave now.'

'Really?' His eyebrows rose. 'The show's over for the moment. Let the boys in blue work their magic. I promise you'll be the first to know if they find anything.' He started the engine and turned the car around. 'Where to?' His hands were loosely wrapped around the steering wheel.

'Home, I suppose …' Her voice trailed off at the sight of the throng of people now looking in their direction.

'I'm not so sure that's a good idea.'

'Well, as I have nowhere else to go … and I do have to think about Bucket.'

'Bucket?'

'My cat. And what about clothes and things?'

'Look, Izzy, you can't go back there at present. What about Rebecca? She'll put you up in a heartbeat.'

'Oh, but I couldn't possibly impose.'

'You know you wouldn't be imposing,' he said with a frown. 'You've always been thicker than thieves with my sister.'

'No. Really. Mam and Dad will find me a bed or even Bethan.'

'Don't you think I haven't thought of that? With that reporter sniffing about, staying at either isn't going to be a deterrent. And anyway, she'll be glad of the company. Jake's just left for his stint on the oil rigs and you know she's always complaining about how lonely she is when he goes away.' He shot her a look before returning his gaze to the road ahead. 'You don't really have a choice here. It's Rebecca or a hotel and I'm sure you'll be happier with my sister.'

'But what about my cat and …?' She was starting to cave in. Spending time with Rebecca was exactly what she needed right now.

'Izzy, let me worry about your cat. If you give me the keys, I'll make sure he's looked after. And as for your clothes … I'm happy to collect your toothbrush and a few essentials when I'm there but I'm not prepared to rummage through your drawers,' he said, his colour rising. 'You're not too far off Rebecca's size. I'm sure she'll be happy to lend you anything you need. It should only be for a few days.'

The A487 was deserted; there was nothing to distract from the empty road in front of them and, into the sudden silence, he finally spoke.

'So, what was it about the car that upset you so much?'

Chapter 26

Gaby
Thursday 9 January, 2 p.m. Swansea Police Station

The incident room was heaving, the smell of hot bodies and stewed coffee steaming up the windows and adding to the overall feeling of anticipation. The chase was on after a hiatus of five years. No one present liked the idea of failure and the Grant case had been failing within days of Alys's disappearance.

Gaby opened her notebook with a sigh, trying to dampen the excitement building underneath her Marks and Spencer navy trouser suit. She was almost shaking with the hope of having something concrete to focus on. But she also knew the stats. The best opportunity for finding Alys had been in the first forty-eight hours. What they were doing now was damage limitation. They wanted to end the case, tie all the ends off in a neat little ribbon of explanation that would please Detective Superintendent Holmes, a man she'd only heard rumour of because he sure as hell didn't come into the squad room.

'Right people. Can I have your attention please?'

Gaby looked up from her notes and to where DCI Brazil-North was standing, her sharp grey suit and plain white shirt complimenting her blonde hair, brushed to a glossy sheen around her cheeks. She'd earned every one of her *steps up the ladder* the hard way, but still managed to exude the impression that she was just about to head out to have coffee with friends instead of head up a murder investigation.

Her attention wandered while the DCI droned on about how successful an operation it was. *Blah de blah de blah.* She didn't want to listen to all that tosh. She wanted to be back behind her desk searching for clues, not that clues could help. Now it was a waiting game while the forensics team worked their magic, step by painful step. Gaby didn't have to listen too closely anyway. After all, she knew what was coming. She'd been in the car, hugging the back seat, her eyes and ears pinned to Rhys and Izzy when he'd questioned her gently about what she'd seen that no one else had. The car was one huge weed-covered mass of stinking green and, even with all her skill and training, she could barely make out the shape of the interior and certainly not anything inside, which made her all the keener to hear Izzy's take on it.

Gaby turned to where Rhys was propping up the radiator. He'd spent the last fifteen-minutes holed up in the office with *her ladyship* and Gaby would bet her only pair of Manolo Blahnik's that he'd just had the dressing-down of his life. It was easy to see in the way he'd immediately moved from her side when they'd entered the room, his arms folded, his chin set, his lips drawn into a thin line. It couldn't be because he'd arranged for Izzy to stay with his sister. While a little over and above, it probably wasn't a bad idea to get her out of the way of the media shower that was heading her way. No. There was more to it than that. Gaby's mind headed back to the conversation she'd had with Amy on that first day.

There was something she couldn't work out, something at odds with the case, something more than the rumour he fancied the mother. But that was just gossip. Rhys was an experienced officer who surely wouldn't allow his feelings to interfere with an investigation. Her frown deepened. Growing up on a housing estate in Liverpool, she'd learnt from an early age to trust her instincts. She wouldn't be alive today if she hadn't developed a heightened awareness of when trouble was about to happen and she smelt it now.

Brazil-North had finally come to a halt. Clearing her throat, her gaze flickered over the room, pausing deliberately on each pair of eyes that stared back. Gaby squared her shoulders. She was one of the few people there who knew what the guv was going to say. She'd suspected as much as soon as Izzy had mentioned the car seat. But knowing still didn't stop the hand of fear trailing over her skin and tinkling down her spine. She loved being in law enforcement. It was the very best of jobs: different and challenging in a range of ways with no two days the same. This was the only part she hated.

'As we all know by now, the car pulled from the Blue Lagoon has been formally identified as belonging to Isabelle Grant.'

'I don't think she'll have a pig in hell's chance of getting it past her MOT this year,' Bill said, his chins wobbling with unsuppressed laughter. The room dissolved into sniggers and snorts only to be silenced at the sound of DCI Brazil-North's next words.

'Ha ha. Very funny. Just for that I'll schedule you in to accompany DI Walker when he has to break the news to her that both her boyfriend and baby were in that car.'

Chapter 27

Gaby

Gaby had always wondered what a deathly silence would sound like. Now she knew. She glanced around at the sea of faces, her gaze finally landing on Bill and where his chins were heading for his knees.

'But—?'

The DCI ignored him, instead turning her attention to the forensic pathologist, lounging at the back. 'Wayne, what can you tell us?'

'It's far too early to say at this stage, ma'am. The team have spent the morning at the site and we're in the process of moving the bodies. They should arrive back here later on today – I'll start on them ASAP.' He put his hands in his pockets, jingling his keys. 'The bones indicate that we're dealing with two bodies, one a grown male and the other …' He paused, giving a little cough. 'And the other a baby. But at this stage, I can't tell you anything more.'

'Is there any indication as to what might have happened?'

'Not a clue. Nothing obvious but, who knows? We'll do the usual and get back to you. The team is reviewing the car. They'll strip it down and send the report directly, but it might take a while. Five years submersion has turned it into a rust bucket that crumbles at the touch.'

'That's not what I want to hear,' she said on a sigh. 'What about personal effects?'

'Again, not a lot to go on. The male had a wallet in his back pocket with a credit card in the name of Charles Anthony Dawson. The fabric remnants suggest a T-shirt and jeans. The baby was also dressed in what was probably a Baby-gro; it's hard to be sure after all this time. I'm sorry I can't be more specific but …' He shrugged his shoulders.

'No, that's fine.' She turned back to face the room. 'Right. Rhys, you take Amy along with you and go see the mother. We need to get to her before the press.'

'What about me? I thought you said I was to break—?'

'Bill, I wouldn't trust you to break wind without cocking it up. You can take Gaby and interview the two poor devils who found the car. Then, I want you to go back over the initial search and tell me why we didn't find it five years ago.'

'But that will take days.'

'Well, the sooner you start the better.'

Chapter 28

Izzy
Friday 10 January, 10.30 a.m. Rebecca's flat, St David's

The knock on the door did little to disturb the wall that Izzy had surrounded herself in since yesterday. She'd spent the last twenty-four hours waiting for news but, with each successive hour ticking by, she'd finally managed to convince herself that the police weren't coming. It had all been a mistake. There was a reason why Charlie had left both the car seat and the car behind. Perhaps he'd thought it was an extra trail that would lead the police to him. Perhaps he hadn't wanted any reminders of what he was trying to leave behind. Perhaps ... Since yesterday a million and one reasons had blossomed in her mind only to be discounted one by one.

When the knock finally came, she stayed in the lounge, hugging her knees to her chest. She didn't even raise her head when the door creaked open. It took the sound of her name on Rhys's lips to drag her out of the dark place she'd been hiding.

'Hello Izzy. You might remember Amy Potter, our FLO?'

Raising her head, she looked straight into his eyes and knew immediately that it wasn't going to be good news. His face was a bland mask but no amount of training could hide the fine lines and lengthening shadows pressed into his skin just as his calm demeanour couldn't lift the pallor from his cheeks. She dropped her gaze to his highly polished shoes and back up over his grey suit and pale blue shirt, which looked as if it had been slept in. Even his conservative blue and black striped tie wasn't tied with its usual precision. And, at the sight of that knot, she wanted to run. She wanted to flee the room, the house, the country. She didn't want to know what they had to tell her. Hearing their words would make it true somehow and the one thing she couldn't run from was the truth.

She was up on her feet before she even had time to think. She didn't want them here but, heaving a sigh, she decided to stay all the same. What had started all those years ago needed to end – it needed to end now. After all, she knew the news. There was nothing to be gained by them drawing it out.

'Go on.'

His expression said it all. She was being abrupt, rude even, but she didn't care. All she cared about was getting the next five minutes over with.

'Izzy—?'

'Rhys. Please don't do this to me. I can't—' She swallowed hard, her gaze flicking to Amy. Pleading, imploring, begging.

Amy placed a hand on his arm. 'Just tell her. She needs to know.'

He sat down abruptly, gesturing for Amy and Izzy to follow his lead. Izzy remained standing; her gaze riveted to his face.

'There's no easy way to say this but I can confirm that the car contained the remains of a man and a baby.'

She closed her eyes, swaying back into the chair. She'd been hoping … She'd even been praying, to whatever God might be listening. But her prayers had gone unanswered. Curling her fingers, she dug her nails into her palms, not caring if she drew blood and, staring down at the red wheals marking her flesh, in a funny sort of a way, the pain helped. Now she knew. Now she could move on. She opened her eyes wide, remembering.

Charlie. The person she'd blamed for stealing her baby. She'd stamped out all memory of him. Charlie, the man she'd loved and then hated, dead all those years: dead and forgotten.

She sat up, her nails finding a greater purchase, her eyes turned to Rhys. 'Can I see them?' she said, her voice barely a whisper.

She watched Rhys shoot Amy a look before meeting her gaze. 'No. No, I'm afraid that's not possible. They're … they're still being … they're still across at the—'

'What he's trying to say is that the team is still examining them,' Amy said. 'They're still part of an active investigation, you see, and there may be clues as to what happened.'

'Clues? What sort of clues?'

'We need to find out why it happened and if there was anyone else involved,' Rhys said, dragging his hand through his hair.

'So, what you're trying to say is that they could have been murdered?'

He paused, his gaze shifting from her face to his feet. 'We can't rule that out. We can't rule anything out at this stage.'

Izzy stretched her arms out in front of her. An hour had passed, or was it two? Ten hours? It didn't matter how long it had been since the door closed on their backs but, by the feel of her muscles, a very long time. But didn't she have all the time in the world? She didn't have to worry about where the next meal was coming from or how she was going to cope through a fog of inertia. She didn't have to worry about trying to find Alys. She had all the time in the world, all the months, days and seconds she could ever wish for. Time stretched before her – time she no longer had any need of.

The layer upon layer of memories flickered past like pages in a book and, between the pages, the silent memories that could never be expressed simply by words: the tilt of Alys's head, the hue of her dark blue eyes, the warmth of her body as Izzy held her close, her baby-soft hair tickling her chin. Charlie's smile … The guilt, lurking just under the surface since their visit, exploded in a cacophony of thoughts causing her heart to splinter into a thousand shards. The pain clawing through her insides had her gripping her stomach, the intensity as sharp as if someone was twisting a blade. All along, all these years her baby and her man had been lying on the bottom of the cold hard seabed hidden from sight by a mass of water. All the times she'd blamed him and with only a couple of crappy postcards to support her worst fears. Her Charlie, the man she'd entrusted with her hopes, her dreams and finally with her heart, hadn't deserted her. He hadn't stolen their baby. She didn't know what had happened that day in the car but presumably the police would sort it out. Maybe he'd been distracted by Alys's cry and lost control of the car. She didn't know and, at this juncture, she didn't care. The explosion of feeling ripping through her veins made no allowances. It wasn't concerned with extenuating circumstances or what ifs and maybes. It didn't care that an explanation would be found now the police had again picked up the baton of the investigation. It had Izzy in its icy grip and she couldn't see past it's slithering tentacles invading every corner of both her body and mind.

She stumbled out of the chair and away from all the images pinning her to the seat. Making her way through the silent hall her eyes slid towards the kitchen. She hadn't eaten since breakfast, because a couple of digestives and a cold cuppa couldn't be considered food. But she didn't pause. There was nothing for her there. Hunger would come later, if at all.

Walking into the spare bedroom, her bedroom now, she flung her jumper over the comfy chair in the window recess before removing her watch, placing it in the little ceramic dish on the dressing table. Her blouse and jeans came next, landing on the floor for the first time in living memory, but she didn't care. Normally fastidious in everything, she didn't care that the denim would be creased by the morning just as she didn't care where her knickers landed when she threw them in the general direction of the linen basket.

Turning her head, she stared again at the dressing table and the memories scattered across the surface. The bottle of perfume Charlie had bought for her nineteenth birthday. Perfume she'd never worn but Rhys wouldn't have known that when he'd collected her washbag from beside the sink. The bundle of clothes piled on top: a higgledy piggledy mass plucked at random from her meagre wardrobe.

Her attention shifted to the bed, a different bed to the one she'd shared with Charlie, and a sudden rush of emotion crumpled inside, dragging her with it. Letting out a cry she collapsed onto the mattress, swaddling the duvet around her bare skin, her thoughts shattering around her.

Chapter 29

Gaby
Friday 10 January, 11.30 a.m. Swansea Police Station

DS Bill Davis was just one of those blokes. Gaby could be six-foot-three with legs up to her armpits and a smile to sink a thousand ships and it wouldn't make a bit of difference to the way he treated her. All he saw was her sex but that was his problem and not hers.

They'd settled down opposite the first of the two boys in the interview room. Yes, boys because neither of them was more than eighteen – nineteen at a push. David Prestwich and Arthur Norman, both studying geography at Swansea University and both fanatical cliff divers.

'So, run it by me again, Mr Prestwich,' Bill said, picking up his pen and tapping the centre of his pad, making a fine series of random dots. 'Why cliff diving and why Abereiddy's Blue Lagoon in particular?'

Gaby raised both eyebrows but there was little she could do other than add to the list of questions she'd already jotted down earlier. It was clear that Bill hadn't made any effort to read up on the topic, her mind swinging back to the hasty, albeit, thorough search she'd just carried out on cliff diving – something she'd known nothing about until half an hour previously. She settled back in her chair, stretching her feet out under the table, her eyes trained on the lad opposite.

'The where is easy. The Blue Lagoon is a world-famous cliff diving site. The why? Why not? The world is full of risk-adverse behaviour. Throwing ourselves over a cliff is our way of raising a couple of fingers in the air, pardon the inference, ma'am.'

'Right! Moving on,' Bill said, his brows beetling. 'Can you tell us in your own words just what happened on the day in question?'

'There's not a lot to tell, actually. We'd been diving about half an hour and had one jump each under our belts. It was just a normal jump, you know.' He started playing with the silver ring on his thumb. 'We're used to cold water dives and the great thing about this time of year is the bonus of not having your heart stop when you plunge it into ice-cold water,' he added with a smile.

Gaby hunched forward, her gaze trained on his face. *He's a clown with his winks and jokey ways but, underneath it all, he's anxious or nervous, or both.* Shifting in her seat she stared across at Bill, willing him to ask the kind of questions he should be asking instead of this drivel. Questions like why the Blue Lagoon at this time of year when the world diving championships were months ago? Abereiddy, while pretty, wasn't the centre of the universe and even less so in January. So, why would two lads shift from the heady nightlife to be found in and around Swansea for a weekend in St David's? If it was just for the diving then surely they could have done the return trip in a day instead of having to make a weekend of it. She flipped over to a new page of her pad and added a final note before lifting her head. While his explanation on paper looked fine, she was as sure as she could be that he wasn't being completely honest.

'A normal jump,' Bill said, his colour rising. 'I certainly wouldn't call finding a couple of dead bodies ordinary.'

'No, well. I didn't see the bodies, not then. Not at all.' His voice was not quite as confident as moments before. 'All I spotted was the car. In fact, I very nearly landed on the roof. We didn't think anything of it, not really. We decided to memorise the number plate just in case it was stolen,' he said, a lopsided grin on his face that didn't quite reach his eyes. 'There might have been a reward, or something.'

Gaby narrowed her gaze. He might be quite cute-looking with his man-bun and scruffy denims. He was certainly running rings around poor old Bill and they still had to interview the other one!

'So, you're telling me that the only reason you came over to the lagoon was the thrill of the dive? It's all very well in the summer but at this time of year?' she said, planting her elbows on the table and ignoring Bill completely. 'Go on. We promise we won't rat on you.' Her voice was whisper-soft. 'Who told you about the reward?'

Excuse me?'

'Come on, Mr Prestwick. There's bound to be a reward for making such a huge discovery. The whole world has been on tenterhooks for years about the whereabouts of baby Alys. I can't believe that an intelligent lad like you hasn't heard about the disappearance and international search, not to mention the two-hundred-thousand-quid reward for any information leading to their discovery.'

'No, really. We didn't know about that,' he said, turning pale. 'If you must know, officer, it was Arthur's idea. He was on *Clift'd,* the UK forum for cliff jumpers, and someone mentioned Abereiddy and as we'd never been …' He lifted his head from where he'd been studying his hands and stared straight at her. 'We didn't know about the reward, but we do now.'

Chapter 30

Izzy
Monday 13 January, 2 p.m. Swansea Police Station

Izzy didn't recognise the interview room but then, she remembered little from the early days of the investigation. All she knew was that she still appeared to be the number one suspect if the questions they were throwing at her were anything to go by. She didn't recognise the men sitting across from her and, if they'd told her their names she certainly couldn't remember them after an hour of questioning. There was no sign of Rhys, Gaby or Amy and she wondered if that was a good thing or a bad thing.

'How well did you know Charlie Dawson, Miss Grant?'

'We've gone over this before.'

'I know, but please answer the question.'

'Well, as much as anyone knows the person they've shared everything with for the nine months of their relationship.'

'Was he depressed? Did he give any indication that he might do something like this?'

How the hell was she meant to answer that?

Were you ill, Charlie? Were you hiding something from me, something dreadful, or maybe not so dreadful but life limiting? Were you crying out for help, unable to carry on despite the precious gift we'd made together?

'I thought that he was really excited about the baby,' she said after a pause. 'His disappearance was the very last thing I was expecting.'

'And what about you, Miss Grant? Were you depressed after the birth?' the fat one on the left said, scribbling something on the top of his notebook and shoving it under the nose of the dark-haired thin one.

She stared at them, her mouth compressed. She knew they were asking, in that roundabout way of theirs, if she'd killed them and she could feel her stomach heave at the thought. But it wasn't their fault. They didn't know her, and their question had to be answered.

'Yes, I was depressed after but not post-natal, or whatever it's called. There'll be records somewhere ...' Her voice trailed off.

'Tell us about the postcards, Miss Grant,' he said, changing the subject after a quick look at his colleague. 'There were two of them but with a five-year interval. A little strange, don't you think?'

The postcards worry them. They worry me but, out of all this mess, it's the only thing that gives me a sliver of hope. They think it was a prankster preying on the sorrow and unhappiness of others, someone who'd heard about the missing baby and decided to cause as much upset as possible. I don't agree. I still think there's more to this than they're saying. They may think he took his own life but to murder our child ...? It's unthinkable. There's something inside me that hopes, despite the evidence, that somehow the police have got it wrong. Somehow it was another man and baby in my car – it could have been stolen or used as a decoy or anything. Surely to God there must be another solution.

After another hour of covering the same ground, they accompanied her out of the station to where they'd arranged for a constable to drive her home. It was as if, now they'd finished with her, they were scared she'd stay. Glancing over her shoulder she watched as they made their way back into the building, their heads bent together. She knew they were talking about her just as she knew that she was the main topic of conversation stretching out across St David's and beyond – there was nothing she could do about that other than stay out of sight. Rhys was right about Rebecca's flat being the ideal place to hide.

Three days had passed since the discovery of their bodies, the longest shortest three days of her life. Alys and Charlie were dead; their bones had been tagged and measured on some forensic pathologist's metal table, with one of those fancy high-powered lights dangling overhead. There were no other clues, at least, that's what the papers were saying. Time had done its worst by dissolving everything into the spume of flotsam that remained. They wouldn't let her see them, despite her repeated pleas. She was expected to pick up the strands of her life while the police got on with whatever they were doing.

The feeling of inertia was worse than before. Now, all she seemed to do was hug the sofa with a box of tissues by her side. Rebecca had even suggested calling in her doctor but what help could a medical man offer at a time like this? He wouldn't be able to bring them back and there weren't enough drugs in the world to make her forget.

'Do you want to talk about it?'

Rebecca settled down on the sofa beside her, placing a hand on her knee.

'There's not much to say, is there?' she sniffed. 'I'd resigned myself to losing Alys a very long time ago but … I can't get it out of my head that I was wrong about Charlie,' she said, squeezing her hand. 'I'm ashamed that I thought he'd steal our baby. He loved her so much.'

'And you, Izzy. I remember the way he used to look at you whenever I saw you out together. I used to be jealous, if you must know – those dark eyes of his always trained in your direction even when you weren't looking.'

She managed a smile. 'Thank you, that means so much. I'm trying to stay positive if I can. Maybe Charlie changing from the villain and into one of the victims will, in some way, push the investigation forward – who knows?'

Chapter 31

Izzy
Tuesday 14 January, 3 p.m. Rebecca's Flat, St David's

Time shifted, taking Izzy out of the dark hiding place where she'd been wallowing in grief. Grief was the pervading feeling of the day. Grief was the pervading feeling every day.

Another day had passed; six days since the discovery of the car, not that it mattered.

She twisted on the sofa, aware that Rebecca must have placed a fresh mug of tea on the coffee table without her even noticing.

Izzy needed to do something – something useful – or she'd go mad. She was probably halfway there already, her eyes on the jumper she'd worn continuously since dragging it over her head before heading out with Rhys to watch the crane in action. It had been one of Charlie's, one of the only things of his left at the cottage. It was something she should have binned along with the rest of his kit. But it was such a beautiful jumper – Welsh cable-knit in rich cream and one of the only items she'd gotten around to knitting for him. If she'd bought it instead of staying up late to finish in time for his birthday it would have been relegated to the charity shop pile. But it remained and now she was pleased she still had one thing that had belonged to him. He'd been a sweet lad really. Her hatred over the last five years couldn't change that fact, no matter how hard she'd tried to pollute his memory. Something had happened on the edge of the Blue Lagoon to cause him to slide into that murky pool and she was determined to find out what.

She pulled the jumper over her head and bundled it under her arm before following the sound of out-of-tune singing coming from the kitchen.

'Thanks for the tea. I'm really grateful to you for putting me up like this.'

'That's what friends are for.' Rebecca crossed the room to stand in front of her, her gaze on her crumpled T-shirt. 'I'm about to put another load in the machine if you'd like me to throw in some of your things too? I have tons you can borrow. You know how Jake is always nagging about the amount of clothes I buy.'

'I don't want to be an inconvenience.'

'Izzy, if I was in your situation, would you be there for me?'

'You know I would.'

'Well, then. There's nothing more to say although I do think you should take advantage of the shower facilities.' Rebecca's eyes were now on her greasy, rat-tail of a hairstyle. 'Rhys is coming around for supper – perhaps he'll have an update for you.'

Izzy flicked her a look. Was she giving her a hint or a warning? Had she heard something or was this an attempt at trying to act Cupid?

'Okay,' she said, heading out of the room and towards the bathroom.

She decided not to add to the confusion by asking what she'd meant by her words. She'd have a shower because it was the right thing to do and she'd be nice to Rhys because he'd always been kind back. But that was all. Her life, all of it, was on hold until she found out exactly what had happened inside that car.

'What time did you say you'd invited him?' Izzy said, sneaking a carrot from the pile Rebecca had chopped to go with the hummus. Rhys liked hummus apparently just as he liked chicken tikka masala.

'In a couple of hours, just long enough for the chicken to marinade.'

Rebecca had given her the task of chopping chicken into bite-sized chunks before smothering it in the spicy yogurt sauce she'd made earlier. Cooking wasn't something Izzy was any good at but she'd do anything to keep her mind off the case and what Rhys might have to say.

They didn't talk, not really. There was nothing to say outside the obvious and, as much as she loved her, there was no way Izzy wanted to talk about her current predicament with Rebecca let alone think about it. Now that the story had moved from the front page to the third, she'd decided it was time to think about returning home. She knew that both Rebecca and Rhys wouldn't be in favour. So, instead of mentioning it, she carried on chopping and stirring, the sound of the radio burbling in the background. There'd be time enough when Rhys arrived.

'I hope Rhys's partner doesn't mind him spending the evening,' she finally said, when the silence had changed from comfortable to awkward. But she wasn't prepared for Rebecca's snort of laughter.

'Ha, whatever makes you think our Rhys has a partner?'

'Well, his girlfriend then.'

'Nope. He's as free as fresh air,' she said, waiting for Izzy to elaborate.

'I sort of assumed. When I bumped into him before Christmas he had a trolley full to the brim of every festive concoction known to man, including a raft of toys …'

'That will be our Rhys – the kindest, most generous uncle but far from married. It was his turn to cater but we all took pity on him, as long as he bought the turkey and all the trimmings. You remember that girl I told you about a while ago? A PC on the force. We were hoping it would work out. She moved to Somerset in the end.'

'What happened?' Izzy said, nibbling on a stalk of celery.

She frowned. 'I'm not sure, if I'm honest. We all thought her lovely and were all set on going out *en masse* in search of "kick ass" hats. One day she was there and the next she'd been transferred to the West Country.' She shook her head, as if dislodging a memory. 'Anyway, enough about her. The main thing is he's not attached and, if I know my brother like I think I do, he likes you. He likes you a lot.'

The sound of the doorbell halted the conversation and, as far as Izzy was concerned, it didn't come a second too soon. It was kind of Rebecca to put her up but not if Rhys came as part of the package. She couldn't even begin to think of looking at another man until she knew what had happened to Charlie and Alys. To someone like Rebecca, it must seem that, with the discovery of their remains, it was the end of a five-year mystery. But, for her, it was just the beginning. Finding a man, any man, wasn't in any of her current plans. She just hoped that Rebecca didn't have other ideas – ideas that included her brother.

Rhys walked into the kitchen, a bottle of red wine under his arm, which he placed on the worktop before propping himself against the wall.

'Hi Izzy, how are you doing?'

She ignored the question. After all, how did he expect her to answer? *I'm fine* really didn't hack it. Instead, she shook her head and concentrated on her wine glass. She didn't know why he was here, not really. He was still heading up the case but was he here as a detective or just as Rebecca's brother? She eyed him over the rim of her glass. While part of her felt that he should still be at the office, looking under every stone for clues, he had to eat. He had to rest. He had a life outside of the case even if she didn't. She felt like an outsider suddenly. She was an outsider, there under sufferance despite their assurances to the contrary. There wouldn't be any talk about the case, not with Rebecca in the room and she wasn't in the mood for the small talk they'd launched into. She turned her back and pulled open the cutlery drawer.

'I'll just lay the table, shall I?'

Rhys sat back with a groan of satisfaction. 'That was lovely. I don't know why I don't move in.'

'Ha, because you're not invited. One man here is one enough, thank you very much although, I might as well make use of you while you're here. It's bin night!' Rebecca said with a chuckle. 'I'm just about to make some coffee. Did you want me to parcel the rest of this up in a doggy bag? Izzy's thinking of heading back to her own place tomorrow and I'll never be able to eat this lot.'

'Isn't that a little soon?'

Izzy tilted her head. 'No. I need to get on with my life,' she said, struggling to keep her voice even. She wasn't in the mood for an argument and she'd already made up her mind that tonight would be her last, whatever he said. 'As much as I appreciate everything you and Rebecca have done, it's time for me to stand on my own two feet.'

'But the press—?'

'The press can go to blazes. If they want to hound me, I'm sure you can find a couple of boys in blue that will come to my rescue,' she said, starting to gather the empty dishes together with a clatter.

He wasn't happy. She could tell by the way his eyes bored into her as she reached across the table. But she'd had enough of being told what to do.

'Leave those,' Rebecca said.

'No, I like washing up,' she lied. She'd do anything if it meant being able to keep her back to Rhys. After a moment of silence, she heard the scrape of a chair.

'I'll just go and take out the rubbish. I'll be back shortly and Izzy … I'd like a quick word before I go.'

A few minutes later, she walked ahead of him through the door and out to his car.

'I won't keep you long,' he said, resting his hand on the side of the roof. 'It's too cold to be outside.'

'I'm fine, really.' She pulled her coat around her body as if to emphasise the point. 'Look, I know you couldn't say anything in front of your sister and I also know that I'm probably the number one suspect but …'

'No! How could you even think that?'

'Well, whatever. Just – please. I need to know if there's any news.'

She watched him lift his hand, rubbing it across his jaw. 'Are you sure you want to know, really sure?'

She stared back, her heart squeezing inside her chest. A car door slammed, the sound drawing her attention away from him and to the sudden arc of light as the driver switched on his lights before starting the engine. She only turned back when the noise trickled into silence. She opened her mouth to speak but the words wouldn't come. Instead she nodded her head. She had to know.

'It looks as if there was foul play of some sort. There are signs that the male—'

'Oh, for God's sake, at least call him by his given name, why don't you.'

He threw off her snappy comment with a shrug. 'Preliminary results confirm that Charlie Dawson received injuries not consistent with those normally sustained when a car has been involved in a crash. While the airbag was deployed, the team believe this was only after the vehicle hit the water.'

'So, all that means precisely what?' she said, her gaze pinned to his.

'I'm afraid it means that there's conclusive evidence that it wasn't an accident. Charlie was murdered.'

Chapter 32

Izzy

Izzy leant against Rebecca's front door, her forehead resting on the smooth surface of the wood. She couldn't move if her life depended on it. Her thoughts had taken her full circle to this moment, a moment where the last five years had finally caught up with her. All along she'd been hoping to see Alys again but news of her and Charlie's accidentally death had padded her emotions against any feeling other than that of guilt. She'd done her grieving. She'd more than paid her dues on the River Styx in coinage of tears. Nothing could change the fact that she'd lost them both. What she regretted now with a fierce passion was the betrayal of her love for Charlie. She'd allowed that pure clean love to disappear under the weight of her sorrow for her child. Now a new story would have to be written. She knew the start. Rhys had just told her the ending. But the middle—

A shout from the lounge pulled her out of her reverie and back into the lounge and where Rebecca was waiting with a fresh mug of coffee but, despite her entreaties, she made her way to her room and started to pack.

She couldn't stay another night, not now. She welcomed the

respite she'd been given but things had moved on. She'd been shielded for far too long. Now that she knew the truth, or part of the truth, she wouldn't stop until she knew it all. Her feelings of grief and guilt had been brushed aside by a very different Izzy to the one that had followed Rhys out to the car. Now a blood-red anger flowed through her veins, sweeping away all other emotion. All her energy had one focus: to find the person or persons responsible for their murder.

Within the hour her taxi was pulling up outside her house, her mind in tatters.

There was no sign of anyone, no indication that the media had been camped outside her door, apart from a flattening of the grass and a few discarded butt ends. But inside was a different story. The letter box was jam-packed with notes, fliers and business cards from all the people wanting a piece of the action. She threw the whole lot on the table for the morning before crossing to the phone and where its green light was blinking in quick succession. She ignored the messages, all of them. She ignored everything apart from Bucket who wrapped his warm body around her legs as if she'd been gone weeks instead of only a few days. He looked well, fat even, her gaze drifting to his overflowing food bowl. She was pleased Rhys had kept his word.

With Bucket trailing behind, she unplugged the phone and drifted up the stairs to her bedroom, discarding her coat, beanie and shoes along the way. She still had one more task to carry out, something she was dreading. Not bothering to undress, she rested back against the pillows and pulled out her mobile, scrolling down for the right number.

'Hello Ma, I don't know how to tell you so I'm just going to blurt it out. Someone murdered them ... oh Mam ...'

She couldn't sleep but then she couldn't be expected to after information like that. Lying there, staring at the shadows crossing the ceiling, her mind hopped from one thought to the next. The worst thing, of course, was the lies. The postcards had taken her down a rabbit hole very much in the vein of *Alice in Wonderland*. Someone had deliberately gone out of their way to make her believe that there would somehow be a fairy tale reunion with Alys – and she'd fallen for it.

She watched the light at the window changing from black to grey and, at the first glow of orange she knew it was time to get up, if only to fill the kettle and feed Bucket. Scooping up her phone, she switched it back on and made her way downstairs and into the kitchen. She wasn't hungry but she knew she had to eat.

With a plate of toast in one hand and a mug of tea in the other, she wandered into the lounge and sat at the table, the post in front of her. Junk mail, a couple of bills and slips of paper ripped from notebooks with requests for interviews. Apart from the bills, which she stacked neatly under the fruit bowl, she bundled the rest into a neat pile for recycling. They could whistle if they thought she was going to comment about what the police had found.

On her way back into the kitchen and the recycle bin, the sound of her mobile ringing made her forget what she was doing, the pile of paper slipping through her fingers and scattering at her feet.

'Izzy, for Christ's sake. Why haven't you been picking-up? I've been trying since last night.'

'Bethan? What's the matter?' she said, a coldness clutching at her heart. Bethan, her sensible and in-control sister sounded anything but.

'It's Dad. He … he heard Mam and you speaking on the phone. She didn't know what to do. You know what he's like. He made her tell her there and then about Alys and Charlie. He … oh Izzy.'

Izzy gripped the edge of the phone, willing her to hurry up. It could only be bad news, but how bad? If she was honest, she'd known something like this was going to happen, just not when. He wasn't a well man. He hadn't been well since the day Alys had disappeared. Something had left him on that day – something unquantifiable, something vital. Something irreplaceable.

The phone was quiet, too quiet. Izzy sank down on the bottom stair, trying to put herself in her sister's position. She'd obviously had to deal with whatever it was on her own – their mam wouldn't have been any good and Oscar, for all his well-meaning ways, was always useless in a crisis.

'He's …?' she prompted gently.

'He's had a heart attack.'

Chapter 33

Gaby
Wednesday 15 January, 8.05 a.m. Swansea Police Station

'Thank you all for coming in early,' DCI Brazil-North said, scanning the room. 'There's a press conference at eight-thirty and I want to make sure that I have all the information I need.'

It was a repeat of last week's meeting except now they had the preliminary findings from the pathologist in front of them. It wasn't pretty reading and, even after eleven years in the force, Gaby still felt her stomach heaving at the gorier elements.

She sat, perched on the corner of the nearest desk, examining the woman in front of her with an impartial eye. The DCI looked as if she'd come straight from the hair salon, while the rest of the team, following a week of living off coffee and sandwiches, looked decidedly the worse for wear. Today the DCI had swept her hair back off her face with a couple of tortoiseshell combs, her freshly ironed blouse in sharp contrast to Gaby's crumpled offering but that was hardly surprising. Gaby's jacket was disguising the sight of her clearly un-ironed shirt.

Last night, when the rest of the team were at home with their families, she'd headed back to the office. There were never enough

159

hours in the day to do even half of what was needed and the only extra time she seemed to have was always at the expense of sleep. She'd finally crawled into bed at 3 a.m. and, as a result, missed the alarm clock banging about on her bedside table. She'd had to prioritise a mug of black coffee and toast over assembling the ironing board, a decision she was yet to regret.

'DI Walker, would you update the team on what's been happening with the Grant case?'

Gaby turned her attention back to Rhys. By the look of the shadows bruising his skin and the mark from where he'd cut himself shaving, he'd also spent an indifferent night. He'd barely said a word to her when she'd been expecting, at the very least, a comment about her shirt. There was obviously something niggling him, her gaze now on where he was holding his notebook in a tight grip, the knuckles gleaming white.

'We have a murder investigation on our hands,' he said, placing his pad down on the desk before hiding his hands in his pockets, the bunched outline of his fists still visible. 'Charles Dawson, nineteen, suffered a fracture to the hyoid bone, which, as you'll know occurs during mechanical asphyxiation, indicating that Dawson was strangled prior to immersion in water. We also found the remains of a baby still strapped into the car seat – a car seat which, on the surface, fits the description of the one bought by Isabelle Grant for her daughter, Alys. At this stage in the investigation the pathology report is inconclusive. There's no sign of asphyxiation or indeed other trauma to the baby and it's difficult, without tissue samples, to make a positive case for drowning. But that's the most likely scenario.'

He took a step back. 'The car has been stripped right down to the engine and there's no sign of a collision even though the airbag was deployed. After all this time it's unlikely that they'll find much of any use but then again it's too early in the investigation to make that assumption.' He paused, surveying the room briefly before continuing. 'I've set up a preliminary murder book with relevant photographs and the pathologist's initial findings but, at this stage we have no definite leads. All we have is a list of suspects that, in light of this recent development, will need to be re-interviewed.'

'Sir,' Gaby interrupted, 'there's something odd about how they found the car.'

'Go on.'

She threw an uneasy look across at Bill but when she spoke her voice was strong. 'David Prestwich and Arthur Norman, the two lads that found it, heard about the Blue Lagoon from a conversation on a cliff diving forum. We're trying to chase it up now.'

He laughed. 'Well, I'm sure they could have as easily been directed to a thousand other jumps. Surely a coincidence?'

Her brow wrinkled into a frown. 'I'm not so sure that's correct, boss. I've been on the phone to the marine biology department over at the University. During the summer months, when this kind of sport is at its most popular, the lagoon sees hundreds of thrill-seekers and yet no one discovered the car. Apparently, that's because Algae thrive in warmer waters and the boffin I was speaking to suggested that it would have been almost impossible to find the car during the summer. It's only now, with the temperature at seven degrees that the water would have been clear enough.' She met his gaze head on. 'Whoever dumped the car did their research, which makes the posting on that forum of high importance. Why now, after all these years would the killer want the car to be found?'

'Why indeed? I think you've answered your own question, DC Darin. It's not likely, is it? But, if you're that keen on wasting your time, get one of the lads in IT to look at the web address and see what they come up with.'

'What about Isabelle Grant?' DS Bill Davis said.

'What about her?'

'Surely she's the obvious suspect? Most crimes are committed by someone known to the victim so who better placed than the girlfriend?'

'Indeed? It's certainly not something we can rule out at this stage but what would you suggest her motive was? Filicide isn't the most common of crimes, after all,' he said, rolling his eyes at the sea of blank faces. 'Filicide, the killing of one's son or daughter.'

'Post-natal depression perhaps? She was under the care of the psychiatrists for months after,' Bill mused. 'Or the other option is that she found out he was having a fling and decided to do something about it.'

Rhys glowered, clearly unhappy with his comments. 'All we have to go on is one unsubstantiated comment from her friend about a possible affair, a friend who went missing around the same time ...'

'Well, there's your answer. Find the friend and take it from there.'

Chapter 34

Izzy
Thursday 16 January, 6 p.m. Withybush Hospital

You think that life can't get any worse. You think that the worst thing possible has already happened.

Her father was in a bay of six but he seemed so much worse than the other patients. There was no response when she clutched at his hand. There was no flicker under his eyelids or around his mouth that, as long as she'd known him, had always twitched into a ready smile. The old man in the bed opposite, propped up by a thousand pillows, sipped his tea, his hand crazed in tubing. The teenager in the adjacent bed was asleep but with a biker magazine on the bed cover beside him. Her dad wasn't doing any of those things. He looked as if the Grim Reaper had marked his card and was, even now, knocking on his door with a steady fist.

Mam and Bethan had disappeared for a quick cuppa and a sandwich but they'd be back. The doctor had been and gone, her face set into one of those fixed smiles that never quite reach the eyes. There was nothing else they could do except wait. The next couple of days were crucial. If he could survive those, there was a good chance he'd be okay.

'Go on, love. It's your turn now.'

Izzy had been so engrossed in her thoughts that she hadn't heard them return until they were almost on top of her. Mam looked a little better. Still pale and with new lines etched deep but that was to be expected after a marriage that spanned thirty years.

She stood and stretched, unable to meet her mother's gaze. It was her fault he'd been taken ill. If only she hadn't phoned. If only she'd gotten into the car and driven over to their house. If only … They'd needed to know before the news hit the papers but she should have thought of a kinder way.

'I'm so sorry. I should have waited to tell you—'

'There you go, blaming yourself,' Bethan said, her voice sharp. 'It's not your fault, Izzy. If anything, it's the fault of the bastard that did this to you,' her hand squeezing her arm. 'Go get a cuppa, love. I'll look after Mam.'

'Only if you promise you'll let me know if anything happens. I'll switch my phone back on as soon as I'm out of here.'

The canteen was nearly empty now the dinnertime rush was over. There was no one behind the counter so she headed across to the wall of vending machines and finally decided on a tuna and mayo sandwich and a cup of what was meant to be coffee. Finding an empty table she settled in a chair and, lifting the plastic cup started to take a sip, only to return it to the table and reach for her ringing phone, her heart in her mouth.

'Izzy, its Rhys.'

She let the air out of her lungs in a sigh before speaking.

'What can I do for you, Rhys?'

'I need you to come down to the station for another chat. I'm afraid that in light of recent events, we have to revisit everyone's witness statements.'

'I'm sorry but now's not a good time.'

'I can come and collect you if transport is a problem. We really need to move on—'

'Rhys, you don't understand.' She pushed her sandwich away and, cradling the phone to her ear, wrapped her fingers around her coffee cup for warmth. She didn't want to tell him about her dad. That would make it real somehow when the one thing she couldn't cope with was the reality of the situation. The reality was far too cruel to share. Once it was out, once everyone knew, they'd all swarm around the honey pot waiting to sting. They didn't care about her or her family. All they cared about was themselves. One of the most unsavoury truths, a truth she'd known for the last five years, was that people relished in the misery of others.

'Listen, please. I'm at the hospital.' Her voice was flat, devoid of emotion. She gripped the phone even tighter, the plastic covering biting into her chin. 'My dad … he's had a heart attack. I can't do anything about either Charlie or Alys but I sure as hell can be here for my father, if and when he needs me.'

'I'm on my way.'

Chapter 35

Izzy

It was getting late and time for her to think about heading home to feed Bucket. There was nothing she could do here. There was nothing anyone could do. If her father could just survive the next few hours … She left Mam beside his bed, while she went outside to wait for Rhys, because that's where her mother wanted to be. She couldn't have budged her even if she'd wanted to and who'd want to, now that Dad had woken up just long enough to curl his hand through hers.

Within moments of pushing open the heavy double doors, Rhys was upon her, almost running down the corridor, his grey coat flapping around his legs, the expression on his face impossible to read.

'You didn't need to come.'

'It's no trouble. I feel partly responsible as it is. Your dad is a nice bloke, one of the best. For this to happen now …' His voice trailed off, his attention shifting to the painting of rolling hills that hung on the wall beside the entrance to the ward, his hands tucked into his trouser pockets in a stance she was becoming familiar with.

'Come on. Let's get a bite to eat and after I'll drop you home.'

'I'm driving and anyway I've already eaten.'

'Really? One of those sandwiches they sell downstairs?' He raised his eyebrows. 'I'll bet you the price of a meal that you took one bite and stuffed the remainder unfinished back into the carton and then into the bin. And as for their coffee ...'

She noticed the grey tinge to his skin and the fine lines radiating out from the corners of his mouth and, for the first time, she wondered if she was being selfish refusing his offer. If the last few days had been tough for her they must have equally been tough for him. Perhaps, instead of making a fuss, she should just let him take her out for a quick meal; somewhere quiet, somewhere where they could both get something to eat, only that. He was right about the sandwiches. She wouldn't cry a single tear if she never saw another sandwich again and there was a much better chance of her drifting off to sleep on a full stomach than the toast she'd been planning in the silence of her mind. She opened her mouth to accept only to close it again, another thought ricocheting.

'What about your work colleagues, hmm? I thought you said that coppers weren't allowed to fraternise with members of the—'

'Izzy.' His hand was now resting on her arm. 'I started out as a bobby on the beat, which included taking an oath to protect and serve the public. There's nothing wrong with dropping a key witness home especially after the day you've had. Now, come on, or are you too scared of what people might think?'

She stared back. It was the only thing he could have said that was guaranteed to have her falling in with his plan – that and the thought of food.

'What about my car? I'll need it in the morning.'

His hand gripped her arm, his fingers exerting a light pressure 'You're forgetting I still live in St David's for my sins. I can easily drop by on my way to work in the morning. This way if you fancy a glass of wine or two there's nothing to stop you.'

'Nowhere posh then,' she said, gesturing to her jeans and trainers.

'Ha, you should know by now that I don't do posh. What about the Purple Frog? I haven't been for a while, but I hear they do a mean steak and ale pie?'

The Purple Frog, situated on the outskirts of St David's, was the ideal place for a quiet meal and they soon found themselves tucked away in a corner, the flames from the log fire adding texture and atmosphere to the otherwise white-washed walls.

Izzy placed her knife and fork neatly in the centre of her plate with a sigh before reaching for her wine glass. 'I feel guilty sitting here, stuffing my face, with everything that's going on.'

'Well, don't. You need to eat and your father wouldn't be much of a man if he thought twice about you leaving his side when your mam is there,' he said, taking a final chip from his plate before pushing it aside. 'You'd have only gone back to a cold house and spent half the night worrying. As it is, you'll probably drop off as soon as your head hits the pillow.'

'Thank you, then. It seems it's just what I needed.'

'You're welcome. Sometimes the brain needs to shut down for a while and a good meal and a couple of glasses of wine can help put things into perspective.' He picked up the menu, propped up between the salt and pepper pots. 'What about a slice of apple pie for afters?'

'No, I can't manage another thing,' she said with a laugh. 'But go ahead. I'm happy just sitting here nursing my wine.'

'No. Pudding really isn't my thing.' He dropped his eyes to the table and started fiddling with his fork. 'I know it's probably not the right time or anything but with you there never seems to be a right time … There's something I need to say.' He dragged his hand through his hair before continuing. 'You do realise that we may never find out exactly what happened in the car? After five years any clues that may have been there won't be there now.' He looked up, his jaw clenched. 'There's only so much we can do. Only so many people we can question. Only so much evidence we can expect to find after so long. You know more than most people the importance of grabbing life with both hands and holding on tight, especially now with your dad being ill. So, what I'm trying to say is to make the best of what you have now and not invest everything you have in hoping for a truth that may never be discovered. You're worth more than that.'

She closed her eyes. This was his way of trying to break it to her gently. He wasn't interested in her as a person. He was a copper on a case in the game of damage limitation. Great! She snapped her eyes open. The one thing he seemed to have forgotten was that she wasn't stupid. She knew that the chances of finding out what happened were slim at best but that wasn't a reason to give up.

'Look, Rhys. We've known each other a long time, perhaps too long.' She leant back in her chair, suddenly reluctant to meet his gaze. 'I know what you're trying to say here but it won't work.' She stood suddenly, lifting her jacket off the back of her chair. 'I've spent the last five years hating Charlie, the sweetest of boys. I've spent the same years searching for our baby. I've looked in every pram and pushchair, under every hat and bonnet when all the time she was—' She ran her hand across her face, shoving back any trace of tears. 'I can't talk about this now. Please, just take me home.'

Sometime during their meal, the rain had set in and they had to race to the car, their feet drowning in puddles.

'Bloody weather! When it rains in Wales, it certainly pours,' Rhys said, throwing off his coat and flinging it across the back seat before switching on the engine and fiddling with the dial of the heater. Soon hot air was streaming up to clear the windows and the wiper blades were working overtime.

They didn't talk. He'd said more than enough words to last the rest of the evening and more. Resting her head back against the seat, she took refuge behind her closed lids. If that was his attitude she'd just have to try and avoid him like she used to.

He pulled up outside the house and, reaching in the back, dragged his coat across his shoulders.

'No, don't bother,' she said, holding up her door key like a prize. 'I'll be inside in a couple of seconds anyway. There's no point in you getting wet.'

But she might as well have saved her breath for all the notice he took. Ignoring her words, he plucked the key from her fingers before making a run for the little porch area that overhung the front door.

Izzy followed with a sigh, the thought of the comfort of her own bed fading into the distance because she now felt obliged to ask him in for a coffee. Bucket met her just inside the door, entwining himself around her legs in a bid for food but that wasn't what caught her attention. It was the sight of Rhys picking up a card from where she'd tossed the post last night.

The noise of the door slamming on its hinges was indication of Izzy's rapidly changing mood.

'I thought you said they shouldn't be touched even if you are wearing gloves.' But Rhys simply ignored her, not bothering to reply.

She headed into the kitchen, blindly pulling open one of the cupboards and plucking out a sachet of cat food, before squeezing it out into Bucket's bowl and replenishing his water. Next, she flicked on the switch and reached for a couple of mugs: anything to keep her mind off the reality of yet another card. She couldn't handle much more: first her dad and now this. It was all too much. The card must have been sent by some crank or other, someone who took joy from the misery of others. If she could get her hands around their scrawny neck, she'd show them a thing or two about misery.

'Don't you want to know what it says?'

She'd been so wrapped up in her thoughts that she hadn't heard him follow her. Without a word, she pulled out the same drawer as last time and handed him a see-through freezer bag, before picking up the mugs and ushering him back into the lounge. It was far too cold but she was damned if she was going to turn on any heating just for his benefit. With a bit of luck, he'd be gone in a few minutes – him and that blasted card.

'Well?'

'I expect you're going to tell me whether I want to know or not,' she said, picking up her mobile and checking it for messages.

'Izzy, this is serious stuff. If you could just put down your phone for a minute.'

She placed her mobile on the table, her mouth dry and suddenly she wanted him gone. She wanted him to leave her house and take the rotten card with him. It didn't matter what it said, not now that she'd lost the two most important people in her life. A card wasn't going to bring them back and, with her dad ill, she had more important things to concentrate on. Picking up her mug, she settled on the sofa before replying.

'Go on, I'm listening.'

Instead of answering he placed the plastic bag on her lap before heading towards the window and pulling back the curtains to peer outside. 'You just couldn't stay at Rebecca's? No one would have known you were there. This is a serious threat to you, something that we hadn't foreseen although we probably should have.'

'I don't understand?' she said, her gaze shifting from his rigid shoulders and back to the card.

The card was plain white, the kind that people popped through letterboxes when you were out. There was no signature, no clues of any kind, not even a stamp. She flipped it over to read the writing on the back.

You're next

She felt the colour drain from her face at the words even as she tried to come up with some kind of a comment.

'It's obviously some kind of pervert trying to frighten me.'

'Perhaps,' he said, picking up his mug before joining her on the sofa. 'But, whatever the motives, we can't discount the seriousness of the threat,' his eyes watchful. 'You can't stay here, that's for sure. There's someone out to get you and …' Lifting the mug to his lips, he drained it in one before setting it down on the coffee table. 'Come on, get your coat. I'll take you back to Rebecca's.'

'Now just hang on a minute. There's no way I'm going to turn up at your sister's this late at night,' she said, standing to her feet before turning and facing him. 'What about what I want for once or doesn't that matter, hmm? What about the hospital and if my sister tries to phone? The reception out here isn't that great so they usually use the landline. What if someone wants to contact me urgently?'

'The fact still stands that until we find out who sent you this,' he tapped the card, 'it's not safe for you to stay here.'

'Well, the fact still stands that I'm staying, so there,' she snapped, pleased beyond measure that she'd managed to put together a decent retort despite everything going on in her life right now.

'Okay, have it your way,' he said, and before she could think of anything else to say he'd removed his jacket and draped it across the back of one of the spindle-backed chairs before bending down and starting to untie his shoelaces.

'Hey, what do you think you're doing?'

'What does it look like I'm doing? Getting ready to go to the disco? If you continue to act like a stubborn little fool when all we're trying to do is protect you then so be it. I'm staying and –' he held up his hand in the air, palm facing her '– I don't want to hear any paltry excuses, Izzy. You've got me for the night so just live with it like I'm going to have to,' he said, pressing his hand down on her too-hard and far too-short sofa.

She didn't reply. In truth, all her words had dried up at the start of his little speech. She didn't want him to stay but, apart from trying to man-handle him out of the house, she had very little choice. Turning her back she headed up the stairs and to the bathroom to find a spare toothbrush and a new bar of soap, which she carried into the spare room. The south-facing bedroom was dominated by heavy oak furniture with a large wooden bed pitched right in the middle that still had the old-fashioned patchwork throw Gran had hand-worked for her wedding. She stripped off the covers and replaced them with fresh sheets and thick blankets before heading downstairs to where Rhys was sitting on the edge of the sofa like a spare part, all his clothes apart from his open shirt, boxers and socks, folded in a neat pile beside him.

'Come on, you'll freeze to death like that. You can have the spare room at the top of the stairs. I'll go and make us another drink.'

'No, you're falling asleep on your feet, let me do it,' he said, walking into the kitchen, the door whispering shut behind him.

She felt hysterical laughter build at the ridiculousness of the situation. Rhys had put himself up as her self-proclaimed bodyguard. But, with a killer on the loose and no leads to go on, perhaps he was exactly what she needed right now.

Chapter 36

Izzy
Friday 17 January, 7 a.m. Abereiddy

Sleep had crept through the house, pushing away grief and tears with its dark all-consuming presence. She didn't dream. As soon as her head touched the pillow, the wine on top of the heavy meal had the desired effect of dragging her under the cover of darkness. She was aware of a dip in the mattress sometime in the small hours when Bucket shifted his position, but it would have taken an earthquake to wake her. Feeling both warm and safe, she slept on until the ring of her mobile dragged her back from the depths, twisting her heart in her chest.

She finished the call but, before she'd even had a chance to process the news, there was a gentle knock on the door, which had her sitting up in bed, a hand to her hair and the duvet dragged right up to her chin, her gaze following Bucket as he jumped onto the floor and slunk towards the landing.

'Ah, only me. I heard the telephone and thought you could do with a cuppa.' Rhys walked in, mug in hand which he placed on the bedside cabinet with a steady hand, studiously avoiding looking in her direction.

Now wasn't the time to break down with him in the room, especially after last night, but there was nothing she could do to staunch the sudden flow of tears other than dip her head.

'Oh, Izzy, I'm so sorry.' He sat on the edge of the bed and, cradling her in his arms, his hand rubbed her back, smoothing over her hair.

Time paused for a second, just one, as a thought flashed across her mind only to be discarded as unworthy of her. There was no way someone like him would take advantage of such a situation, not if he valued his career. After a moment she returned his hug before pushing him away and dragging her hands over her cheeks.

'Thanks for that, just what I needed.'

'What did they say?'

He was still sitting on the bed, so close that she could smell the trace of lemon shampoo coming from his hair, her shampoo.

'Silly me. It's not bad news,' she said, a smile breaking. 'It's good. The very best. They've moved him back onto the general ward and there's talk of him being discharged soon. He'll need further investigations and a possible stent in the future but he's out of danger. Isn't that great news?'

'It couldn't be better. Come here. You shouldn't be crying if it's good news, silly.' And he dragged her back inside the wall of his arms for a second hug.

Something shifted between them. She didn't know if it was the way his hands tightened around her back, or the way his breath hitched in the back of his throat. But what began as a brotherly hug quickly lost all trace of innocence. Now, instead of being tucked against his shoulder he was leaning back, his hands on either side of her face, his eyes asking a question. She stared back, almost mesmerised by the blue of his iris.

Would it be so wrong to kiss him? Would it be so wrong for it to stop at just a kiss? After everything he's done already I probably owe him.

She blinked. Not the best of reasons for sex but, at least, she'd finally know if he was someone she could see herself with in the future and, if she was being completely honest, she needed this. Her emotions had almost unravelled to breaking; the thin strand of reason the only thing stopping her descent into the same mental chaos she'd suffered before. Surely it wouldn't be wrong to accept what he was clearly offering. The comfort of a man's arms was a rapidly fading memory and suddenly she wanted that to change.

Chapter 37

Izzy

'Put it on,' he said, draping her dressing gown around her, his hands pressing against her shoulders before heading back to lean against the door of the bathroom, his gaze never leaving her face. 'So, I take it what we've just done was all a mistake? You didn't really mean for us to make love?'

She felt for the sleeves of her dressing gown and belted it tight around her waist before attempting to stand, well aware of his gaze tracing the outline of her body under the thin fabric, his hands fiddling with the top button of his shirt before starting to work on his tie. She was pleased that he'd taken the trouble to dress before following her into the bathroom. The conversation was going to be awkward enough without the added complication of nudity.

With her hands on the edge of the sink she allowed her mind to dip into the difficult problem of what to say. What reason could she give for scrabbling out from underneath him within seconds of allowing him to …? She closed her eyes, aware of the cloud of colour blooming under her cheeks, even as she tried to find a way out of her current predicament. But wishing the ground would swallow her whole wasn't the best use of what few seconds she had to come up with an explanation. The one thing he deserved was the truth but that was the one thing that would hurt him the most. While her experience of men was limited, she was pretty sure admitting to thinking about another man during sex was taboo as far as post-coital conversations went. In fact, it would be cruel of her to tell him that while he'd been grinding himself into her flesh, all she could think about was how it had been with Charlie.

'Rhys, I owe you an apology. I've obviously done something incredibly stupid.' She tightened her hold on the sink, her finger-tips pressing into the ceramic until pain caused her to loosen her grip. She'd made a huge mistake and, by the dour expression glued to his face, he wasn't prepared to leave without a full explanation. She tried again. 'Please don't think it's you. I'd feel the same with any man. After Charlie … after everything that's happened, sex just isn't relevant anymore.'

'What, you're going to die a born-again virgin?' His laugh was harsh.

'Hardly! You're not being fair.'

'No. It's you who's not being fair, Izzy. One minute you're in my arms and the next … What the hell am I meant to think?'

'You can think what you like, Rhys,' she said, turning back to the sink and catching his gaze reflected in the mirror. 'You won't believe anything I say but it's the truth.

'You wouldn't recognise the truth if it jumped up and bit you on the arse.'

'You're probably right.'

She felt weary all of a sudden, the weight of all her troubles pressing down hard. She'd obviously made a mistake, but mistakes happened all the time and, in the long run, she was the one that had to live with the burden of what they'd just done. She had to know what had happened that day in the car and only then would she be able to start thinking about a future but not with him.

He wasn't in the running. He'd never been in the running, but how the hell did she tell him that without ruining the chance of the case ever being solved? She couldn't.

She stayed by the sink, reaching for her toothbrush with an unsteady hand. Everything was out of focus, blurred around the edges. She tried to concentrate on squeezing the toothpaste out of the tube in an effort to blot out the sound of the door opening and his footsteps on the stairs. It was only when she heard the front door slamming that she allowed her tears to fall. Tears for Charlie and Alys. Tears for her father and finally tears of self-pity for her. What a bloody mess.

Chapter 38

Izzy

The sight of him standing in the kitchen rinsing out his mug nearly had her heading back upstairs.

'I thought you'd be long gone.'

'Well, you thought wrong. I know that I'm probably not one of your favourite people right now but, after what we've just done, I feel responsible somehow.' He spread his hands. 'Perhaps I should have said no when you crawled into my arms. But it would have taken a better man than me, Izzy – a far better man.'

So he's blaming me for what just happened. I don't remember initiating things but whatever. I can't be bothered to argue. The simple truth is we had sex and now I want him gone.

She flicked on the kettle and reached for a couple of fresh mugs, trying to inject some normality into what felt like the most bizarre of situations. Instead of picking up on his conversation all she said was. 'Do you want tea?'

'Only if you promise not to make the situation more awkward than it feels?'

'I can't lie and say I feel anything other than uncomfortable at the moment, but I'll try to forget what a complete idiot I've been,' she said, throwing him a quick look over her shoulder before reaching for the tea bags. 'I wouldn't want to hurt your feelings for the world.'

'But you still can't see us together anytime soon despite what we've just done?'

She shook her head. 'I'm sorry. I just don't think of you in that way.'

'Not as sorry as I am,' he said, rubbing his hand across his chin.' He picked up his mug from the counter and carried it into the lounge, leaving her to stare after him with a frown.

She heaved a sigh as she untied the top of the bread and popped a couple of slices in the toaster. Sorry was such an ineffectual word in these kinds of situations. All she wanted was for their relationship to shift back twenty-four hours, but that ship had sailed. The irony of it was if it hadn't been for that stupid card, she'd never have agreed to let him stay.

Knife in hand, she concentrated on buttering the toast and placing marmalade and homemade blackberry jam on a tray before carrying it into the lounge. She'd delay all thoughts of last night until after she'd gotten rid of him – as much as she wanted him gone she was still relying on him keeping his promise to drop her back to her car.

'I thought you might like something to eat before we have to leave.'

'Thank you,' he said, his face pulling into a lopsided smile. 'I didn't think you'd want to spend any more time in my company than absolutely necessary.'

His words, almost mirroring her thoughts, caused her face to flame. 'We're both grown-ups, Rhys. I know it sounds trite after … well, after what's happened but I'd like, if possible, for us to remain friends.'

He took a bite of toast, brushing the crumbs off his top lip, his gaze unwavering. 'I had thought that too but now I'm not so sure.'

Izzy stared back but, instead of trying to conjure up the right sort of reply, she continued sipping her tea, any thought of food turning her stomach. She'd done her best. She'd bent over backwards trying to apologise. She wasn't prepared to apologise again.

His plate empty, he reached behind the chair for his jacket. 'If you want that lift I need to leave now.'

'Of course.' She placed her mug on the table and collected her keys and purse from the bowl and an old jacket from the coat rack. 'I'm ready.'

She reached the door and her hand curled round the handle when someone's shadow appeared through the etched glass and the sound of the doorbell reverberated across the room.

'Don't answer that,' he said. But it was too late, she'd already twisted back the lock and pulled it open.

'Hello Miss Grant, I know it's early but I just thought I'd—' Gaby's voice dropped away into silence.

Chapter 39

Gaby
Friday 17 January, 8 a.m. Abereiddy

'Morning Gaby, two great minds and all that,' Rhys said, shifting the door from her grasp and obstructing her view into the lounge. 'Izzy has had some bad news about her father,' he continued, walking her back out to her car. 'I thought I'd pop in and see how she was doing and it's a good thing I did.' He reached inside his pocket before handing her something wrapped in a freezer bag. 'Go on, flip it over. It's another card.'

Gaby watched him drag his hand through his hair before returning it to his pocket and jingling his keys.

'I don't like it one little bit. I'll speak to her about increasing security and the possibility of her staying with her sister for a while. I have to tell you I'm seriously concerned for her wellbeing.' He waited for her to get in the car before continuing, his hand resting on the roof. 'If you can drop the card back to the lab – I'm going to be out of the office for the morning. I'll let the guv know but, in the meantime, I'd like you to work with DS Davis.' He smiled briefly.' I know you don't see eye to eye but I don't want to hear any negative feedback. In this job you'll come across all sorts and it's part of your responsibility to make it work even if you can't stand each other.'

Gaby stared up at him, barely hearing a word. Her mind was on other things like the flustered look on Izzy's face and the image of the table set for two; evidence enough of what must have happened. There were other clues too, clues that it didn't need a copper to analyse. She'd never known Rhys so verbose. He was the strong silent type, only speaking when he had something to say. Now he was positively chatty. But chatty in the wrong way. She'd, at least, expected him to question her as to the reason for her visit. Not that she had a good reason other than a hunch that Izzy wasn't telling everything she knew.

With one hand adjusting the rear-view mirror and the other controlling the steering wheel, she continued to watch them as she negotiated the drive, the feeling of bitter disappointment raw in her gut. Was every man she came across going to let her down so spectacularly? First Leigh and now Rhys. Leigh, the man she'd given her heart to and … She blinked, suddenly realising that he didn't have the power to hurt her anymore. She'd thought at one point that he was her future. Now, with the upheaval of her move to Swansea closely followed by the search for Alys, he'd been squarely relegated to her past. She'd learnt a tough lesson along the way and it would be a very long time before she'd allow herself to be taken in so easily. Her heart, once a fragile thing, was now coated with impermeable steel.

Rhys Walker's betrayal of everything she stood for felt somehow worse. She'd come across bad detectives in Cardiff. Coppers who'd decided that crime was a better career path. But there'd been an air about them. They'd been men she hadn't liked from the offset and men she'd certainly never trusted. She'd liked Rhys. She still liked him even though he'd put her in an impossible position. How could she allow him to continue to act as lead officer on the case having just compromised the key witness? But after what had happened to her in Cardiff how could she not?

She was already on her second chance. She'd been told that there wouldn't be a third.

The DCI led the later than usual morning catchup instead of Rhys, albeit reluctantly. With no real excuse for why he wasn't there and a less than honest reason for her impromptu three-hour round trip to Abereiddy, the air was thinner than the hair on the top of DS Davis's head. Car journeys had to be logged. Reports had to be made and going on a fishing trip wasn't a good enough reason for what the DCI had termed 'wasting police time'. It didn't matter that she'd worked late into the night at the station and, on returning back home, found then that she couldn't sleep. Choosing to leave the house at six-thirty instead of the usual eight was her choice and therefore didn't count as part of her working week.

With no news other than the card, it was a very short briefing. Gaby would have been quite happy to carry on where she'd left off yesterday. There was still work she wanted to do surrounding the discovery of the car in addition to finding someone to speak to about Eurostar passenger lists. DS Davis had other ideas.

He wandered over to her desk and, picking up her notepad, started flicking through it without comment. He didn't need to – the snigger on his face said it all. 'So, you say that DI Walker handed you the card this morning?'

'That's right.'

'That's right, sir!'

'That's right, sir,' she repeated, assuming a bland look.

'And?'

'And what, sir?'

'Don't come the innocent with me, Darin, or you'll be smiling on the other side of your face. And how come you saw the DI this morning and how did he come to be in possession of the card?'

Because he spent the night shagging Isabelle Grant's brains out.

But what she said instead was, 'We met at her house first thing and that's when she passed it over.'

She spread her hands, hoping her expression didn't give away the fact that she was telling him a fairy story. Although she very much doubted that there'd be a *happy ever after* to the end of this tale. If the body language she'd spotted between Rhys and Izzy was anything to go by it had all been a huge mistake – career-wise it was catastrophic. Gaby had heard of incidents where police officers had crossed that emotional line with members of the public, but to form a dalliance with a witness in an active case had only one outcome. A misconduct hearing closely followed by dismissal. The worst of it was he'd put her in a very vulnerable position. As a junior officer she had a responsibility to notify a senior officer of her suspicions, not least because of the potential effect it could have on the running of the case. On the other hand she liked Rhys and she was pretty sure he wasn't the type to let his personal feelings compromise an investigation. Thoughts of what had happened in Cardiff, when she'd tried to share her fears about a fellow officer, swept into the forefront of her mind. Was she about to tell Bill Davis? Was she hell!

'You met at her house?' He glared at her from under bushy eyebrows. 'Why did you meet her there? As the number one suspect surely Walker should have brought her in for questioning?'

'With all due respect, sir, there's no way Miss Grant murdered her boyfriend and child. I just don't buy it,' Gaby said, leaning forward in her chair.

'With all due respect, DC Darin, I don't give a damn what you think. From where I'm looking it's very likely she's involved. Post-partum psychosis is a medical fact. There's a heap of literature on post-natal depression and other associated disorders. The postcards are her way of trying to deflect suspicion when things started to unravel. I think these postcards are a complete red herring.'

'That's as may be,' she said quietly. 'But I still know she couldn't have done it.'

'That's a complete load of bollocks,' he hissed through clenched teeth, colour creeping over his collar and up his neck. 'The only way you'd know that would be if you killed them yourself. Did you?'

'Of course not! But I still know she couldn't have done it, Bill.'

'DS Davis to you, babes.'

'I am not and will never be your babe, DS Davis.' Her voice was calm, the two bright spots visible on her cheeks the only sign that she was angry beyond belief.

'No, that's true.' He scanned her from head to foot. 'There's a Weightwatchers running every Tuesday in the church hall.'

Gaby paused, her attention on the buttons straining his shirt before sliding her gaze up to his double chin.

'Why? Would you like me to give you a lift?'

Chapter 40

Izzy
Friday 17 January, 7 p.m. Abereiddy

Izzy was at a loose end.

With her father still in hospital and the media attention still shining in her direction, she was keeping a low profile. She'd been in touch with her web designer and placed an extra two weeks onto the current delivery dates, which should give her enough wriggle room to get part of her life back in order.

So, with her business on hold, apart from the orders that she'd passed over to the girls, she'd been spending most of her time at the hospital propping up Mam.

'It's best you go home before it gets too late, Pearl. You know you hate driving in the dark,' Dad said, managing one of his famous smiles.

'I'm happy to stay.'

'No, come back in the morning, love,' he said, closing his eyes.

Outside, the rain had started up and they both paused on the top step to search for their keys.

'Why don't you come back with me to Bethan's?' Mam said, her face etched with tiredness. 'It's not right that you should be by yourself. Bethan and Oscar won't mind and there's plenty of room for all of us. At times like these, families stick together.'

Izzy walked her mother to her car before drawing her into a deep hug. 'I know you mean well, but I just need to be alone for a bit,' she said, trying to inflect a note of reassurance into her voice. She just couldn't cope with the wealth of questions heading her way and if that meant she had to spend the night alone at the cottage, then so be it.

She didn't remember the drive back and dusk had already settled by the time she pulled into the drive and switched off the engine. She'd been dreading arriving home just in case a lone-wolf reporter was still staking out the cottage. But for once, luck was on her side and any journalist that might have been hanging around earlier must have decided the likelihood of her returning home wasn't worth a night spent on her doorstep.

The lounge was cold, but she didn't bother with the wood-burner. Instead, she headed into the kitchen and popped a couple of slices of bread in the toaster and, while the kettle was boiling, sorted out Bucket with a little tuna snack. It was far too early to think about bed but she hadn't slept well last night so it wouldn't do her any harm to tuck herself up with a good book. Rhys hadn't been in touch, but she wasn't really surprised. What was there left to say? It was best if she stayed out of his way in future.

Bucket, with a deep meow, followed in her footsteps as she made her way up the stairs, a mug of chocolate in one hand and a plate of toast and peanut butter in the other. Resting her impromptu supper on the bedside table she stripped the sheets off the bed before quickly remaking it with clean linen from the closet, the smell of fresh bedding helping to drown out the memory of his scent. She wished that it was as easy to drown out the memory of those few moments of passion. With a little shake of her head she removed her clothes and flung them in the wash-basket before reaching for her nightdress and, within seconds, she was propped up in bed and searching her Kindle for the latest thriller by Valerie Keogh.

She was dragged out of her unconscious state by a set of claws, fully drawn, spiking into her shoulders.

'Ouch!'

One second, she'd been in the land of oblivion and the next … the next she was sitting up in bed with her heart in her mouth, struggling to breathe. The room was a hazy mist of fog. No, not fog – smoke. Smoke that filled the air in hues of grey to black and, in that second she realised the cottage was on fire.

She jumped out of bed, grabbing a suddenly passive cat before racing for the door, the sight of smoke seeping in through the cracks stopping her in her tracks. But it was the only way out. The windows on the first floor were too high from the ground and, with nothing to break their fall, they'd be seriously injured or worse. Taking a deep breath, she gathered Bucket to her chest and, pulling open the door, walked into a wall of black. There was no landing. There was only billowing black smoke and a flicker of orange creeping out from the corner of her eye.

Finally her fingers stretched out for the bannister but the heat had her pulling back. There wasn't time to think about the cause of the fire or even where it was coming from. There wasn't even time to think about the silent smoke detector outside her bedroom door that screeched every time she turned on the grill. All she thought about was making it to the front door without taking a breath even though her lungs felt fit to burst. She bumped against the dresser, rattling the china on the shelves before stumbling into the centre of the room, the back of a chair helping to guide her way.

The front door was hot, the paint blistering under her finger-tips and she had to use the corner of her nightdress to unhook the security chain and unlock the door. It only took a second but, by the time she'd worked the lock the bright flames had spread, licking towards the ceiling and beyond. Flinging the door open, the hot metal of the handle ripped through her nightdress down to the skin, searing flesh with a blinding heat. She stumbled forward, still clutching onto Bucket, and headed for the safety of the van, a van she couldn't open as she'd left the keys in the bowl. She couldn't even phone anyone, her thoughts now on her mobile still sitting on charge in the lounge.

Outside was cold, so cold despite her warmest nightdress. She was freezing suddenly, all apart from her hand which was red hot. She fell to the ground, reluctant to let Bucket go but, with one wriggle, he was out of her grasp and racing round the side of the house despite her screams. With her left arm cradling her hand, she rested back on her heels, watching all her dreams collapse into a pile of stone and cinders.

Her cottage, her beautiful cottage, filled with so many happy memories until grief crept in. Sadness oozed out of every pore and even with the sound of sirens wailing in the distance, she knew that it would be too late to save. She suddenly remembered her thoughts of a couple of days ago when she'd first heard the news about her father. She'd thought then that the world was doing its damnedest to make life unbearable … If it hadn't been for Bucket she'd be dead by now. She'd have suffocated to death by the smoke flowing in a steady stream. Turning, she watched the flames take a hold, burning and destroying everything they touched; all the memories of her gran, all her clothes and belongings. Alys's first baby outfit and her photos, all lovingly preserved. All destroyed, leaving her with nothing.

Chapter 41

Gaby
Saturday 18 January, 4.05 a.m. Gaby's cottage, Mumbles

It was the ring of the phone that woke her.

She ran a hand across her face, before peering at the clock. It wasn't unheard of for a copper to be dragged out of their bed in the small hours. In fact, she counted herself lucky if she managed two or three uninterrupted nights on the run.

'Darin?'

'Speaking.'

She frowned. It sounded like DCI Brazil-North but why the hell would she be phoning her at this time of the morning?

'You need to get your bum back in here, right now. There's been a development in the case.'

'You what?' she said, wide awake and sitting on the edge of the bed.

'There's been a development in the Dawson/Grant murders. I'm pulling everyone in, including you.'

'I'm on my way,' she said, cradling the phone to her neck while she gathered together a clean blouse and underwear before heading into the bathroom. She knew better than to ask questions.

'Gaby, don't be too long.' The DCI's voice was softer than she'd ever known it. 'It looks like you may be right about Isabelle Grant's innocence.'

The desk sergeant stopped her as she ran into the building, directing her to the DCI's office even though it was still only five. Gaby tried not to consider the implications, but it was difficult to swerve her thoughts away from the worst possible scenarios playing out in her mind.

After a cursory knock she found herself seated beside Rhys while the guv stood by the window, fiddling with the blinds.

'The fire brigade was alerted, at twenty-three-hundred hours, to a fire lighting up the sky over Abereiddy.' She must have noticed Gaby's expression because suddenly her voice changed. 'She's all right, Darin. They have her in hospital for smoke inhalation and minor burns. We, or rather I, underestimated the seriousness of the case.' Her hand unbuttoned the top button of her blouse as if the neck was suddenly too tight. 'I take full responsibility for not putting Miss Grant under twenty-four-hour surveillance; something that has been rectified with immediate effect.' She sat down behind her desk, reaching for her phone. 'I need you both over at the crime scene but,' she turned towards Rhys, her expression for once kind, 'if you need to check in at the hospital first, that's fine by me.'

They'd admitted her overnight for observation but, apart from a brief look at her sleeping form huddled under a pile of blankets, they weren't allowed to see her.

Gaby stared across at Rhys where he was pulling his car keys out of his pocket. He looked as if he hadn't slept, the five-o'clock shadow scoring his chin almost merging with the dark hollows under his eyes. There was also a smell, a trace of something she recognised, an odour that wrinkled her brow. Digging round in her pocket, she pulled out a packet of mints.

'Here.'

'What?' He stared down at the packet with a frown of his own. 'The very last thing I need right now is a sweet.'

'Really? I thought it would disguise the smell of whiskey or is it brandy? Whatever it is, I'll drive, thank you very much,' Gaby said, stretching out her hand.

There was a pause, his gaze hovering between the pack of mints and her face. 'Oh, for God's sake,' he said, taking a couple before handing her the keys. 'The first thing we need to do is get a cardboard box.'

They pulled up outside the house, on a squeal of breaks. Rhys barely waited for the car to stop before pushing the door open and jumping out, leaving Gaby to follow on behind.

The place was deserted apart from a solitary policeman protecting the pale grey outline of a building, which had been stripped back to roof joists and a pile of rubble at the base; all that was left of the beautiful stone cottage. The air, redolent with smoke had her pulling her scarf higher up over her mouth and nose, thankful she'd had the foresightedness to spray herself liberally with DKNY before tearing out of the flat.

She watched as Rhys lifted the box from the boot and placed it on the ground. Instead of following, she took a moment to say hello to the officer, huddled in a corner with his arms folded across his chest.

'You've picked a very short straw tonight,' she said, holding out her hand. 'I'm Gaby Darin.'

'Ben Michaels.' He gripped it briefly before refolding his arms. 'The missus is expecting again and it all helps.'

She threw him a smile, offering her congratulations. 'So, what did the fire brigade say?'

'They'll be back at first light but it's increasingly looking like arson. A couple of oil cans flung through the kitchen window at the back.'

She shook her head, her gaze never leaving his face. 'Just who the hell would do something like that?'

'There's plenty of weirdos out there, isn't there – take your pick.'

She moved away with a small smile and, squinting into the darkness, tried to place the muffled sound of Rhys's voice as he shouted for the cat. The sharp blade of her torch picked out the odd shape; a wheelbarrow, a spade, a stoneware planter. She kicked over the remains of a blackened chair, the legs disintegrating at her touch. Izzy would be lucky if she was able to salvage anything. She'd have to pick up the fabric of her life from the small pile of belongings the fire brigade had managed to cobble together before the fire had ripped the heart out of the place. It wasn't a lot to start a life with. An armchair, a coffee table, an old spinning wheel, a clutter of china from the dresser.

Her eyes snagged on a movement in the corner and, just for a second, her heart lurched until a decidedly blackened Bucket shifted from the shadows to come and curl round her feet. She crouched down and, reaching out a hand, stroked his sleek fur before scooping him up under her chin, his little body snuggling against the fleece of her jacket.

The case wasn't about finding Alys Grant anymore. It was about finding a murderer.

Chapter 42

Izzy
Saturday 18 January, 2.20 p.m. Withybush Hospital

'What are you doing here, Rhys?'

'Charming. I come to find out how you're doing and that's the response I get.'

Izzy knew she was being rude but she couldn't seem to help her behaviour around him, not with the memory of their last encounter lurking like a bad talisman. Their relationship had deteriorated to such an extent that she found it difficult to even look him in the eye, her gaze instead resting on the top button of his shirt.

'Thank you for checking on me,' she finally managed, propping herself up on the pillows, her bandaged hand stretched out in front of her. 'I'm fine. They're discharging me after the nurse has the time to renew my dressing.'

'To where?' he said, his voice sharp.

She stared back; swallowing the sudden lump in her throat because, of course, now she was homeless.

'Bethan is going to put me up for a few days until I decide what … what I'm going to do.'

'Great idea. I would have suggested it if you hadn't,' he said, balancing his left ankle on his knee and resting back against the orange plastic chair. 'While Rebecca would love to have you, security is tighter at the farm with all those prize heifers.' He stretched out his hand and touched her fingertips. 'How are you really, Izzy?'

She swallowed again, the feel of his hand on hers bringing back a whole host of memories she was desperately trying to forget. 'Oh, you know. I'll live and all that. It's a great opportunity to start afresh. I know I'm lucky to be alive. In fact, if it wasn't for Bucket—' She squeezed her eyes tight at the thought of her cat, a single tear escaping and tracking down her cheek.

'What about Bucket, love?'

'He … he woke me. If he hadn't—'

'Shush, it's all right.'

'No, it's not,' she said, snatching her hand away, her gaze hardening. 'He was all I had left and now …'

'No, not all.' He pulled back, rubbing his hand over the back of his neck, not quite meeting her gaze. 'I should have told you first. I didn't think. We have him or, at least, Gaby, DC Darin does. We'll bring him back whenever you want.'

He leant forward, thrusting a pile of tissues into her hand before opening his notebook.

'I'm afraid it's not just a social call. I do need to ask you some more questions.' He looked at her briefly before settling his gaze back on his pad. 'I'll try and keep them brief. There's obviously something that you're not telling me. It might even be something so insignificant that it hasn't registered on the scale of important things that cops have to know about, but I'll be the judge of that.'

She balled up the tissues into a tight wad. 'I don't really know what you want from me?'

'I want everything. From what you've bought to who you've talked to, from your online activity to all your phone calls. In fact, that's a good place to start,' he said, his eyes bright. 'Try to remember who your contacts are, who you call.'

'You're sure that this will make a difference?'

But all he did was stare back, his pen poised, waiting for her to speak.

'There's nothing, really. I use it primarily for work; emails and messages to wool shops and my team of knitters. Messages to and from Rebecca and Bethan and there's no way they're involved. Some stuff from Amazon … that's it.' Her life was an open book, an open boring book. She didn't do anything risqué. She didn't say anything risqué. Her mind froze because, of course, that wasn't true. Having sex with the person leading the case must be the riskiest thing she'd ever done.

'What are you thinking?' he said, the sound of his voice interrupting her thoughts.

'I think my thoughts are my own business.'

He dropped his eyes back to his notebook. 'So, tell me about these other knitters then?'

'There's not much to tell. I put an advert in the *Echo* at the start of last year and I got five replies. We meet every couple of weeks around at mine for a stitch 'n' bitch.'

'A what?'

'A stitch 'n' bitch,' she said, a small smile pulling at the confused expression tattooed across his face. 'It's an American term, coined I believe as far back as the Second World War. You know, no idle hands and all that. A group of like-minded individuals meeting regularly, usually around at one of their houses to knit and chat but stitch 'n' bitch is a much better term, don't you think?'

'I think that if you keep distracting me with pointless observations we'll be here all morning.'

'Well, you did ask.'

'Hmm.' His voice was dry. 'So, what about these women? Who are they and just how well do you know them?'

'As well as I know anyone, I guess. I've known Marjory Williams the longest. She lives the nearest too, in a small house next to the city hall. I can't really see that she'd have anything to do with it. It would take too much time away from her soaps. Then there's Paula Edwards and Mary Collins,' she said, throwing him a look. 'They're widow sisters and need the knitting money to supplement their pension. They must be touching eighty. Janice Smith is somewhere in her forties, happily married with two teenagers at University. In fact, now that I think of it, her husband works with your lot. She's always moaning about the late nights when he trips over his feet while taking his socks off. He wakes her up every time.'

'That's our Gary Smith,' he said with a laugh. 'So, who else?'

'That only leaves Pat.'

'Pat? I thought it was only women who knit?'

She rolled her eyes. 'Pat is short for Patricia. Patricia Caruthers and she's an accountant for Blackstock and Greene, I believe. I'll agree she's not what you'd term your typical knitter in that she obviously doesn't need the money but she's nice. I count her as my best friend after … after Bethan,' she said, suddenly remembering Grace.

'Okay, so we'll start by visiting Pat.' He pushed his notebook aside and folded his arms across his chest. 'Izzy, you do want me to help you find out about Charlie and Alys, don't you?'

'What sort of a question is that?'

'It's the kind of question I have to ask anyone – especially a witness that I think might be concealing something. Look, I'm not in this for me, all right,' he said, a look of exasperation on his face. 'Okay, so I made a mess of things but if I could put the clock back, I'd still have stayed. That postcard was threatening and I was worried. I'm still worried. What happened after was obviously a mistake and one I gather you don't want to discuss?'

She shook her head, annoyed at the shift in conversation. He was trying to make her feel guilty when that was the very last emotion she needed right now. She felt guilty enough about her dad as it was. 'There's no need to worry about me, Rhys. I'll be safe at Bethan's.'

'How do you know that? They've already killed …' He paused, his eyes scrolling over her face before pinning his gaze back to hers. 'The question here is one of trust. Do you trust me, Izzy?'

Did she trust him? She had, right up until she'd found herself in bed with him but now wasn't the time for that discussion. Instead she chose to lie.

'Of course. After all, I've known you since we were kids.'

He smiled. 'Indeed. I remember you as a—'

'Spotty kid with braces and pigtails?' She pulled a face.

'No! I remember you as a …' He jerked back, all his attention now on his notebook. 'You just carry on trusting me. I promise not to let you down. So humour me for a moment, I want to go back over that day, the day they went missing. But I also want you to try and remember anything strange about the days and weeks leading up to their disappearance,' his eyes back on her face. 'But first, Izzy, I want you to tell me what you were thinking about when you mentioned Pat and Bethan being your best friends?'

She had to tell him. She'd known as soon as he'd started asking all those questions that it would come out. The problem was that it looked bad, bad for her. He was bound to think that she was obsessed with trying to find someone who obviously didn't want to be found.

She met his look head on. 'The woman I told you about that day in the supermarket. Grace Madden? I thought we were friends, maybe even best friends.'

'But you said you'd lost touch?' he said with a frown.

'I … I found her,' she stuttered, brushing her hair back from her face. 'After Christmas I managed to track her down.'

'Quite the little detective, aren't you?'

'I wouldn't say that.' Turning her head away she told him the rest: the midwife, the trip to Swansea and finding Geraint's grave.

She even told him about Grace admitting to having slept with Charlie.

She watched him stare down at his notebook, twisting his pen round and round his fingers as if deep in thought.

'Okay, let me do some digging to corroborate the facts. We started to look into her before but, I seem to remember we got waylaid by the arrival of the second postcard and then the car …' He lifted his head. 'What was her husband's name again?'

'Geraint Madden.'

Chapter 43

Gaby
Monday 20 January, 9.40 a.m. St David's

It took a lot to surprise Gaby. She'd always thought she was the most open-minded of individuals. The last time she'd been surprised had been when Leigh's wife had interrupted the usual nine o'clock briefing, her large swollen belly protruding out through her check maternity top. Although that had been more of a shock than a surprise.

It took one look at Patricia Caruthers's long blonde plait and she had to reset her databanks to stop her jaw dropping to the floor. This lady was a revelation. Dressed in a pillar-box red suit, which fit where it touched, and with high-heeled shoes to match, all her previous thoughts about accountants flew out the window as did her thoughts about the case.

Gaby reached out to shake her hand and felt lacquered nails scrape her palm. There were many questions she wanted to ask this woman, all of them listed in her illegible scrawl in the notepad tucked in the inside pocket of her jacket. But the one she really needed to know the answer to was probably the one she wouldn't be able to ask. How the hell could she manage to knit anything with nails like that?

'Thank you for agreeing to meet us both at such short notice,' Rhys said.

Gaby frowned her annoyance. By the glint in his eye and tone of his voice, Izzy Grant now had competition for his affections. She would never have thought him a player but that's all she knew. With a sigh she dragged her boring jacket across her bosom, trying and failing to make the edges meet in the middle. The smart, sassy woman in front of them was having an effect on her too, but not in the same way as Rhys. Blinking rapidly, she promised, yet again, to give dieting a go.

'No problem, detective. Izzy phoned me from the hospital earlier,' Pat said and, without further comment, led them into a bright shiny office full of smart office furniture and the kind of wood flooring sold by the inch.

She sat down, gesturing for them to take a seat opposite. 'Fire away. I have a ten o'clock that doesn't like to be kept waiting.' Her nails tapped against the polished wood of her desk.

'I did have a list of questions,' he said with a pull of his lips. 'But there's really only one that's relevant. Why would an accountant with all this –' he waved his hand around the room '– decide to take up commercial knitting for what must be a pittance? What's in it for you?' His gaze flickered to the sign on her desk with Senior Accountant etched onto shiny steel.

'That's two questions, why and what, not that I'm counting or anything.' Her blood-red lips drew into a pout, her eyes now fixed on her nails as they continued their relentless tap tap tapping.

The one thing that always made Gaby nervous was when someone didn't meet her gaze. It usually meant they had something to hide, something they didn't want other people to know. Would she lie? She wouldn't necessarily know if she did, despite that two-day training course on body language last summer. The silence lengthened and just when she'd written the interview off as a waste of time, Pat leant back in her chair, her gaze now lingering on the ceiling above their heads.

'I'd like to tell you both a little story, if I may?'

Oh, here we go. Another timewaster.

But instead of sighing or folding her arms across her chest, Gaby simply rested back in her chair and composed her face. She'd thought she'd heard it all before – obviously not.

'Once upon a time there were twin girls with long blonde hair and cornflower-blue eyes.' Her hand reached up to pat her smooth plait, tied with a matching red ribbon. They lived far far away in a place called Innisborough. You might have heard of it?'

Gaby froze, her mind making the connection straight away. Now there was no need to pretend. Now she was leaning forward in her chair and hanging onto every word, all her attention fixed on the woman in front of her.

'I don't know if you've ever been,' Pat continued. 'Innisborough is a lovely place, idyllic even. I still have some very happy memories of it from before we moved but I wouldn't go back, not now, not ever. It's never the place that's bad, just the people that reside there. After my sister's disappearance, we tried to stay but her memory haunted us, so we moved and finally settled in St David's – far enough away not to be the topic on everyone's lips but, sadly, not far enough away to forget.'

Rhys raised his hand, halting her speech, his eyes touching Gaby's. There was no need for her to continue – the case of the Mitten twins had stretched across borders and continents.

The tapping had stopped and in its place there was complete silence, which no one in the room knew how to break.

The Mitten twins. Sweet little five-year old girls with the prettiest of faces forever immortalised in that last photo taken at some party or other, a photo that made its way round the globe. The last photograph before one of them was snatched. *Snatched in plain sight* the headline ran; a headline that was still used today during police training. Snatched and never to be seen again; missing all those years and still missing to this day.

'I'm sorry … I …' Rhys finally said, and now it was his turn to not quite meet her gaze.

'There's no need for an apology, detective.' She looked at him for the first time since the interview began. 'You weren't to know. After all, it was a very long time ago and people forget, don't they? I think that probably answers both of your questions.' Standing up she held out her hand, offering them both a brief smile. 'All I ask is that you keep it to yourself. I've made a sort of life here away from it all. My parents and I have accepted that she's dead. I hope you understand that being there for Izzy is just something I have to do.'

There was no doubt in Gaby's mind that Pat Mitten/Caruthers was speaking the truth but that didn't prevent her from booting up her laptop on her return to the station and searching up old newspaper articles on the case, her notebook open in front of her. She'd only been a child at the time, more interested in football than the news but she'd have had to have been living on Mars to fail to notice the media coverage on the disappearance.

Scrolling over the faded-to-yellow online archives her first thought was that Pat took after her mother, her mother as she'd appeared in that TV interview; the same hair, the same mouth, the same face although, without the red-rimmed eyes and tormented expression. Turning her head away from the screen, she picked up her mug and took a deep sip. She had no need to read any more. Just one look and the story had come flooding back: Two little girls playing happily in the garden. Rachel, the older by fifteen minutes and decidedly the braver, climbing in beside the stranger, leaving Patricia to watch as the car sped away. Two girls' lives changed forever with that one act. There were no clues. Not one. To this day no one knew exactly what had happened to her.

She placed her now empty mug back on the desk and picked up her notebook, peeling back to the previous page. There was still work to do. Pat was only the first of the team of knitters to be interviewed. She only hoped that the other four meetings wouldn't be as traumatic. Glancing at the clock, she started searching up their contact details just in case Rhys popped into the office. She didn't know where he'd disappeared to. She just hoped it wasn't in search of a quick snifter. Obviously, the fire on top of his liaison with Izzy had hit him harder than he was prepared to admit but now was not the time to turn to drink, not when they had a case to solve.

Chapter 44

Gaby
Monday 20 January, 2 p.m. Swansea Police Station

Gaby ran into the squad room, dumping her bag on the floor under her desk with only seconds to spare before the afternoon briefing. It was difficult enough finding the time to cram in lunch but now she had a cat to feed and a litter tray to clean before racing out the door – all achieved at the expense of food. As it was, she'd left Bucket guarding the centre of her bed, his sharp claws doing untold damage to her Egyptian cotton sheets.

'Thank you for taking time out of your day to join us, DC Darin,' the DCI said, throwing her a speaking glance before starting to address the rest of the room. 'Now that we're *all* here … As you know, the fire brigade was alerted at ten to midnight by a passing taxi to a possible out-of-control bonfire at Abereiddy. By the time they arrived the fire had already taken hold and it was only by luck that Miss Grant managed to escape. DI Walker attended the scene and it's not looking good. A preliminary walk around the property indicates that it was arson – the fire brigade has already commented on the strong smell of petrol fumes when they arrived.' Annette Brazil-North pressed the palms of her hands flat on the table, her gaze pausing on each of their faces, her expression neutral. 'So, it looks as if the Grant saga is turning into an epic. I want to hear your ideas, all of them, even the most stupid. Rhys …' She gestured for him to take the floor.

'A brief recap of what we're looking at.' His eyes scanned the group. 'Alys Grant and Charlie Dawson; missing now for five years and recently turned up in Miss Grant's old Mini at the bottom of the Blue Lagoon. We're still waiting for the full forensic report but, as you're already aware, Charlie was strangled before submersion, suffering a fracture to his hyoid bone, this being the cause of death. The team are still working on Alys Grant but it's possible that it was a straightforward drowning. Jumping forward five years, Miss Grant has fashioned a new life for herself and apart from a couple of recent postcards, the first allegedly from her boyfriend, there's been no indication of activity with regards to the case. The postcards are key here. Either we have a nutter trying to interfere or someone, possibly Miss Grant or one of her family, has inadvertently done something that may have triggered recent events.'

He paused, looking down at his notes while he allowed the news to sink in.

'I've met with Miss Grant and revisited her initial interview. She's also compiled a list of people that will require further investigation,' he said, tearing a page from his notebook and, reaching forward, handing it to Bill. 'Gaby and I have already ruled out the first name on the list – take Michele and interview the remaining four. It's unlikely that any of them are involved but they still warrant investigating.' He turned slightly, looking at the couple of men standing at the back. 'Muir, I'd like you to catch up with the fire brigade crew and Andrew, if you could chase down that taxi driver for his witness statement. We'll also need to check any CCTV even though it's unlikely there are any cameras in the area.

'What about Miss Grant? Will she need police protection?'

Gaby interrupted; surprised that he hadn't suggested it already.

'Good point. The DCI has provided an officer on her door at the hospital until she moves out to her sister's farm. The security is already pretty tight with Oscar at the helm. It would take someone pretty stupid to try and break into that set-up and stupid is the one thing this killer isn't.' Rhys leant against the side of the desk, gathering his thoughts. 'This is a high-profile case with lots of media interest. If I find anyone breaking the rules and getting in touch with the newspapers, you'll be out of here before your feet touch the ground. We'll reconvene back tomorrow morning at eight when hopefully the forensics report will be through. I'll be out of the office until then, but you can contact me on my mobile,' he said, swinging round to face Gaby. 'How do you fancy a trip to church?'

Chapter 45

Gaby

Gaby was happy to be left with her thoughts on the hour-long drive to Carmarthen, not that she had much choice. Rhys, while never the chattiest of individuals, hadn't said more than a couple of words in all that time. She flicked him a covert look, under the pretext of changing gears, only to wonder at his grim expression. He hadn't even acknowledged her presence other than to ask which radio station she preferred. The man had something on his mind, at a guess something to do with the investigation. But he wasn't sharing, which of course had her mind buzzing with ideas. He couldn't still be concerned about Isabelle Grant's welfare because she was now more closely guarded than the Queen. So, it had to be something else and she could only assume it was something to do with his spending the night … It was almost a relief to pull into the drive outside the manse and give her thoughts a well-earned rest.

'Well, this is a nice surprise,' Reverend Simpson said. 'I was all set for a quiet afternoon struggling with my sermon and instead I have a couple of nice officers to break the monotony.' He gave them a gentle smile. 'I hope It isn't another one of those speeding fines; I did explain the urgency of getting to the hospital that last time. Poor Mrs Watkins, I only just managed to make it …' He shook his head.

'No, sir. It's nothing to do with fines although I do recommend you let us know if you have any intention of, er, breaking the law again in the future. We do on occasion turn a blind eye to this sort of thing if we're made aware of it first,' Gaby said, struggling not to catch Rhys's eye.

With the vicar's balding pate and rotund stomach, he wasn't one of the usual speed merchants they saw at the station on a regular basis. She was suddenly desperate to ask him what he'd managed to get out of the vintage Rover sitting out front – she'd just have to look it up as soon as she got back.

'That's a relief.' He passed out mugs before continuing. 'I don't normally go above twenty-five unless it's life and death. Would you like a Rich Tea to go with that?' he asked, neatly changing the subject. 'I'm afraid there's no cake, Mrs Le Marchant only bakes on a Monday and a Thursday, more's the pity.' He settled back in his chair, crossing one leg over the other. 'Right then officers, what can I do for you both?'

'You might remember a young woman who came to see you, a Miss Grant? She was looking for a grave,' Rhys said, breaking his silence.

'Ah yes. The pretty young woman with the weight of the world on her shoulders. Deep sorrow always shows, you know. It's there in the back of the eyes, lingering like a bad memory.' He took out a freshly laundered handkerchief and, carefully unfolding it, proceeded to blow his nose. 'Of course, I've been in this job far too long to ask prying questions. I might just get back an answer I don't want.'

'She lost both her baby and her partner.'

'Oh dear. The poor woman. And you're here to help find them?'

'No, not exactly.' Gaby swallowed hard before continuing. 'We found them ... you might have read in the papers about the bodies in the Blue Lagoon?'

He picked up a teaspoon and stirred his tea, all the while shaking his head. 'What a terrible business. Absolutely terrible. If there's anything I can do to help?'

'Reverend ... could you tell me everything you know about a Grace Madden? Even the tiniest little thing might be important.'

Back at the station the first thing Gaby did was to turn the radiator up in the squad office, her hands lingering against the warm metal. Rhys had zoomed off again, she didn't know where, but she had more important things to think about than the vagaries of her boss. She couldn't remember the last time she'd eaten anything apart from one measly biscuit. It certainly wasn't at 4.05 a.m. when she'd been woken up, and there hadn't been time when she'd rushed back to check on Bucket at lunchtime. What she really fancied was a deep-pan pepperoni pizza with a side order of fries, instead of the cheese sandwich and black coffee on offer But that would necessitate a trip to the supermarket and the time in which to do it unless she treated herself to another takeout, something that was becoming the norm.

The sandwich had long gone as had the black coffee. Pushing away from the desk, she stood and stretched, her fingers reaching for the ceiling, her shoulder muscles aching from the forced inactivity. What wouldn't she give for a hot shower and bed but with the clock heading towards six that wasn't going to be for quite a while. She had so much to do and no idea where to start. There was a puzzle to be solved, her gaze wandering again to the top sheet of notes that she'd highlighted in yellow. The police department was a great one for lists and notebooks. If it wasn't written down and recorded in some way it was never going to stand up in court. That's the reason why Rhys had transcribed word-for-word everything the vicar had said, her attention shifting back to the computer screen.

She had a name, the same name she'd had before. Grace Madden. She even had a description and quite a good one, so good that she could almost picture her in her mind's eye. Grace Madden, erstwhile friend of Izzy with chin-length, bluish-black hair and the palest of skin. Mid to late thirties with a slim, boyish, five-foot-six figure, give or take. Someone sophisticated, someone that was always smartly dressed and had an aloof manner to match.

Her gaze fixed, she continued staring at the screen, trying to work it out. She was confused. No. Baffled was probably a better word – baffled at what Grace ever saw in a possible friendship with Izzy. She frowned at the thought but the two words she'd never have associated with Isabelle Grant were smart and sophisticated. So, what exactly would have been in it for Grace? Squeezing her eyes tight, she let her thoughts drift over the case, trying to piece it together. Rhys had told her that Grace had admitted to sleeping with Charlie. Could guilt have come into it? Two pregnant women striking up a relationship as their bodies burgeoned out of control, one with a secret she couldn't share. It just didn't make sense. She picked up her pen only to throw it back down in disgust. The only way to get to grips with Grace Madden was to speak to her in person and that was the reason for her sudden unrest. She'd just spent the last two hours searching for someone that didn't appear to exist.

Chapter 46

Gaby

Tuesday 21 January, 9 a.m. Swansea Police Station

'The bad news is that the bakery has run out of doughnuts.' Rhys held up his hand to deflect the groans and sighs. 'The good news is they had an order cancellation so ... who's for a butterfly cake?'

With another early start it was shaping up to be an horrendous morning, but that didn't stop Gaby from rustling up a smile at the sight of grown men and women ripping the wings off the pretty little cakes Rhys had bought to sweeten their mood. She caught the eye of Amy Potter and threw her a wink before turning her attention back to DCI Brazil-North.

'If you've all finished stuffing your faces, we have work to do,' she said, slowly scanning the room, 'As you all know by now, we're focusing our attention on Isabelle Grant. So, not only are we trying to solve the mystery surrounding "the bodies in the Blue Lagoon" we're also trying to solve an attempted murder.' She took a step back. 'There's not much to go on at this point. The site has been secured and I've sent a team in to scour the area but, it's not looking hopeful. Early thoughts are someone swung by sometime before twenty-three-hundred hours and heaved a couple of oil cans in through the kitchen window. Even if there were any footprints they'll have been long obliterated by our colleagues from the fire department. DI Walker interviewed the victim yesterday, but she had nothing to add as to why someone might want her dead.' She perched on the edge of the table while Rhys took the floor.

'Darin, I want you to search all the relevant databases for any and all information on Grace Madden. I'm still not sure how relevant she is to the investigation but, as her name seems to crop up a little too frequently, we need to rule her out of our enquiries.'

'Actually, I started on that yesterday, boss. There isn't a trace on any of the usual ones we use but I'll continue looking. I also have the results back from *Clift'd*, the cliff diving forum, if now's the time?'

He stared across the room at her before nodding his head.

'It appears we were right. Something fishy is definitely going on. The boffins in IT traced the original message. I have the typed transcript, if you're interested?'

'Just tell us what it says.'

Gaby regarded him. She was used to abrupt but not from him and not in front of a packed incident room. In truth, she'd expected more, spotting the knowing look that passed between Michele and Bill. To hell with them – to hell with them all. She was a good copper; now she was going to prove it.

'It looks as if a new member, Jumper19, stormed into a conversation between David Prestwich and Arthur Norman on the 23rd December at 10 p.m. They were discussing which sites to tackle over the Christmas holidays and to quote Jumper19, "The Blue Lagoon is situated in one of the loveliest parts of South Wales and within sniffing distance of St David's where the Welsh girls are at their prettiest."'

'How sexist is that!' Amy glared at her from the other side of the room.

'Quite,' Gaby replied, casting a smile in her direction. 'But it did the trick. They came hurtling down the A48 as quickly as their Honda 50s would let them only to find Charlie and Alys in their watery grave.'

'Surely that's a coincidence?' Bill said, dragging her attention away from Amy and back to the rest of her colleagues. 'A couple of lads looking for a good time and the Blue Lagoon is well-known internationally for cliff diving.'

She returned his stare with one of her own. Bill had been gunning for her from day one, but she'd learnt her lesson the hard way in Swansea. Being prepared was the only way to win against men like him.

'I know all that but how can you explain why Jumper19 deleted his or her part of the conversation on the same evening?' she said, raising an eyebrow in Bill's direction and, after no reply, she continued. 'Deleting the email was the first red-flag. They also deleted their account, which was the second. It was only thanks to the boys upstairs that we've been able to find out more about Jumper19. They used a shield before joining the forum, the third red flag. They encrypted their address and in effect masked it from all eyes. But Dan has managed to drill down to the ISP and an internet café situated locally.'

'What a waste of time,' Bill interrupted. 'A public access computer with a generic IP address – good luck with that.'

'Thank you, DS Davis. Yes, as you've so rightly highlighted – a public access computer,' she said, turning to face DCI Brazil-North. 'Jumper19 had something to hide, something so important that they went out of their way to mask their identity. So, the question I asked myself yesterday was how could we trace them? It turns out that Jumper19 made one mistake and it's a real doozy. They chose the EXTM café over at Oriel y Parc.' She let the words sink in for a moment before heading for the jugular. 'That's right,

216

a little out of the way and ideal for the purpose of setting up a fake account except for one fatal error.'

'Wasn't that where they made all those drug busts last year?' Amy asked, catching her eye.

'Exactly, thank you Amy. The owner, Dai Jones, decided to set up a hidden CCTV camera. So, who's up for spending next week looking at boring old farts playing Grand Theft Auto then?'

Gaby sat back in her chair, one hand kneading the back of her neck, before returning to the spreadsheet in front of her. She had no idea when she'd started the search just how many Grace Maddens she'd have to eliminate from the investigation. She'd found a whopping ninety-eight. But not one of them was the right Grace. She'd spent most of the morning checking birth and death certificates. Marriage certificates and property registers. She'd even looked into social security contributions. The nearest she'd managed to find was a fifty-five-year-old divorcee living in Aberdeen.

Rubbing her eyes she only raised her head when a sharp hello heralded a welcome interruption.

'All right Gaby,' Rhys said, his hands full of sandwich packets. 'There's egg and cress or cheese and pickle?'

'Anything, thank you.' She sat back and watched as he demolished his in a couple of bites. 'Hungry, were you?'

'I missed both breakfast and lunch. So, any luck finding her then?'

'Nope.'

She eyed the egg and cress with dismay. The egg was fine but the cress … She opened the soggy white bread only to shut it again. It would take a better person than her to pick out each strand of revolting green, especially with Rhys's gaze boring down. She took a bite and swallowed with barely a chew before speaking.

'Have you heard back from Bill yet?'

Rhys had sent him off straight after the update to visit all the hardware stores and garages within a ten-mile radius that sold jerry cans. It was always going to be a longshot that they'd remember an individual sale or whether the customer had paid by card instead of cash.

'Another complete waste of time.' He threw his sandwich wrapper in the bin before standing and stretching, his hands meeting in the small of his back. 'God, what a morning. I was pinning my hopes on Grace Madden being the key. If she exists why the hell can't we find her?'

'Maybe she doesn't,' she said, taking another bite from her sandwich and almost choking when the tangy taste of pepper hit the back of her tongue.

'Repeat that.'

She tilted her chin only to find his gaze pinned to her face. She swallowed hard, clearing the back of her throat before speaking. 'All I said was maybe she doesn't exist. After all, if we can't find her, what other reason could there be? Everyone, without exception, has a footprint these days.'

'But how could she not exist?'

'I don't know but I think that we should probably go back and interview Miss Grant again. I've a feeling she's hiding something.'

She rested her hands on the desk, pushing her half-finished sandwich out of the way, her mind playing with all the possibilities. People took on pseudonyms all the time for a variety of reasons. Maybe Madden had a criminal record or was hiding from something in her past. Or it might be something as simple as not wanting to admit that she was only a common-law wife. More importantly, maybe this was what they'd been searching for all along – the certain something that didn't make sense. She picked up her pen and started clicking the end, remembering back to the beginning of the case. What was it that Izzy had said – something about having spotted her by accident after a gap of five years? Was that the reason for the second postcard appearing out of the blue?

Grace Madden, a woman who didn't exist.

Where and what was she hiding?

Chapter 47

Izzy
Wednesday 22 January, 7.15 a.m. The Farm

Izzy knew she was both safe and secure hiding out at Bethan and Oscar's farm situated just outside the town of Llandeilo and yet she'd never felt more vulnerable. All she wanted was to be back at the cottage, where she knew every creak and groan and every shadow and outline. She'd asked Bethan to swing past on the way to the farm, not that she needed reminding. She wouldn't listen to her pleading voice telling her in no uncertain terms that she was still too ill to deal with any more upset. Instead, she closed both her ears and her mind to any thought other than the need to see her home. It was irrational. Seeing it again was only going to bring a tide of grief – but she'd insisted. It was the wrong decision.

Sitting up in bed she pummelled the pillow with her left hand. She'd have liked to use her right hand but she wasn't meant to use it for another few days, her eyes trailing a path to the large, white padded bandage that would need to be changed in the morning. They'd wanted to keep her in for another night. They'd wanted to do some more tests, on lung function and what have you, but she'd told them she'd discharge herself if they didn't let her go. The nurses were kind as was the young officer guarding her door. But they didn't make her feel safe and that was her number one priority. She would have died if it hadn't been for poor old Bucket and with that thought her eyes started to fill. She never thought she'd miss him so much and, as soon as she could, she'd make sure they were reunited.

Dragging the duvet further up her shoulders, she resolutely closed her eyes but sleep wouldn't come. Instead of sleep all she could think about was Rhys.

She opened her eyes and stared at the wall, papered in geometric stripes in tasteful blacks and silver to match the metal bedstead and grey carpet, her mind refusing to be quietened. She'd only run into him once since that night but ever since, she couldn't stop thinking about him, just not *in that way*. Sleeping with him had made her determined never to see him again unless she had to, which made it all very awkward, considering. She knew it was irrational but she couldn't help how she felt.

Her eyes continued wandering over the paper, automatically following the lines where they tangled and stretched across the wall to the window, the swathe of black curtain fabric bringing her thoughts full circle. Instead of Rhys her mind took her to a place she rarely visited; her time with Charlie. The bright glittering light from the disco ball on their second date, the loud music pulsating off the walls, the feel of Charlie's warm lips against hers as they smooched in the corner, his hand sneaking up inside her jumper. She blinked and the image disappeared only to be replaced by another – the image of Charlie and her in bed, his legs wrapped around hers. The night Alys was conceived. A night so different to the time spent with Rhys … Those few short hours, ruined for so long, now assumed an importance more precious than diamonds.

She jerked upright, her good arm propelling her forward, her feet stretching to the floor, her right arm clutched to her chest.

She couldn't stand another second with her thoughts even though it was still only seven-thirty. In borrowed dressing gown and socks, she padded out of the room and headed downstairs to the warmth and comfort of the kitchen, a room that was always warm due to the vintage Aga, which took pride of place along one wall.

The sight of the teapot in the centre of the table had her reaching for a mug. There was always a teapot on Bethan's kitchen table. The tea might be stewed but it was hot and wet and, until the kettle boiled, perfect. Drink finished she wandered over to the fridge and gathered together the makings of a fry-up. With thick rashers of bacon and chunky sausages arranged in the pan she refilled the teapot before taking a seat at the end of the scarred pine table. Apart from Gareth and Dylan, who'd already left for school, breakfast was always at nine on the dot, so she still had plenty of time left to mull over her options – not that there were many. She was homeless, pretty much friendless and, with no business apart from a few quid in the bank, penniless. Okay, so the cottage was insured but she had no idea if she'd be able to afford to have it rebuilt.

Time shifted as she continued musing over any and all possibilities for her future, a future now without any hope of finding Alys. If it wasn't for Dad, she'd consider leaving – America. Australia. South Africa. All appealed for very different reasons and all were discounted as a wild fantasy with Dad still lying prostrate on that hospital bed. She'd love to move somewhere different; somewhere anonymous where no one knew her and, more importantly, she didn't know anyone. But that was impossible now. No, it looked like she was stuck in St David's with no way of going either back or forward.

A knock on the door dragged her out of her reverie and she hurried to pull it open, hugging Bethan's borrowed dressing gown a little tighter around her waist. She was safe enough with one of Oscar's farmhands guarding the gate but that didn't stop her from worrying.

'Hello, Izzy. I know it's early but Oscar said it would be all right to see if you were up,' Rhys said, gesturing to Gaby standing quietly by his side.

'Yes, of course. Come in. You'll have to excuse the state of me, my clothes …'

'There's no need to apologise.'

With a nod of her head she directed them to the table and, gathering up crockery from the dresser, started pouring out mugs of tea. She spent a couple of minutes fussing over sugar and spoons before sitting down opposite, laying her hand on the table in front of her.

Rhys studied her before speaking and she just about managed to hold his gaze, her mind flicking back to her thoughts of earlier. Would she ever feel comfortable in his presence?

'Right, as you've probably guessed, there are some questions.'

'When is there anything else?' she said with a sigh, moving her mug to make room for her elbows and turning to face Gaby. 'But, before you start, tell me how Bucket's doing?'

'Bucket has completely taken over. But I'm more than happy to have his company. Just let me know when you're sorted, and I'll drop him off.'

'Thank you, I'll speak to Oscar.' She turned her attention back to Rhys. 'Go on then, let's be having those questions.'

'I'm afraid it's about Grace Madden again. I know we spoke about her yesterday and you told me everything you knew but there must be something else, no matter how trivial you think it might be,' Rhys said, his continued stare making her uncomfortable.

'But I directed you to the church? She's devoted to Geraint even after all this time. The vicar said that …'

'Yes, quite. But, you see, we've visited the church. We've seen the grave – the flowers dead in their pot, the leaves and petals brown and withered. She hasn't been back since you met up with her. So, where has she gone or, more importantly, why?'

'What, you think I had something to do with her disappearance? Give me a break.'

'No,' he said, his smile brief. 'I don't think you're involved. I don't think you're involved in any of it. But it's not up to me and the truth of the matter is that the one person currently of interest to the investigation can't be found.'

'What about her daughter, Daisy? Surely she's at school or something. There must be records?'

'That's what you'd think. My team is looking into it. Madden is just one of those names that's common enough to take time in rooting out the right one and Grace and Daisy, as first names go, are far too popular to narrow the search.'

He picked up his mug and took a sip. It must be cold by now but he didn't seem to notice and she wasn't going to offer to make a fresh pot. The longer he stayed, the higher the chances of Oscar, Bethan or her mother bursting in and that would be disastrous. It would only take one look from her sister to realise something had happened between them. Izzy couldn't allow that – she'd never hear the end of it.

'What about the husband, boss?' Gaby interrupted.

'Go on.'

'I've been going through the files and, during the original investigation, the search stopped when they found his grave,' she said, flicking a glance towards Izzy. 'I think that was a wrong call. Geraint Madden must have had a life outside of his wife. You know, parents, siblings. Most people keep in touch, don't they? Even if it's only a card at Christmas and this Daisy. She'll be their granddaughter so—'

'Good point, Gaby,' he said, turning his head to stare again at Izzy. 'Anything to add about parents?'

She shook her head. 'We didn't talk about things like that. I barely knew her husband's name let alone anything about him. We talked about babies and being pregnant. Stuff like that mainly.'

She started fiddling with the end of her hair for something to do, her mind in turmoil. She had no idea what his true thoughts were on the case, but he was wrong to think Grace was involved. After all, what could her motive have been to murder both Charlie and Alys and then burn her house down? The reality was that Grace's world had crashed down on her with Geraint's death, and Rhys looking in her direction for a possible link was the wrong thing to do. There was someone else involved – the only problem was she had no idea who.

A sound from the floor above broke her train of thought and had her staring down at her watch. Was it still only ten-to-nine? It felt like hours had passed since she'd opened the door to Rhys's knock. Now she wanted to tell them to go. She wanted to stare Rhys straight in the eye and tell him she didn't want to explain his presence to her mum. She deserved a lot better than a kitchen littered with coppers after the few days she'd had. Izzy opened her mouth to put her thoughts into words, but he didn't give her a chance to speak.

'Thank you for the tea and your time,' he said, pushing back from the table and gathering the mugs together. 'We'll be in touch.'

Gaby walked over, pressing a card into her good hand. 'I'm here if you need me for anything, even if it seems the silliest thing,' she said, dipping her head, her mouth next to her ear. 'I'll make sure he keeps you up to date. As soon as we hear anything, anything at all, we'll be in touch.'

They'd gone and just in time. As soon as the door closed on their backs, her mum ambled into the room, her slippers sliding on the terracotta tiles.

'Who was that, dear?' she asked, heading for the teapot.

'Only the police and no, there's still no news,' Izzy said, catching the sudden look of hope on her face. 'No, don't drink that. I'll make some fresh.'

She refilled the kettle before joining her at the table. 'Oscar and the lads will be in shortly looking for their breakfast. I've already started—'

'There's time enough for that. You just sit there and tell me what the police wanted. There must have been a good reason for them to come out all this way and at this time of the morning too.'

'They seem to be harping on about Grace again. They want to know anything I can remember, no matter how silly it seems – but there's nothing. I've told them everything. There's no way she's involved.'

'That's as maybe but there has to be a reason for their interest. I suppose it was that nice DI Walker, was it?' she said, her eyes twinkling.

'Not you as well, Mam. For the very last time, I'm not interested.'

'I've made no secret of the fact that I'd like you to settle down. Charlie was okay but what you really need is a proper man to take care of you and who better than a copper? Is it wrong to want you to be as happy as me and your dad? It's time to let go of them both and relegate them to the same place we put all the other special people in our lives, like your gran. It doesn't mean that you love them any the less. At the moment you're allowing them to take up all the room in that generous heart of yours. They wouldn't want that, either of them.'

She was right, but not about Rhys. Just the thought of him and what they'd done turned her stomach but how was she meant to tell her mother that? One-night stands and the like weren't even in her parents' vocabulary. She remembered back to how they'd very nearly disowned her when they'd found out about her pregnancy and, if it hadn't been for the timely intervention of Bethan, they probably would have. So, instead of making any promises she couldn't keep, she gave some non-committal answer and started making the tea while her mother made a start on breakfast.

'Right then. They'll be in shortly and I'm just in the mood to rustle up one of my fry-ups. When your dad comes out of hospital I'll have to watch what he eats so I might as well get my cholesterol fix while I can.' She threw her a broad smile. 'I've been reading up on the benefit of porridge oats for breakfast.'

'Mam! You know Dad hates porridge nearly as much as I do. Are you trying to make him live longer or just make it seem like he is?' Izzy said, trying not to laugh at the thought of her dad doing anything that was good for him.

'Ha, very funny.'

She watched in amusement as her mother filled the pan with enough oil to fry chips before turning her attention to the pile of eggs. 'Two eggs each I think, don't you? There's nothing more nutritious than a freshly-laid egg.' She flicked a tea-towel over her shoulder before reaching for her still-full mug. 'Why don't you make yourself useful while I'm doing this? There can't be that many Maddens in the phonebook and just think how grateful Rhys will be if you help solve the case for him.'

'Surely that's the first place they'd have looked?' Izzy said, starting to collect plates from the dresser.

'Not necessarily. They'll want to check it's the right Madden before bothering God-fearing people with nuisance phone-calls and all that checking takes time.'

'Mam, I still don't think—'

'No, well, that's always been your problem. I want us all to move on with our lives so, the sooner this mess is sorted out the better,' she said, flipping the bacon with a steady hand before rolling the sausages over and spooning them with hissing fat. 'Go on now and bring me that fresh loaf from the pantry while you're at it. I can get that sliced and fried while you're sorting yourself out.'

Oh, God, fried bread and a runny egg sitting on top just like the old days. But, instead of watching as her mother spooned more oil into the sizzling pan, Izzy went in search of the phonebook, which was conveniently situated under the phone. With a sigh she headed into the lounge for a bit of privacy, having to shift two dogs and a cat in order to make room on the sofa.

Madden, what had Rhys said? Too common a name not to cause problems and all she had to aid her was the Pembrokeshire directory.

Chapter 48

Gaby
Wednesday 22 January, 2 p.m. Swansea Police Station

The squad room was packed. It was probably due to the rumour of doughnuts, still warm from the bakery, but she wasn't complaining. The more brains they had on the case, the better because, from where she was standing it looked to be going absolutely nowhere.

With the DCI away the mood was lighter, irreverent almost, the jokes coming thick and fast.

'Right then, settle down. I know it's nearly time to knock off but the Prof shouldn't be long and for God's sake, someone save him a doughnut or he'll probably go ballistic,' Rhys said, his gaze specifically targeting Bill who was reaching into the box for what must be his third.

She had no idea whether eating cake was something Professor Percival Pounder usually did. She'd only met him the once, if you could call attending a lecture on forensic pathology meeting someone. What concerned her more was the reason why he'd decided to leave his microscope in favour of the squad room.

'While we're waiting, are there any updates on the CCTV

footage and what about the fire? Any news from the watch commander?' Rhys continued, his gaze now resting on Muir.

'Nope. Not a dicky bird. No cameras in and around the area and it's as we thought with regards to arson. The cans are with forensics but it's unlikely they'll find anything,' he replied. 'Standard issue from any local hardware store – hundreds are sold each week so impossible to trace.'

'Now, there's a surprise. We interviewed Miss Grant earlier. She seems to be recovering well after her injuries and has nothing to add to her original statement,' Rhys said, pausing to stare above their heads and towards the back of the room.

Gaby's brow puckered at the sight of Professor Pounder strolling through the door in mismatched jacket and trousers, a pair of glasses perched on top of his bald dome and a sheaf of paper tucked under one arm. Was the whole room thinking what she was thinking, she wondered?

Either he's decided to take a few days off in rural Wales in the depth of winter or something's up with the case.

'Thanks for coming all this way, sir,' Rhys said, offering him a chair.

'Not at all, my boy. You've got an interesting case on your hands.'

'Interesting?'

'Yes indeed.' He stretched his fingers, his eyes now on the last doughnut, which Gaby pushed in his direction with a little smile.

'There's nothing I like better than a pile of bones and this lot will certainly set the cat amongst the pigeons.' He reached across to the cake box and they all watched while he took a huge bite before brushing the back of his hand across his mouth. 'I did have a report somewhere?' He stared at the desk with a frown.

'Under your arm, sir.'

'Ah yes.' He started patting his pockets.

'Your glasses? On top of your head, sir.'

Gaby managed to avoid bursting into a fit of the giggles by

staring at her shoes, which were in dire need of a polish. She only raised her head at the sound of his voice.

'Right then,' he said, hardly glancing at his notes, his glasses now perched on the end of his nose. 'The CSI team retrieved two skeletons from the interior of the car. The adult skeleton was pretty straightforward despite the lack of significant features such as jewellery or clothing remnants. A male between eighteen and twenty-five. Estimated height 185 centimetres. I'm happy to say that we've also managed to match dental records so I can confirm that the body is that of Mr Charles Dawson.' He offered a quick smile very much in the vein of a magician sharing the finale. 'It's the other skeleton that isn't quite so easy to explain but I'll try to keep it simple. This is also a human skeleton and, using Pearson's formulae for long bone length, we've been able to narrow the age to less than two months. This is in part confirmed by the skull where both the posterior and sphenoid fontanelles failed to unite. I'm afraid I can't be more specific at this time. With regards to the time submerged – the absence of soft tissue, cartilage and bone marrow mean I can only estimate in years as opposed to months.' He lifted his head, pushing his notes aside. 'The main area of concern is the lack of credible evidence as to the sex of the child … morphological methods are the gold standard for such a determination however, given the age of the infant, there are no hard and fast rules about the identification.'

'But I thought that women had that extra rib in addition to an extra wide pelvis?' Bill interrupted. 'That's the excuse the Mrs keeps giving for not being able to squeeze into her size-ten jeans.'

The whole room broke into laughter only to be silenced by a tilt of the Prof's head.

'Young man, you've fallen into the same trap set for under-graduates entering this esteemed medical profession.' His eyes shone. 'Either that or you've been reading too much of the bible. Notwithstanding the role of Adam and Eve, both men and women have twelve pairs of ribs. The disparity in the size of the pelvis between the male and female is however true enough, but not noticeable prior to puberty so your question, both parts, is irrelevant. But then I think you knew that already,' he added, pinning him with his gaze. 'With regards to your comment about your wife, I'm afraid you're on your own as women have never been my strong point and I gather a larger size in denim isn't the answer?' His eyes wandered down to where Bill's belly was spilling over the top of his belt.

It took a moment for the room to settle down again and for Gaby to ask the question that was suddenly on everyone's mind. 'So, in effect, you're saying that we could have a male baby on our hands?'

'No, far from it, young lady. In the absence of reliable morphological elements in such a young victim we had to change our tactics. Using molecular genetics we examined the amelogenin gene using a polymerase chain reaction, something that's guaranteed to provide a certain degree of certainty on this issue ...'

'The amelogenin what?' she asked faintly

'Oh dear,' he said, pulling out a handkerchief and dragging it across his brow. 'I do keep forgetting to whom I'm speaking. Using advances in DNA technologies we are 98 per cent certain that the baby in the vehicle is a girl.'

Why was I hoping otherwise? It would have been the most unlikely of discoveries. Of course, it's a girl. Of course, it's Alys. I feel bad in hoping that, by some fluke it was someone else's child. But there it is. Game over.

'In addition, using the same DNA, extracted from the infant's clavicle, we were able to do a paternity test and have been able to conclusively state that Charles Dawson was the baby's father.' He blinked rapidly before refocusing on her face. 'Although, to be accurate we would of course need to acquire a DNA sample from the alleged mother.'

'Excuse me?' Rhys said, his eyes trained on the professor. 'So, what you're saying is there's still a possibility that the baby isn't Alys?'

'All I'm saying, officer, for accuracy's sake, is that proving Charles Dawson is the father of the infant hasn't really added anything – after all, queries over paternity are two-a-penny these days.' He slid his gaze around the room. 'In order to determine if the infant is indeed Alys Grant we need to match it to a sample of maternal DNA. But that's not why I'm here today.'

Chapter 49

Izzy
Wednesday 22 January, 4 p.m. Carmarthen

The historic town of Carmarthen was situated on the river Towyes but, instead of faffing about with taxis and trains, Izzy decided to take the van. It was a little difficult but now that they'd reduced the dressing to just around her thumb and forefinger i t w as manageable.

There were other differences to the journey, differences she was trying not to dwell on. Differences like the fact someone was hellbent on trying to ruin her life and, up to now, they'd nearly succeeded. It was only by luck more than anything that they hadn't managed to damage the van. It was only by luck that she hadn't gotten around to unloading the back of the large supply of fleeces and it was only by luck that she was still alive.

Izzy didn't believe in luck or chance or whatever it was called. Some people would say that falling pregnant on a first date was unlucky but how could she ever think that having Alys was a bad thing? She was the very best thing that had ever happened to her and she wouldn't change a second of the time they'd spent together.

Without the satnav, she'd never have found the elegant, stone-built mansion surrounded by formal gardens. While only a little over an hour from St David's she hadn't visited since a child and the roads were all new to her.

She struggled out of the car, her heart dropping at the sight that greeted her, the stunning gentleman's residence a wealth away from her parents' Sixties bungalow. There was nothing she could do about the ill-fitting borrowed denim skirt and sloppy jumper. She couldn't even put a hand up to smooth her hair with the sight of the door opening. So, instead of wasting time, she walked towards them, apologising for being unable to shake their hand.

'You have a beautiful home,' she said, following them both across the marbled hallway and into the lounge, complete with wood-panelling and thick cream carpets that she was almost scared to walk across in her borrowed boots.

'Thank you, it was built in the 1920s by Edwin Lutyens. When we bought it back in the Eighties it had sadly fallen into disrepair.' Mrs Madden tugged on the tapestry bell-pull beside the fireplace. 'It's been a labour of love getting it back, hasn't it, Jack?'

Mr and Mrs Madden were as far removed from Izzy's parents as it was possible to be. Both tall and slim, they were dressed in that effortless way that only comfortable wealth allowed. Their wardrobes … no. Their walk-in-closets … would be packed with Burberry and Erdem as opposed to the George and Primark she was used to. Even their shoes were immaculate and, in Mr Madden's case, polished to a military sheen. In fact, that's what he reminded her of with his straight back and clipped moustache; one of those old-school army colonels with a military record to match his bank balance. Everything was muted, understated and, quite frankly, she was frightened to death. After all, she had no right to be here. She had no right to interfere and certainly no right to ask the first in the list of questions queuing up since Rhys's visit to the farm.

She took the seat offered, placing her borrowed bag on the floor beside her chair and tried not to feel overwhelmed by the impressive artwork dotted around the buttercream walls. Instead, she turned her attention back to the couple sitting opposite on the button-back, champagne-coloured sofa with cranberry throws draped across the arms. Mr and Mrs Madden, for all their poise, appeared awkward and uneasy, their eyes not quite meeting hers. But before the interrogation could begin in earnest there was a soft knock on the door – a welcome interruption where cups, saucers and matching side-plates, with thin slices of the softest jam sponge, were handed out. For a few moments the silence was only broken by the chink of bone china as social niceties took precedence.

'Thank you for agreeing to see me at such short notice,' Izzy said, her cup safely resting back in its saucer. 'It's difficult for me to know where to begin.'

'How about from the beginning, m'dear? I have to admit we were surprised by your call but also intrigued,' Mr Madden said, his smile uneasy. 'We welcome any information that might ease the pain of our loss.'

'I'm sorry.'

'There's no need to apologise. You never met him,' he said, standing abruptly and heading to a small table in front of the window where he picked up a sliver frame. He stared down at the photograph briefly before handing it to her. 'Geraint was such a special young man. He had everything: good looks, a super brain but also a kindness that marked him out as different.

She took a long look at the picture, a sigh escaping but, in this case a sigh of relief. The face was a handsome one with bright, storm-grey eyes and unruly, blond hair – a face, if she was honest, that resembled her Charlie even down to the tone of his skin and colour of his hair. But, more importantly, it was the face of a stranger.

'Well, this is difficult in addition to a little awkward,' she said, placing the photo on the coffee table, before lifting her head and meeting their gaze.

'You mentioned Grace Madden. In truth, that's the only name that would have gotten you through the door. My wife ...' He paused, his hand now covering that of the women at his side. 'It's been harder on her. Up until recently I've had my work to drown in but ...'

In the nicest possible way, they're telling me to get on with the reason for my visit. Taking a swallow, she chose her words carefully. 'I don't want to upset you but—' She swallowed again before taking a deep breath, her next sentence coming out in a rushed jumble of words. 'I thought that Grace was my friend. We were pregnant around the same time.' She spread her hands wide. 'I didn't even know about her husband's death.'

Mr Madden held up a hand. 'Now, just stop there, young lady.' His smile froze on his face. 'I do hope you're not insinuating that Geraint and *that* woman were ever married? They weren't even engaged and as for dating ...'

Her attention shifted to his wife and her sudden change in posture. Now, instead of staring at her fingers, she was leaning forward, her chin thrust out, her eyes pinned to hers.

'I don't understand?' Izzy said.

'Well, understand this.' Her voice dripped with anger. 'That woman is nothing but a fraud. She ... she—'

'What my wife is trying to say,' he interrupted, 'is that her name isn't even Madden. She only adopted it after his death.' The knuckles on his right hand, where he was gripping the arm of the chair, gleamed white through the skin. 'She was obsessed with our son to the extent that he was planning on taking out an injunction against her. If it wasn't for the fact he was a lawyer and thought that he could handle her he would have. He went out with her only a handful of times and in return she spent the last months of his life stalking him all over Wales. He couldn't escape. That last time, the day of the crash, he was going to have it out with her once and for all. He left here full of hope that he'd be able to persuade her to move on. Who knows what happened after? That night my son had an accident and never spoke again. He never even opened his eyes. She got to walk away scot-free and we got to turn off his life support machine six weeks after the crash.'

Izzy felt the colour drain from her face as all her thoughts, apart from one, remained.

She lied – if she lied to me about that what else has she lied about?

'But the baby?'

'Oh, yes. The baby. The baby we had to demand a paternity test for. Our son was a fool, Miss Grant. That woman walked all over him when he was alive and now she's trying to walk all over us.'

Chapter 50

Gaby
Wednesday 22 January, 4.50 p.m. Rhys's Office

'Are you sure you're all right, guv?' Gaby said, plonking a cappuccino on the desk in front of him before taking the seat opposite and booting up her laptop.

'I'm fine – just all these sleepless nights getting to me.' He scrubbed his hands over his face, which looked as if it hadn't seen a razor in days.

'It's certainly an interesting case, that's for sure. Who'd have thought Professor Pounder would discover something like that, not that it makes any difference really but it might make it a little easier on the mother in the long run.'

'Yes, who'd have thought?' His tone dropped.

Gaby looked across at his face before glancing away. She recognised the grey skin and dark shadows embracing his skin – didn't she see them every time she stared in the mirror? The late nights and early mornings along with a diet lacking in any of the major food groups were starting to take their toll. She was starting to break out in spots and as for her waistband … She'd had to start leaving the top button of her trousers unfastened. And yet instead of planning a mercy dash to Tesco's on the way home for fresh fruit and veg, all she could think about was the case. The news that Charlie had been suffering from an incurable neurological condition, one that would have eventually led to his premature death, had no bearing on the investigation. The only way it could have been in any way relevant was if he'd taken his own life but that fracture to his hyoid bone was indisputable.

She concentrated on her screen, pulling up Charlie Dawson's birth certificate, closely followed by that of his father's, not quite able to suppress the long sigh at what she found.

'What is it?' Rhys said, his hand shaking slightly as he picked up his mug again and took a long sip.

'Nothing exciting, just an obituary notice for Paul Dawson, Charlie's dad, although it does seem to confirm the Prof's findings.'

'What does it say?'

'Oh, just the usual. Father of one, died at the age of twenty-nine after a long illness bravely born …' She eyed him over the top of her laptop. 'What a bloody shame.'

'I couldn't have said it better myself.'

She stared at the sharpness of his tone, but he'd withdrawn back under his shell, his attention now on his phone. She had no idea what he was thinking or who he was thinking about, but she was pretty sure it wasn't about Paul Dawson. She watched him reach behind his chair for his jacket, his phone still in his hand.

'Thank you for the coffee but I'm not very good company at the moment. Too much on my mind. We're at a crucial stage of the investigation and I need to be left in peace to think things through.' He made for the door. 'I'd like you to trace Geraint Madden's family and see if they have any ideas as to the where-abouts of their daughter-in-law. While you're doing that, I have a couple of leads I need to follow up – we'll compare notes later.'

What leads and how much later?

There was so much she wanted to say to this man about his relationship with Izzy Grant, but she wouldn't say any of it. The last time she'd spoken her mind about how a drugs investigation was being handled she'd been drummed out of the area. Oh, it wasn't obvious or anything. She wasn't sacked or even suspended. Their way of getting rid of an awkward and unwanted officer was more subtle than that and her catastrophic relationship with Leigh had only added to the mix. Things that they usually turned a blind eye to, like parking offences, soon racked up to the extent that she was in danger of getting points on her licence. Being followed home by an unmarked car and made to take a breath-alyzer test on the flimsiest of excuses, any time she made the mistake of going out for the evening, became the norm. She was soon a prisoner in her own flat, scared to leave in case she was trailed. So she left. She walked away from the job in Cardiff to spend a month licking her wounds back home in Liverpool. It didn't matter that the DS who'd started it all was eventually found out. It didn't matter that the missing drugs led directly back to him. While she had eventually been exonerated of all wrongdoing there was no way she could ever go back. Swansea was meant to be a new start, a golden opportunity for the new girl to prove herself. But she'd already proven herself. No, there was nothing she was prepared to say to him. But that didn't mean she was going to let him ruin the investigation. If he wasn't prepared to get his head back into gear, it certainly wasn't part of her role to make him. She'd play along and, in her own time, continue delving into finding out the truth about what had happened in that car all those years ago.

Chapter 51

She walked to the van in a stupor. She couldn't remember much about the last few minutes of her visit and only hoped she'd said and done the right thing before being shown to the door with firm handshakes and customary smiles. The conversation had stopped for her when they'd told her about the web of lies Grace had woven; a web of lies that far outstripped anything she could ever have imagined.

Before she knew it, she was driving up Dalton Lane and towards the B4312. Twilight had switched from orange to red and then black, the road stretching out before her, empty and uneasy, in a ribbon of murky grey. The sight of the deserted road was, for once, unsettling. The built-up areas had dwindled to the odd house straddling the roadside, the unwavering beam from her headlights picking out a gate, a roofline, a gable – turning them from ordinary and into something dark and slightly sinister.

Premonitions weren't something she was prone to. In fact, Charlie used to say she was the most down to earth person he'd ever met. But that didn't help her now, her mind drifting. It was a foolish idea for her to visit the Maddens and more fool her for agreeing – anything could happen on a deserted road and no one would be any the wiser until it was far too late. She pressed her foot on the accelerator, her heart in her mouth. She was driving along an empty road with no streetlights, the only things visible the edge of the road and the silhouette of bare branches in the distance.

The sudden glare from headlights in her rear-view mirror initially calmed her. She wasn't on the road all alone – if something was to happen there'd be help at hand.

The sound of a hooting horn cut through the stillness like a blade through butter, causing her thoughts to scatter. Blinded by lights on high beam, she scrunched her eyes half-closed, but it made little difference. Her gaze flickered between her mirrors. Surely the car couldn't want to pass here. He'd realise there wasn't room and pull back … Beads of sweat built on her brow as she scanned from right to left for a drive, a lay-by, a gate but there was nothing, nowhere wide enough to let another car pass. The only answer was to press her foot down on the accelerator, her attention now on the speedometer as it jerked from thirty to forty to fifty and beyond. Leaning over the steering wheel, she hazarded looking into the mirror only to look away and press her foot down harder, realisation finally hitting. This was no ordinary motorist, no act of road rage. The car behind was keeping pace, matching and then narrowing the gap, inch by fatal inch.

The first thump jarred straight through and nearly had her in the bank, the front near-side wheel spinning in mid-air as it tried to seek purchase on the soft damp bank. Managing to straighten, she rammed her foot down hard, her eyes almost closed against the blinding flash of light – all she could see was the glare from the other car's headlights ricocheting around her head.

She should have expected the second thump. She should have been prepared but her mind was in shreds. Someone was trying to kill her, again, and this time there was no one to save her.

The second thump reverberated off the bumper, the grinding screech of metal on metal rising to a crescendo into the stillness like some new wave, heavy metal climax. The sudden crunch. The swerve of tyres. The wrench of the steering wheel as it twisted out from her grasp. The sound of the car folding in on itself, mingling with the scream wrenched from her lungs.

The front of the van finally crumbled round her body, only to merge with the silence, black invading all the corners.

Chapter 52

Gaby
Wednesday 22 January, 7.15 p.m. Swansea Police Station

It had been a frustrating day. Outside of the meeting with Professor Pounder, Gaby had spent most of it holed up cross-checking birth certificates and land registries on top of all the other lines of enquiries, finally narrowing down Geraint Madden's parents to an address in Carmarthen. She leant back in her chair and stretched before picking up the phone with a sigh. She could honestly say her afternoon had been a complete waste of time. But Rhys had left her little choice other than to follow orders – she didn't know him well enough to gauge how he'd react if she decided to follow up on some hunches of her own. The only problem was, she didn't have any.

Her brow wrinkled. It was already after 7 p.m. and there'd been no sign of him since he'd strolled out just before midday. Part of her was relieved that he was happy to leave her to get on with it but the other part was worried. There weren't enough mints in the world to disguise the smell of a major bender.

She shelved thoughts of Rhys and concentrated on dialling the right number. It did sort of make sense to finally rule Madden out of the enquiry but it was just all so labour intensive ... She pulled a smile that was more of a grimace. After she'd put the phone down she'd head back to the flat to her 300-calorie ready meal and low fat, low sugar, low everything raspberry yogurt for afters.

'My name is Detective Constable Darin, Mr Madden. I was wondering if I could ask you some questions in relation to your late son.'

'This wouldn't be in relation to Miss Grant, would it?' he mirrored, his voice harsh. 'We told her everything we knew earlier.'

She replaced the receiver with a steady hand when all she wanted to do was slam it back into the cradle. *Of all the stupid, foolhardy things for her to do.* Compromising the investigation when they were so close she could almost smell it, and not only that ... what if his parents were tied up in the deaths? It wasn't likely but stranger things had happened and the name of Madden kept cropping up too many times for her liking.

There was still no sign of Rhys. Should she leave him a note, her attention now on his empty desk? It was doubtful he'd swing by the office this late but ... She smoothed her hand over her hair, flattening her plait before peeling off a new Post-it note. She was convinced there was something he wasn't telling her and the one thing she couldn't abide was a boss who kept secrets. With that thought uppermost, she scrunched the yellow slip of paper and aimed it at the bin. Two could play that game.

With her bag and coat in her hand, she headed downstairs towards reception, her mind scrolling back over the investigation, a frown appearing. He wasn't the only one keeping secrets. She'd thought, right from the beginning that there must have been something Isabelle Grant had done to pre-empt her own misfortune. But what? She didn't seem the type to cause any waves.

She reached her car, still trying to come up with a logical

explanation only to pause and, instead of pulling out her keys, pulled out her ringing phone.

'Gaby? It's Muir, Muir Abraham.'

'We've just had a call from the lads over at Carmarthen station. Isabelle Grant has been in an accident.' The line went quiet for a second. 'It's not looking good.'

Gaby abandoned her car in the nearest parking place before racing up the steps only to learn that they'd just moved her from the emergency department and up to the female medical ward.

Propping herself against the nearest wall she watched the flickering scenes unfold between the edges of the not-quite-closed curtains; a bruised forehead, a twisted arm, a glimpse of leg when they slid her across onto the bed and started attaching her to the monitors. There was nothing the police could do for her now, nothing except ensure it didn't happen again by finding the bastard that kept trying to kill her.

She tucked her phone back in her pocket before heading into the corridor, anger building because, of course, the police had to take some of the blame for this, the second attempt on Isabelle Grant's life. They should have extended the police protection after she'd gone to stay with her brother-in-law and not just relied on the security already in place at the farm. Twenty-four-hour police protection wasn't that hard to arrange. The only hard bit was getting hold of Rhys to agree. After nearly an hour of trying she'd only just managed to track him down, his phone apparently being out of range – a likely story if the sound of chinking glasses in the background was anything to go by. She didn't know what to do with him and this news certainly wouldn't help. What she really needed was advice on his mental state but who could she ask? There was no one except perhaps Amy Potter …

After finally arranging protection, Gaby went in search of someone who could give her news on Izzy's condition and, with Muir agreeing to stay until the relief officer arrived, there was little point in her hanging around. Despite the time, she still had to catch up with DS Davis, who'd been given the unenviable job of breaking the news to Izzy's family. Telling relatives that their loved one was lying in a coma with multiple fractures and possible internal injuries was bad enough but, when all indications were that someone had tried to murder her for a second time, the conversation took on a whole new level of difficulty.

Chapter 53

Lying for hours staring at the same spot of white ceiling was turning her stir crazy. If only she could turn her head but, apparently that wasn't an option until the radiographer confirmed she hadn't broken her back. So, the spinal collar remained, as did the view.

She could live with the view just as she could live with the pain in her leg where the plaster cast was digging into her skin. After all, she'd put up with a lot worse in the last five years, her attention wandering to the person sitting by her side, her mum – the person who seemed to have suffered the most in all of this: a dead granddaughter, an ill husband, a nearly murdered child.

Izzy closed her eyes against the harsh glare cast from the light filament. She was awake and a captive audience with nothing to do other than listen to her mother's snores, and dwell on her thoughts. Someone had tried to kill her again but that wasn't uppermost in her mind even though it probably should have been. No, her thoughts kept returning to that last conversation with the Maddens. There was one thing she didn't understand, a fact that pressed, pushing everything else aside.

Why would Grace have lied about her relationship with Geraint? There could be no reason. Okay, so there'd obviously been some question as to the baby's parentage for the Maddens to have demanded a paternity test but, as for trying to come up with a motive and a reason for all her lies ...

She started to shake her head only to stop, remembering just in time that she wasn't meant to move until she'd had her X-ray results back. Instead, she opened her eyes and stared again at the ceiling, allowing her thoughts free-range. Someone hated her enough to try to murder her twice and, the most frustrating thing was, she still had no idea why. She couldn't remember the crash, not really. Everything had been wiped clean apart from the feeling of impending doom and the arc of light illuminating her rearview mirror with a blinding intensity. She blinked a couple of times but the image of that bright dazzling light still burned bright on her retina, whether her eyes remained open or closed.

The next time she opened her eyes her mother had been replaced by Rhys, a very tired looking Rhys with mussed up hair and red-rimmed eyes.

'Ah, you're awake. You've certainly surpassed yourself this time.'

'What?'

'I hope you'll think twice before deciding to interfere in police business,' he continued, gripping her fingers. 'Actions have consequences and, if that car hadn't come on the scene within minutes of the crash, your poor mother might even now be dealing with the undertakers instead of doctors and nurses.'

She struggled not to shift away, not that she'd have been able to shift very far. When he'd sat down on the chair left by her mum, he'd inadvertently dropped the call-bell on the floor. She was a prisoner for however long he wanted to stay.

'Do you think I don't know that?' she said, managing to keep her voice even. 'It's as if you think I deserved to be run off the road when all I was trying to do was ...'

'Go on, Izzy – why stop now? Just exactly what were you trying to do tracking down Geraint Madden's parents? I'd really like to know.'

He let go of her fingers and sat back in his chair, his arms folded across his chest.

'How did you know about—?'

He stared, his eyes fixed. 'Because they told us. You might have this idea that we're incompetent but we do get there in the end. I'm still waiting to hear what reason you had to go bothering them.'

'Grace is mixed up in all of this. I just know she is,' she said, her voice wobbling. She had no evidence of her involvement in either the devastation to the cottage or the car accident and evidence would be all he was interested in. Instead of shaking her head, she bit down on her lower lip, the salty tang of blood just stopping her from doing some real damage. 'Just go away, Rhys. You're not helping.'

He rubbed his hand over the back of his neck. 'Look, I'm sorry, all right. I should have been kinder when I ... Hell, I didn't even ask how you're feeling?'

'I'm fine, lucky to be alive probably.'

'And it's all our fault, I know. We should have managed to trace her sooner.'

'No, it's mine. You couldn't have done anything to stop me.' She felt tears build but managed to swallow them back.

'If only you'd see sense and—'

'Hello Rhys. Miss Grant.'

They both looked up at the sound of the voice and watched as DC Darin navigated around the end of the bedtable. Rhys sat back in his chair, his face resuming its habitual bland expression while Izzy's face broke into a tentative smile, feeling only a sense of relief at the timely interruption.

Izzy wanted to speak to her, alone. She had so many questions building and no one to answer them. Rhys certainly wasn't going to help. Oh, she was pretty sure he'd do his duty. He'd make sure he dotted all the i's before crossing the t's but, after that night in the cottage, he was different. She couldn't put a finger on exactly what had changed but it was as if his priorities had altered. Now it wasn't about the case anymore. Now it was personal and he was making out with every breath that somehow it was all her fault. She looked at him from under her lashes, feeling aggrieved. There was nothing she'd done to bring this disaster to her doorstep and it wasn't fair of him to blame her. All he was achieving was making her increasingly uncomfortable in his presence. She closed her eyes, suddenly willing them to leave. There was nothing for them in this room.

For once in her life her prayers were answered by the sound of the nurse pushing the door open in a flurry.

'I said only ten minutes.'

'But I still have some questions,' Rhys said with a snap.

'Not today you don't. Now away with you or I'll call the porters to show you the door.'

Chapter 54

Gaby

Wednesday 29 January, 12.30 p.m. Swansea Police Station

'I've found her.'

'Grace Madden? How? Where?' Rhys pushed back from the desk, nearly tipping his mug in the process.

'Yes, Grace Madden – or Grace Edwards as she's officially known,' Gaby said, a broad smile breaking.

A week had passed since the car accident. A full week since they'd had an *all ports warning* out on Grace. In truth, Gaby would have liked it to be an arrest warrant but there'd been no crime committed – no crime they could prove. No, Grace Madden was a person of interest in the case, only that. She'd thought from the onset that there was more to Izzy's story than just a missing friend. Now it was time to prove it.

'Put me out of my misery then,' he said, pulling his chair forward again, his attention now on the computer screen in front of him.

'Well, Geraint Madden's parents didn't have any information that could help us locate her, which got me thinking about who might. So, I decided to pay another visit to the vicar. It was only a hunch that he might know more than he was saying,' she replied, shrugging her shoulders. 'I didn't want to say anything at the time in case it didn't lead anywhere. But, as we already know, she hasn't been back to visit the graveside since bumping into Miss Grant and that puzzled me.'

'Interesting. Go on.'

'It was the grave that finally gave the game away.'

'The grave? How could a grave—'

'Well, you could say it's all your fault,' she said on a laugh. 'I remember you once telling me it's often the simplest of mistake that leads to a case being broken. The vicar, nice man that he is, was no use so, in desperation I popped along to the graveside for some last-minute inspiration.'

'You're killing me.'

'Flowers, boss. She visits the graveside every week for five years and each time brings a ready supply of fresh flowers. Gerberas, no less.'

'What the hell are gerberas?' he said with a frown.

'Big, flashy daisy thingamabobs. Apparently, there were always five and always blood-red. Now, the thing about gerberas is they hail from South Africa so getting a ready supply in the depths of winter isn't going to be easy unless …'

'Gaby! If you don't get a move on I'll—'

'Okay – all it took was a quick call to all the florists within a thirty-mile radius to come up with a Ms Grace Elizabeth Edwards who, up until recently, had a standing order on her credit card for five blood-red gerberas.'

'Bloody brilliant,' he said, offering her a brief smile. 'Well done, Gaby. I mean that. I can count on two fingers the number of uninterrupted nights I've had in the last week trying to work out just how the hell to move this forward.'

She opened her mouth to speak but he stopped her with a wave of his hand. 'We really need to act on this now in case she's thinking of doing a moonlight flit. We might be too late as it is.'

'I know. That's why I came straight here instead of heading for lunch. Oh, and it looks like there's possibly good news too from EXTM café,' she added, pointing to the carrier bag on the floor beside her chair. 'After a week of trying I've finally managed to catch up with the owner in person. He's been in the Canaries since before Christmas – it's all right for some! But there is good news. He normally wipes the CCTV camera on a weekly basis so, somewhere in that lot is a potential killer. Our lucky day.'

'Indeed.' He stared at the bag briefly before picking up his mobile and checking his messages. 'Actually, go and ask DS Davis to accompany you. We can check out the footage on your return,' he said, his eyes glued to the screen.

'But … I thought you'd like to be in on the interview?' she said, confused at his sudden lack of interest. 'After all, it's your case. Five years is a long time.'

'A very long time.' His gaze flickered to meet hers before returning to his phone. 'But I'm in the middle of something here. You and Davis will do just as well. Go on now. We don't want her to run scared now, do we?'

'No, I'll get straight on it.'

'And Gaby.'

'Yes, boss?' she said, pausing, one hand on the door handle, her body half-turned back in his direction.

'Whatever happens remember that you're a good cop. Follow your instincts. They haven't let you down yet.'

Chapter 55

Gaby
Wednesday 29 January, 2.30 p.m. Llanelli

Grace Elizabeth Edwards was easy to find in the end. All they had to do was follow her trail of debts right across Wales. A woman who clearly lived beyond her means with a lifestyle that wasn't serviced by her job as a typist at one of the local health centres.

They pulled up in front of her delightful white cottage situated on the outskirts of Llanelli only to pause a moment at the sight of the carefully manicured lawns and topiary box hedging that must have cost a pretty penny. The flower beds were empty but, no doubt, would soon be stuffed full of spring flowers. If Gaby had taken the time to imagine Grace Madden's house it would have looked exactly like this. The only question as far as she could see was where all the money was coming from.

The door was opened on the third ring by a carefully coiffured woman decked out in designer gear, a small smile planted on her lips, a smile that faded as soon as they presented their ID badges.

'Come into the lounge. I've just boiled the kettle.' She waved them through the first door on the left.

Gaby was used to being invited into an assortment of homes

for lukewarm tea conveyed in a variety of cups and mugs but what she wasn't expecting was the cold clinical room with less character than a dentist's waiting room. She took a seat beside Bill on the snow-white leather sofa and continued her visual tour. There were no photos or ornaments, no books or plants. There was nothing to indicate the personality of the owner; Gaby hated it on sight.

Of course, there was something else missing – or should that be someone? Grace had a daughter but there wasn't a trace. It could quite happily be the house of an upwardly mobile singleton except she knew that it wasn't.

'We believe you know an Isabelle Grant?' It was as good an opening line as any.

'Izzy? Sure. We spent some time together before I moved out here.'

'Ms Edwards, could you tell us where you were on the 17th and 22nd of January, between the hours of 5 p.m. and midnight?' Bill interrupted.

'And this is in relation to?' she asked, her gaze hovering between them, her hand tucking her hair behind her ear.

'Please answer the question, Ms Edwards or, if you'd prefer, you can always come down to the station to help us with our enquiries.'

'What am I meant to have done?' She stood up and walked over to the window, fiddling with the white voile curtains.

'Just answer the question, Ms Edwards.'

'It's Madden, you know – the name I go by. I'd appreciate if you'd use it. In answer to your question, I was here on both occasions.'

'You don't need to check your diary?'

'No, there's no need. I'm either at home or at work and, as I don't work late, I would have been here. My daughter is only five and too young to be left alone,' she said, her hair swinging around her neck in a swirl of black.

'Ah yes. Your daughter. Where is she?' Gaby said, glancing down at her watch. She was becoming increasingly concerned by the lack of evidence of a child. There was that adage children should be seen and not heard but, for a parent to be able to hide all evidence that a child lived in their house, was worrying to the extreme. After all, it wasn't the sort of house that could afford the luxury of a playroom. It was little more than a two-up-two-down so, unless the child's belongings had to be kept in her bedroom … Suddenly Gaby wanted to see that room more than anything.

'She'll be on her way home from school by now, officer. She's … being dropped off.'

Gaby glanced across at Bill, his frown echoing hers.

'Could you tell us something of your relationship with Geraint Madden?' Bill said, taking charge of the interview.

'You have been busy, haven't you!' She reached for the packet of cigarettes on the table. 'I won't offer you one; filthy habit. I'm always trying to give up.' She threw them a thin-lipped smile before lighting up and taking a heavy drag. 'Geraint was the love of my life. If it hadn't been for Daisy, I think I'd have gone completely mad when he died. She's the only thing that keeps me going.'

'But that's not quite right, is it, Ms Madden?' he said, his eyes meeting hers. 'What about the injunction he was planning to take out on you?'

'A lovers' tiff.' Her dark eyes glittered. 'Something, I'm sure, you'll know all about.'

'It's funny how the memory is such an unreliable resource,' Gaby said, her voice unnaturally soft. 'Mr Madden's parents have a completely different interpretation of your relationship with their son.'

'Well, that figures. No one would ever have been good enough for their precious Geraint.' She leant forward, flicking ash into the glass dish in front of her.

The interview was going nowhere unless she decided on a

258

different approach. 'Tell me about how you met Miss Grant. It was during your pregnancy, wasn't it?'

'Not that it has any bearing on anything but yes. We attended a few pregnancy classes along with a few others,' she said, squashing her half-finished cigarette out only to reach for another.

'Interesting that there's no record of you having signed up with a GP in the area?'

'It's not against the law to be attended to by your own physician?' Her eyes shifted to the stairs briefly.

'Not in the least, although it is routine to be referred to the pregnancy classes by a local GP as opposed to just turning up to the sessions unannounced.'

'I was new to the area and saw a notice somewhere or other. Look, I don't get on with his parents, so it was an attempt to escape.' Her gaze skimmed her watch briefly. 'But when Izzy lost Alys, I knew I could never escape their clutches so I gave in.'

'You gave in?' Gaby said, mirroring her words. 'I don't understand?'

'Yes, I gave in,' she repeated. 'They get to spend time alone with Daisy and in return she gets to go to the kind of school I could never afford.' She smoothed her hand over her hair. 'They didn't like the idea of her attending the local primary.'

'Don't you have any witnesses to corroborate that you were home on those two dates?' Bill said, changing the subject. 'You know the sort of thing. A neighbour popping around to borrow some sugar?'

'Yes, and while you're coming up with a list I'll just head to the loo. I take it it's upstairs?' Gaby said, not waiting for an answer before standing and heading for the door. 'I'll be back in a jiff.'

'Hey!'

But Bill had the situation in hand. 'The first incident took place late on the evening of the seventeenth of January.'

Gaby heard his voice droning on but all her attention was now on the three doors that led off the tiny landing.

The master bedroom was another virginal white affair; a hotel room would have more character than this pristine prison. There was nothing on show apart from a smooth white duvet and pillow. No pictures. No jewellery dotted round. She took a moment to nip into the bathroom and flush the toilet before pushing open the door to the last room. This time instead of white she was met with girly pink. The mother must have spent a fortune on the frilly-canopied princess bed and matching little desk and chair. The room was a little girl's paradise – the bed laden with cuddly toys, the cute *Frozen* bookshelf packed with the sort of toys and games most children only dreamt of. But there was still no sign of Daisy.

Gaby had only been away a couple of minutes, but you could have sliced the tension in the lounge with a knife. Instead of even attempting to answer any questions, Grace just sat with her arms folded, shooting dagger looks across at Bill.

Retaking her seat, she opened her mouth to speak only to close it again at the sound of the doorbell. Much to her surprise, Grace Madden remained seated.

'Aren't you going to answer the bell?' Bill finally asked, glancing towards the door.

'It's probably only a cold caller. They'll stop in a minute,' she said, reaching for her packet of cigarettes.

'Are you sure it's not your daughter in the company of Geraint's parents?' Gaby guessed, throwing a look at Bill. She watched as he lumbered out into the hall and started fiddling with the lock. 'You did say that your daughter was on her way home from school?'

Within seconds, Mr and Mrs Madden had joined them in the lounge, a look of alarm stamped across their faces, Daisy Madden trailing in their wake.

Chapter 56

Izzy
Wednesday 29 January, 2.30 p.m. The Farm

'Hi Izzy, its Rhys.'

She squeezed the phone tight into her palm and closed her eyes. He was the very last person she could cope with. There was so much to think about. Dad. Bucket. Her house. The van. Her work. Who the hell was trying to murder her? She wanted to curl up into a tight ball and never wake. But he wasn't going to leave her alone, none of them were. There was still the case to solve, a puzzle with so many twists and turns that it was probably heading for the unsolvable pile. She might have a broken ankle in addition to bruising that stretched down through all the layers. She might have lost both her dignity and her sense of humour over the last few days but the one thing she hadn't lost was her marbles. The case wasn't solved, which only meant one thing – more questions.

'How did you find me?'

There was a pause. 'I didn't think you were hiding or, is it just from me?'

'No, of … of course not,' she stuttered. 'I decided to stay with Oscar and Bethan in case they tried again.'

'I know.' His voice was soft. 'Where else did you have to go?'

'What do you want, Rhys?' she said, fast losing her temper.

'What I've always wanted. The best for you.' He cleared his throat. 'And to bring news.'

'News,' she repeated. 'What news?'

'News about the case. What other type is there?'

'Well?' she said, after a moment.

'No, Izzy. This has to be done face-to-face. We've had a bit of luck with some CCTV footage, but we need you down at the station to confirm someone's identity.'

'Grace? I just knew she was tied up in this from the very beginning.'

'Yes, exactly.' His voice had now dropped to barely a whisper and she had to strain to hear his words. 'We'll send a car around shortly. It shouldn't be long.'

Izzy placed the phone back before easing into the nearest chair. She felt numb. She was numb. Numb from the centre to the outside. She was finally about to learn what had happened to Charlie and Alys.

Images flickered across her eyes in a kaleidoscope of colours. Charlie laughing at some joke or other, his head flung back. The little boy grin whenever he wanted something. The love on his face the very first time he'd held Alys.

She laid her head down on the table, the hard wood cold against her suddenly feverish skin. Love wasn't something you could measure or touch. It wasn't something that was disciplined or defined. What she'd felt for Charlie and Alys was unique and, just because they were now gone, didn't mean she couldn't still remember how it had felt. Something blossomed inside at his touch just as something flowed straight from her heart at the feel of Alys's fingers clutching her thumb. Knowing what happened wouldn't change any of that. It wouldn't make them come back. They were never coming back but ... she still needed to understand. She still needed to find out what had happened. It wouldn't change anything. But this not knowing was killing her inch-by-inch.

Chapter 57

Gaby
Wednesday 29 January, 3 p.m. Llanelli

'So, we're back to square one then,' Bill said, slamming his hands down on the dashboard. 'I always knew that Grace bloody Madden was a red herring.'

I wish you'd have said before.

But she decided to keep her thoughts to herself for once. 'One good thing – we've managed to stop her little racket. Extorting money from the grandparents so they can have access to their only grandchild is a nasty business and something the law officers in Llanelli will have a field day with.'

'That's all very well but it's no help to us now, is it?' He snapped his seatbelt closed before crossing his legs.

She shook her head. 'If it wasn't Grace Madden then where do we go from here?'

'You tell me. You seem to have all the answers, along with Rhys's ear … his latest little lady friend.'

'That's not true.'

'No, of course it isn't. He'd have more taste.'

She'd blast him if she thought it would do any good but people like Bill were intransigent. She had to earn her stripes with him the hard way and, as he was her boss in Rhys's absence, she'd best keep her mouth shut. They wouldn't believe her anyway – just his word against hers.

Turning the key in the ignition she decided to change the subject. 'How long have you been in the area, Bill?'

He threw her a look. 'About twenty years. We moved here because of the schools.'

'It's good to know you're a family man,' she said, trying to be friendly. The smile wasn't returned. 'So, you'll know about Rhys then?'

'What about him?'

'I don't know, do I? That's why I'm asking.'

She reversed out of the parking space before pulling into the road, all her attention on the man beside her.

'Look, Rhys is a good copper, all right. He was born in the area and knows more about St David's than anyone apart from Amy Potter.'

'Amy? Why Amy?'

'Because Amy is about the sixth generation of Potters to be born here. What she doesn't know about St David's, or anyone in it, isn't worth knowing. But you're barking up the wrong tree if you think Rhys had anything to do with the case. He's a copper, for God's sake.'

She indicated to overtake a taxi about to pull out in front of her. 'So, there's no truth in the rumour that he has a thing for Isabelle Grant?'

'Why are you asking?'

'No reason. Just something someone said.'

'I don't know why you're so interested. I'm the very last person to rat on a friend.'

'But he's not a friend, is he? He's your boss. All I'm asking is—'

'You're out of order,' he said. 'Completely out of order. Even if I suspected such a thing, I'd never—'

She settled back in her seat and put her foot down on the accelerator, keen now to return to the station. In his own way, Bill had told her exactly what she wanted to know. Scrunching up her eyes against the brightness of the sunlight shining in through the windscreen, all she could think about was Rhys's final words.

Follow your instincts. They haven't let you down yet.

Chapter 58

Izzy
Wednesday 29 January, 4.05 p.m. The Farm

'I didn't think it would be you picking me up,' Izzy said, handing him the first crutch before easing her leg into the car and handing him the second.

'Why not? I could always have asked the copper stationed outside the gates but it's getting late and he happens to have a young family.' He released the handbrake and performed a neat three-point turn under the watchful eye of her father, staring at them out of the lounge window.

'He's looking well.'

'He's nearly back to normal, all apart from the fat-free diet he's on. As far as he's concerned, Mam and the doctor are in cahoots to turn him into the unhappiest Welshman out there.'

'He has plenty of competition.'

She stared at him, her mouth slightly open, watching as he concentrated on driving over the cattle grid at the entrance to the farm. He looked tired, drawn even. The burden of the case must be a heavy one by the look of the shadows under his eyes and the grim set of his jaw. She wondered what the purpose of the journey was. He'd mentioned some footage but he obviously wasn't in a rush to tell her anything, the way he appeared to be focusing all his attention on his driving.

Her gaze landed on the plaster-cast and she set about rearranging her skirt, trying to disguise its ugliness. Now that her burn had healed, she'd managed to bundle her hair up into a tight ponytail. Her face, she'd left. There wasn't anything she could do about the bruises and scratches caused when her rescuer had dragged her out from under the crumpled bonnet.

Her train of thought derailed – something that was becoming increasingly common over the last few days. For some reason she couldn't seem to focus on anything for more than a few seconds. Now, instead of her injuries, she thought about the man who'd rescued her. There had been flowers sent to the hospital, a beautiful bouquet of the palest pink roses and a brief card. It didn't say much, nothing really, but she still knew it was from him. Nat, presumably short for Nathanial or maybe Nathan—

'You're very quiet?' Rhys said, his words interrupting her thoughts.

'Not really.' She lifted her gaze from her hands and where she'd loosely linked them on her lap, the bright redness of the burn still visible. So many scars. More scars than most people had in a lifetime and to what purpose? Who hated her enough to … Her thoughts slipped, wandering again, her attention now on the view outside the window, and the dark outline of the cliff ahead silhouetted against the darkening sky.

'I thought we were going to the station?'

Chapter 59

Gaby
Wednesday 29 January, 4.40 p.m. Swansea Police Station

'Mrs Grant?'

'Speaking.'

'This is the station. Would it be possible to speak to Miss Grant, please?'

'You lot crack me up. Doesn't the left hand know what the right hand is doing?'

'Excuse me?'

'Detective Walker left over half an hour ago, taking my daughter with him. I don't know what the rush is – even if there has been a breakthrough, it could have waited until the morning. If you need to speak to her … I did make her take my phone. You can never be too careful these days.'

Gaby placed her mobile back in her pocket before heading into the squad room, a heavy frown descending. She'd been hoping for Bill but instead all the desks were empty apart from Amy's.

'All right, Gaby, she said, staring at her before continuing. 'So what's with the serious face then?'

Gaby settled on the corner of her desk, trying to work out just what to say.

'Amy. Do you remember telling me a few weeks ago that Rhys had a thing for Isabelle Grant?' she said, not quite meeting her gaze.

'So? What of it?'

'Something's not right.' She heaved a sigh, raising her eyes from where they'd been focusing on her shoes. 'I've just come off the phone to her mother. Apparently, Rhys has legged it over to the farm to bring her back here.' Gaby picked up her pen and started clicking the end, choosing her words carefully. 'Amy, have you heard that there's been a breakthrough in the case because, as far as I know, it's going nowhere. The Maddens, all of them, are a complete disaster as a family and, in truth, they deserve each other. But, now that they've been ruled out, we're back to square one.'

'What are you trying to say?' Amy said, her voice unsteady, her gaze never leaving Gaby's face.

'I don't know what I'm trying to say and that's part of the problem.' She darted her a look before returning her attention back to the pen. 'All I know is that, for the last few weeks, we've been gripped in a frenzy to find Grace Madden. Now that's over and the only thing that doesn't make sense is Rhys's part in it. Why would he instigate such a wide-scale search with so little to go on? Okay, so Izzy saw her in Swansea and there's always been that query about Charlie having had an affair but that's not a case, nowhere near. Common sense must tell us that the likelihood of a nine months' pregnant woman murdering her lover is low at best. Surely, she'd have waited until after giving birth?' Gaby tightened her jaw, before continuing. 'Grace Madden was never in the running, not really. I think we misread that situation totally. Our instincts told us she was a crook and that coloured our judgement. Blackmailing the Maddens for access to their granddaughter, while abhorrent, isn't murder. But what if Rhys really did have a thing for Isabelle? She knew him from when she was schoolgirl, didn't she?'

Amy nodded briefly, her eyes huge in her suddenly pale face.

'So, he had to watch her hook up with Charlie and go on to bear his child.' Gaby continued. 'For some people that's more than enough of an excuse to drive them mad—'

'But this is Rhys we're talking about. The kindest of men and one of the best cops around.'

'So good that he couldn't find one measly car? I've checked the records, all of them. Did you know that the Blue Lagoon was mentioned as a possible place to search in that first week?' she said, leaning towards her. 'Yes, that's right. And guess who decided that it was too much of a long shot to send divers down?'

'Rhys?' Amy's mouth opened wide.

'Exactly. Rhys, and supported by his father, would you believe.'

'But why?'

Gaby spread her arms wide. 'I have no idea, but I can almost taste that something's not right. Bear in mind we're talking about the very start of the investigation so cost wouldn't have come into it then. It was only later, when the search totalled millions, that the purse-strings were tightened. And what about the cards, hmm? The Eurostar only takes thirty minutes and he was off Boxing Day – I checked. Nothing could have been easier. I'm still trying to gain access to the Eurostar passenger list but when I do I'm convinced we'll see his name on it.' She paused, shoving the sleeve of her jacket up and glancing at her watch. 'Why would a DI put himself out to escort a witness when a PC would have sufficed and why leave it until now.' She glanced at her watch. 'The farm isn't that far away and they left over forty minutes ago so, where are they?'

'Come on.' Amy stood and, snatching up her keys, raced for the door. 'If you're right about this – and I don't think for a minute that you are – we have to find them.'

Chapter 60

Izzy

Wednesday 29 January, 4.40 p.m. Limeslade Bay, Gower
Peninsula

Rhys switched off the engine and twisted in his seat, his face
barely visible now daylight, as if by the click of a button,
switched to dusk. 'I'd like to talk to you before I take you to
the station. I think, after the time we spent together, you owe
me that.'

Izzy hadn't been nervous. All the time he'd been speaking
to her mother, all the time he'd been passing the time of day
with her father. Nothing. Not a twitch. Not a quiver. But now
she was scared, scared more than perhaps she'd ever been
before. It was probably irrational but there was just something
about the way he was avoiding her eyes. It was almost as if he
couldn't bear to look at her. No. She lifted her hand to her
throat and there it stayed, frozen. It was almost as if he hated
her.

'I can't remember the first time I noticed you. You've always
been there – little Izzy Grant, the most beautiful woman. The

272

only woman.' He raised his hand to her cheek, stroking her skin, his fingers warm against her suddenly cold flesh.

She wanted to move, to shift away from his hand. She wanted to open the car and run. But, of course, she couldn't, her fingers moving of their own accord to her leg and the hard casing of plaster surrounding her smashed bone. He'd thought of that. He'd thought of everything. He'd catch her before she'd even taken a step. Heaving a breath, she tried to still her senses with rational thought. Surely she'd got it wrong. Surely it couldn't have been Rhys all along? Surely Rhys couldn't have—? Bile rose in her mouth, the acidic liquid burning the back of her throat. She swallowed it back, trying to concentrate on his words in the hope she'd misread the situation.

'The night you went off with Charlie … I'd had it all planned, you know.' His fingers now trailed a path to her lips. 'I was going to ask you out for the first time. I even bought flowers, the most beautiful cream roses that were on the backseat of my car outside the chip shop. I'd been waiting, you see. I'd been waiting on the sidelines for you to turn eighteen. The age difference wouldn't seem so much, or that's what I kept telling myself. But I waited too long. I had to watch him pick you up like a common tart.' His fingers paused, his hand now on the back of her head, the pressure changing from soft to hard. 'And when I learnt what you'd done. My perfect woman, soiling herself with the likes of him …'

A phone rang; the unfamiliar sound of her mother's mobile was a welcome relief. She closed her eyes briefly, shifting to take it out of her pocket but he was too quick for her, his hand now biting into her arm.

'Turn it off.'

Her eyes fixed on his face and, in that second, she knew it was over. The past, her past drifted before her eyes, just like she'd read about in those true-life magazines her mother bought each week – images of Charlie, images of Alys, even images of Rhys. Rhys as a young man, always on the edge of things, always watching.

She fumbled with the buttons, her mind in turmoil, a silence descending. She didn't know what to say to this man, a man she'd known all her life. She blinked. No. she didn't know him, not really. She didn't know the real Rhys, the man sitting so close she could smell the stale alcohol fumes on his breath and see the dilation of his pupils. She could have reasoned with the old Rhys, but this Rhys wasn't someone to reason with. He wasn't the man she thought she knew. He was a man who'd lied all along. Another thought flickered, causing her to close her eyes briefly. The memory of him in her bed and what she'd allowed happen. That memory more than any of the others startled her out of her inertia, pushing adrenaline through her veins like a soaring kite. She couldn't take flight but she sure as hell wasn't prepared to go down without a fight.

'Why Limeslade Bay, Rhys?'

'Ah, I was wondering when you'd ask that, sweetheart.' He let go of her arm suddenly although the feel of his fingers remained.

She felt dirty all of a sudden. The thought of his touch, his voice, his company. She wanted to leave but there was fat chance of that. He'd lapsed into another silence; a silence she was suddenly afraid to break in case she brought the situation to a head.

'My whole life I've only wanted one thing – for us to be together.' He ran his hand across the back of his neck, his gaze turned to the window. 'I tried so hard to let you see how it was. The number of days I followed you round St David's but, for some reason, you always managed to escape. It was only when you came to me that day in the supermarket that I had you in the palm of my hand.' He threw her a glance before returning his attention back to the window. 'It's your fault, of course – the fire, the car accident. All of it.'

274

'My fault? How could it be?'

'Don't you remember what you said to me, my love? Like nectar to my ears. You said you had to know what had happened to them to move on with your life. Up until that point I'd resigned myself to a future without you, but your words changed all that,' his voice harsh. 'So, I decided to give you what you wanted. But finding Charlie and Alys wasn't enough, was it?'

He turned, and in a sudden burst of movement, unsnapped both the seatbelts, all trace of the calm detective displaced by the wild man in front of her. Grabbing the top of her arms, he pushed her back against the headrest, his breath hot against her face. 'You still couldn't get them out of your system, could you? I gave you everything, even my body. To me it was the most glorious, life-fulfilling experience but to you ... to you it meant nothing. You couldn't even bear to face me after. You crawled out from under me as if I was dirt under your feet. How do you think that made me feel, huh?' he asked, his fingers digging deep under her collarbone, burning, twisting, grinding.

She gave a little moan, tears starting to stream. 'But I didn't know. You never said.'

'I shouldn't have had to say anything, Izzy. I loved you. I still love you but it will never be enough. Taking that slime ball and squealing brat out of your life wasn't enough. My body wasn't enough. I don't know what you want but the one thing I do know is it's not me.' He squeezed his eyes tight, lines radiating across his cheeks. 'That's when I decided that you had to die. You left me no choice because I sure as hell wasn't prepared to watch on while you found someone else.' He balled his hand into a fist, ramming it down on the side of the door. 'Why the hell couldn't you have died in that fire? That would have been the easiest option. But no. You had to escape. You had to bring it to the wire. Well now, my love, there's no escape. It's over. It's over for both of us.'

Suddenly his mouth was on hers, his tongue pushing inside,

his teeth biting, devouring. She couldn't move. She couldn't breathe with the weight of his chest heavy against hers. And with that, something snapped. This was the end. This was his way of saying goodbye. He was going to kill them both and there was nothing she could do to stop him.

Chapter 61

Gaby
Wednesday 29 January, 5 p.m. Limeslade Bay car park

'Thank God you had the sense to take a squad car – we must have broken all the speed limits. I just hope we're in time.'

'I just hope we're wrong,' Amy replied. 'I think that's a car up ahead. I'm going to turn the lights off.'

'But we won't be able to see anything,' Gaby said, peering through the windscreen.

'Yes, and they won't be able to see us either. Pull over there.' Amy pointed to a grassy verge, barely visible on the right. 'I know this place like the back of my hand.'

With Amy in the passenger seat Gaby felt no less anxious, just relieved that all she had to do was follow directions. Switching off the engine she leant forward, looking for even the glimmer of a light but there was nothing.

'Why the hell would he take her up here?'

'Because, on a Friday night in January, Limeslade Headland is probably one of the most deserted places in South Wales. It's pretty isolated – if it wasn't for her managing to keep the phone switched on, we'd have had no chance.'

'Okay, I get the picture.' Gaby peered down at her mobile, frustration building. They'd heard the words Limeslade but little else and now, apart from the odd whimper, all was silent.

'We should be able to see more in a sec when our eyes have adjusted to the dark,' Amy said, lifting her hand and turning off the interior light. 'Here, take that, but don't switch it on yet,' she added, dropping a heavy-duty flashlight into her lap.

Gaby watched her place her hand on the door handle, one finger against her lips. 'Shush. I don't know what's going on, but I don't want to announce our presence until we're good and ready.'

Good and ready for what?

Gaby sighed. While she'd been happy to enlist Amy's help in the search for Rhys and Izzy, when they'd failed to turn up at the station, she was the first to admit she was no good at this cloak-and-dagger approach to crime solving. That was what the boys in blue were for. She much preferred a warm office and a pile of complex clues to look at any day. But she kept her mouth closed and followed Amy's lead, her eyes squinting at the dark shape of a car about fifty metres ahead. She was the one who'd started this, so she was the one that needed to finish it.

She opened her door and slid her feet to the ground, a part of her, a very large part, hoping that they'd just stopped off for reason or reasons unknown. That would be the best-case scenario. She wasn't allowing her mind to drift to any worst-case ones.

She followed her along the edge of the cliff path; keeping well out of the sight of the car ahead. She had no plan as to what came next, her gaze swinging back to Amy in the hope that she'd think of something. After all, she knew Rhys. She knew what he was capable of, if anything …

They both stopped at the same time, within a few of metres of the car. But the distance didn't matter. They could have been a metre away or ten – they were still too far away to do anything other than watch the scene unfolding in front of them, their thoughts simultaneously scattering.

The darkness and quiet had disappeared, only to be filled with the light from headlamps on full-beam and the sound of crunching gears. A sound wrenched through the air. A scream? The squeal of tyres seeking purchase on wet grass? Whatever the origin of the sound Gaby knew they were too late. The car staggered forward, lurching towards the cliff edge. There was a pause, just for a second and then they watched, open-mouthed as the car balanced on the edge like a seesaw in slow-motion before juddering briefly and toppling over the side.

Chapter 62

Gaby

'Come on.'

Gaby looked across at Amy. She wasn't sure which one of them had spoken but, as if in unison, they reached for each other's hand and stumbled towards the cliff edge.

There was a silence, a deathly silence. Even the sea seemed to pause for breath. Gaby flicked on her torch, training the beam down over Limeslade Bay. It was funny how small the car looked, mangled and squashed as if by some giant foot and she was suddenly reminded of the box of Corgi cars that her brothers used to play with when they were younger. The car was a write-off, the roof crushed flat and any thoughts of a lucky escape curled up and died at the sight.

'There must be something – there has to be something we can do.' She turned to stare across at Amy, taking a couple of steps back from the edge. 'So, how do we get down?'

'There's no way unless you're a climber or a mountain goat,' Amy said, reaching for her phone. 'Why do you think they use the crag on training exercises? All we can do is call it in to the coastguards. They'll scramble the lifeboat. It shouldn't take long.'

But too long for Izzy and Rhys. The unsaid words left hanging in the air between them.

Gaby moved away to leave Amy to make the call. She felt a failure. She'd suspected something wasn't right with him but she'd done nothing. She'd said nothing. And earlier when he'd almost spelt it out. It was as if he'd wanted her to stop him before it was too late. She dug her hands deep in her pockets, dropping her shoulders. She'd moved from Swansea to try and make a good impression, to try and start again. That was the biggest laugh of all. There'd be no third chance now she'd made a mess of this, her second. All she could do was return to Liverpool with her tail between her legs.

The wind had picked up, the waves rising and shifting against the dark eerie lumps of limestone. She didn't know if the tide was rising or falling. She didn't know even if it would make a difference to the salvage operation. She bent her head, staring down at the shale by her feet, her mind in a tangle. This time there wouldn't be a kindly DCI prepared to sort her out. No, she'd be on the next train back to Lime Street Station—

There was a noise – a different noise cutting through the air and causing her to raise her head.

Lifting the torch, she held her breath to listen, her eyes spearing the cliff edge, searching for anything that might have made the screech. A gull? A goat? A woman. There it was again. A definite sound. A word. A solitary word that took the air from her lips and fear from her soul.

'Help.'

Chapter 63

Gaby
One week later. Swansea Police Station

'Ma'am, you wanted to see me?'

'Take a seat, Darin.'

The office was the same as ever. Everything looked the same but, of course, it was very different. This time there was no man at her side to share the brunt of the DCI's unblinking stare. This time there was no open folder on her desk or unsolved case to discuss. This time there was nothing to distract from the inevitability of the conversation. The case had been closed; the team disbanded. Now, instead of the Grant saga, they were back working on the break-ins along the High Street.

Gaby crossed her legs and adjusted her face into a blank mask, determined to take whatever censure there was without a flicker of emotion.

'Darin ... Gaby,' the DCI started, her elbows on the desk, her gaze unwavering. 'I don't have to tell you that you're a good copper. You have that one essential many coppers lack. Instinct. You knew there was something up with DI Walker. I only wish you'd come and shared it with me. But there's nothing to be done about that now,' she said, dropping her arms and tracing the edge of her coffee cup with the tip of her finger. 'I think you know that it's impossible for you to stay on here. The team blame you for not calling it in. They think they could have done something, intervened before it was too late.' She shrugged her shoulders. 'Who knows?'

'Yes, ma'am.'

'Is there anything you'd like to say? I'll give you a good reference and do what I can to help you secure another post. I may even know of someone prepared to take you on.'

'Thank you. Are you going to tell Miss Grant about Charlie and Alys's medical condition? She has a right to know and it might help.'

DCI Brazil-North stared at her briefly. 'As you say, she has a right to know.'

'Amy!'

Gaby pulled the door open only to find her friend waiting for her, a couple of large frothy lattes in her hands.

'Come on, let's sneak away to drink these. It's not as if we'll be missed,' she said, pressing a mug into her hand.

Outside, they headed as if in unison towards Amy's battered Nissan Micra.

'Well? Spill the beans then? What did the old dragon say?'

Gaby laughed. 'She's only in her forties and more of a pussy cat today,' she said, sighing with relief. 'I really thought I was in for the chop but …'

'But?'

She took a long sip of her drink, noting with a smile the surplus of sugar. Good old Amy. 'She's arranged for me to be transferred onto another MIT.'

'What! Not back to Cardiff? I thought you said they wouldn't have you back even if you were the last cop standing.'

'That's true enough. I wouldn't go back anyway. No, to some-where nearer home although I've never been. St Asaph.'

She turned in her seat, offering Amy a brief smile even though smiling wasn't something she'd done much of over the last few days. If she couldn't eat or sleep then how was she meant to smile? The thing that hurt the most was that she'd liked Rhys as a man, and she'd respected him as a copper. He was good, too good. He'd been able to obliterate almost every trace of the murder. The worst of it was she truly believed that what had happened at Limeslade Bay was all her fault. If she hadn't followed up on David Prestwich and Arthur Norman's internet activities she wouldn't have known about the CCTV footage from the EXTM café. She'd as good as told him on that last day that he was about to be found out, but she'd been wrong. She'd met with the boffins on the next floor up the day after the tragedy only to discover that the tapes were useless, all but destroyed by water damage from the café's leaking roof.

'That's near Llandudno, isn't it? I love Llandudno. My gran used to take me there as a child,' Amy said with a sigh. 'We used to go down the pier to watch the fishermen at the end and she always let me have an extra-large Candy Floss.' She drained her mug and, stretching out her hand, went to take Gaby's cup. 'I wonder if they have any vacancies for an amazing FLO on their team …'

Epilogue

Izzy
Two months later

She was alive.

That was all she could say. That was all she knew. She wouldn't call it living. She'd lost far too much to ever think it that.

They'd all left apart from Mam, Dad and Bethan. She'd asked them to stay. She owed them that much. She owed them everything. They'd been there every day at the hospital. They'd helped to feed and toilet her while her broken bones continued to heal. How ironic that the very injury he'd caused, her broken leg, was the very thing that had saved her. How ironic that, on the trajectory to hell, she'd managed to kick him unconscious with her plaster cast before flinging herself onto the mercy of the gods. She didn't know what angel had been looking down. In truth, she wasn't sure if she believed in any of that stuff. But three times he'd tried to kill her and three times she'd survived. To be caught upside down, her plaster-cast wedged in a limestone crevice the only thing between her and the swirling sea-edged rocks below had to be viewed as some sort of miracle.

She braced her shoulders in preparation for what was to come, her mind continuing to roam. If only such a miracle could have happened to return Alys and Charlie back to her. She'd have embraced them with open arms even knowing what she knew now – that their time spent together was always destined to be fleeting. That didn't mean she loved them any the less. It meant she loved them all the more. The short time they'd shared together, contracted to microcosmic proportions, was still enough to fill her heart to bursting and she knew that, whatever the future held, she'd love them right up to that last breath.

The church had been packed to the rafters, the noise from the hymns she'd chosen, for this her final goodbye to Charlie and Alys, a joyous sound even if there was little joy to be had. But they'd all gone now. All that was left were the four of them huddled round the mound of dark dank earth.

'Let me take you home, love.' Mam squeezed her arm gently. 'There's no point in staying.'

She jerked away, turning to face them, the three people in the world that meant the most. She looked at each one of them in turn, drinking in their faces as if for the last time. And in a way that was what it felt like. After today, in fact, after the next few minutes they could very well turn against her for what she was about to tell them. But her decision was made. It had been made all those weeks ago when she'd let Rhys in, when she'd let Rhys try to ruin the rest of her life. But no more. Rhys was dead. He couldn't get to her now. He wouldn't be able to blight the one thing that was left, the only thing that was left. She was going to turn this into the best thing that had ever happened, with or without their blessing.

She lifted her gaze heavenward, trying to pluck some courage out of the cloud-filled skies.

'Mam, Dad, Bethan. I have something to tell you. I'm pregnant.'

Acknowledgements

Writing an acknowledgements page is always a bittersweet experience. In this case it's the end of a very long journey, which started out as a dream to be a traditionally published writer nearly fifteen years ago. Turning that dream into reality took lots of help.

So my first thanks must go to Abi Fenton, at HQ Digital, for seeing something in my writing that she could work with. I still can't quite believe it. Also a huge thank you to Dushi Horti for helping me through my first HQ Digital copyediting experience and to Christopher Sturtivant for leading me through each step – I wish him well on this, the start of his voyage into publishing.

Thanks, as always to fellow writer, Valerie Keogh, for her unstinting and selfless support. Our daily word-count battles are a great incentive and a game I'd heartily recommend to other writers to help rack up those words. Originally written in 1st person, it's thanks to Val that *Silent Cry* is now written in 3rd.

Thanks too to writer Susie Tullett. I undertook her creative writing course a couple of years ago but not only that. Her advice and support turned this into a much darker read than I'd initially planned – so thank you. I look forward to an Irish meet-up soon.

Jo Robertson, *My Chestnut Reading Tree Blog*, is a lifeline. As a writer I'm forever procrastinating and never think that my work is good enough. Jo, your support and kind words keep me picking up that pen …

I've always tinkered with crafting. I'm the proud owner of a wonky patchwork quilt, more misshapen hand-knits than I can shake a stick at and numerous other unfinished projects. As yet, I've never tried to spin and dye my own yarn. So, thank you, Helen Hickman, who runs *Nellie and Eve* at https://www.nelliean-deve.co.uk/. Your detailed advice about what it's like to run such a business helped make the book what it is today.

As a nurse my knowledge of anything to do with policing is limited to what I both read in books and watch on TV. Whilst I have had advice from members of both the Guernsey and Welsh police teams any mistakes here are all mine. Thank you again for your help and advice. I really do appreciate it.

Whilst there's a disclaimer at the front of the book with regards to the fictitious nature of the characters, there are two that aren't. Thank you to the fabulous Amy Potter and Annette Brazil-North for letting me borrow your names.

I have a fantastic support network of fellow writers, readers and editors that make picking up a pen easy. Thank you Beverley Hopper, Michele Turner, Elaine Fryatt, Maddie Harris, Adele Blair, Natasha Orme, Susan Hall, Clare Wakelin and Pauline Milliward.

An Irishwoman, living in Guernsey and writing a book series set in Wales? My great-grandparents hailed from Pembrokeshire and this is a tribute to them. The next in the series is set in Llandudno – my parents upped sticks and moved there when I was seventeen. I'm always 'popping home' for a catch up.

As always, thank you to my family for all your support. You're the ones that are affected the most by this writing journey – buns for tea x

Dear Reader,

We hope you enjoyed reading this book. If you did, we'd be so appreciative if you left a review. It really helps us and the author to bring more books like this to you.

Here at HQ Digital we are dedicated to publishing fiction that will keep you turning the pages into the early hours. Don't want to miss a thing? To find out more about our books, promotions, discover exclusive content and enter competitions you can keep in touch in the following ways:

JOIN OUR COMMUNITY:

Sign up to our new email newsletter:
http://hyperurl.co/hqnewsletter

Read our new blog www.hqstories.co.uk

 : https://twitter.com/HQDigitalUK

 : www.facebook.com/HQStories

BUDDING WRITER?

We're also looking for authors to join the HQ Digital family!

Find out more here:
https://www.hqstories.co.uk/want-to-write-for-us/

Thanks for reading, from the HQ Digital team

If you enjoyed *Silent Cry*, then why not try another gripping thriller from HQ Digital?